THE STALKING DEAD

EVA CHASE

GANG OF GHOULS

BOOK
1

The Stalking Dead

Book 1 in the Gang of Ghouls series

This is a work of fiction. Any resemblance to actual persons, living or dead, or actual events is purely coincidental.

First Digital Edition, 2021

Copyright © 2021 Eva Chase

Cover design: Yocla Book Cover Design

Ebook ISBN: 978-1-990338-25-0

Paperback ISBN: 978-1-990338-26-7

one

Lily

Near-death experiences have this funny way of putting everything else in perspective. I almost kicked the bucket in five feet of murky marsh water when I was six, and compared to that, nothing at Lovell Rise College could be all that horrifying. Even if this was my first full day back in town after seven years in a mental hospital.

Even if the question of what I'd done to be committed was still a huge, ominous blank in the back of my mind. Even if the only family I had in town had basically disowned me. Even if… there was a pair of frogs getting busy on the steps outside the main administrative building.

I stopped in my tracks before I stomped on the

amphibious lovers, doing a bit of a double-take. I'd always come across frogs regularly in Lovell Rise, probably because the marshlands ran the whole length of town. But I couldn't say I'd ever seen two of them going at it quite so blatantly before. The male had melded himself to the female's back with no sign of ever intending to let go.

Welp, more power to them. *Get them tadpoles*, I thought at them instead of saying it out loud, like I might have if I wasn't starkly aware of the other students meandering around the courtyard and lawns around me. I gave the frogs a wide berth as I continued my way up the steps.

Now that I was back home, it was more important than ever that I looked, talked, and acted normal in every possible way. I'd only get one chance at a fresh start. Just one chance to prove who I really was—and that it wasn't a girl who should be sent back to a loony bin halfway across the state.

I paused at the end of the smaller courtyard at the top of the steps, taking a moment to gather myself. The tapping and thudding of dozens of feet around me condensed into a weird sort of melody in my head. I could almost put lyrics to it, a trudging back-to-class anthem. *Here we go, like it or not, to stuff our brains full of facts and—*

Shaking myself, I pushed the impulse aside. I wouldn't *actually* turn footsteps into a song. That would be the opposite of normal.

I checked the campus map and veered left toward

one of the smaller white buildings that held the first class on my schedule: Juvenile Delinquency taught by Mr. Leon Grimes. My first real step toward a degree in sociology. I'd already done a year's groundwork of general education classes at the community college near the hospital before the doctors had decided I was sane enough to completely fly the coop.

Here was hoping it turned out that I'd gotten enough distance from my own mess to help clean up other people's messiness.

The cool September breeze licked over my face and flicked my wavy, flax-blond hair. I restrained a shiver, wishing I'd brought a jacket or a cardigan to wear over my thin blouse. Laughter rippled across the courtyard, but I ignored it other than as a minor accompaniment to the rhythm of marching feet, until it was followed by a brash voice.

"Hey, it's psycho girl!"

I should have kept walking. But the words were so jarring and unexpected—and so almost definitely aimed at *me*—that my legs locked up and my head jerked around to see who'd said it.

The guy sauntering toward me with a gaggle of friends in tow was unfortunately familiar. The local elementary and middle schools were small enough that there'd only been one class per grade, and so I'd been stuck in the same room as Ansel Hunter from age four through thirteen.

Seven years later, his shoulders had filled out and the angles of his face had taken on harder edges, but he had the same smooth golden hair, unshakeable ego, and supposedly charming grin that'd had most of the girls swooning over him the instant they hit puberty. Five seconds into our re-introduction, I could already tell his ego had only gotten bigger since I'd known him as a middle-schooler.

I'd realized that a number of the kids from town opted to go to Lovell Rise College if they met the entrance requirements so that they could stay on their home turf. It was a small campus, only eight hundred undergrads according to the new student orientation guide, but with several well-ranked programs and high admission standards. I'd busted my ass making the grades to transfer for my second year.

Somehow I hadn't pictured running into anyone who'd recognize me. It wasn't as if I'd been Miss Popular as a kid or, you know, had any friends at all. Real ones, anyway. I'd let myself assume no one would have even noticed I was missing, let alone figured out what had happened to me.

I guessed I hadn't given small-town gossip enough credit.

I didn't recognize any of the guys and girls who made up Ansel's current pack. He'd probably ditched his old hangers-on for shiny new models when he'd had a wider range to pick from. Otherwise he wouldn't have felt the need to "introduce" me to all of them.

"She went batshit right before high school and had to be shipped off to the insane asylum," he said to his entourage with a toss of his hand toward me, still grinning away, and turned his gaze with its malicious gleam on me. "What was your name again? Tulip? Daffodil?"

The girls in the pack tittered. I focused my gaze slightly above Ansel's eyes, where I pictured a tiny crocodile perched on his sun-bleached hair. One of my fellow patients in the psychiatric ward had insisted that everyone she met had an animal of some kind riding around on their heads. She'd told me I had a frog, which figured. She'd also used to talk to those invisible animals—more than to their hosts, most of the time.

I didn't actually see any animals like that—and I sure as hell wasn't crazy enough to talk to them—but I'd found that pretending I did made stressful situations somehow easier to get through. It was hard to get very worked up about the opinions of a guy who didn't even know he had a crocodile camped out on his cranium.

The imagined crocodile started gnawing on Ansel's pretty hair. I smiled evenly back at my former classmate, molding myself into the perfect picture of a totally sane and stable human being. "It's Lily, actually. Well, I'd better get to class."

I turned away, but Ansel shifted into my path, the gleam in his eyes getting fiercer. I started to wish the crocodile was real so it could chomp his nose right off.

"Oh, come on," he said. "How'd you get the head shrinkers to let you go after all this time? I think we've got a right to know how worried we should be. How can we be sure you're not going to show up one day and mow us all down in a hail of bullets?"

Well, for starters, I've never held a gun in my life, so I wouldn't even know how to get the safety off, answered the snarky voice in the back of my head, which I kept tightly under wraps. I'd realized a long time before I even ended up in the loony bin that people didn't like it when I let that voice out. I'd missed out on a lot of recesses before I'd learned that lesson.

"They decided I'm cured," I said evenly. "No threat to anyone. Nothing exciting here." *Except that crocodile that's chowing down on your artful fringe now.*

Ansel snorted. "Or maybe you've got them all fooled. Isn't that what psychopaths *do*?"

The girl standing closest to him, willowy with thick chestnut hair, an arched nose, and a cup of coffee clutched in one hand, gave him an awestruck look and then narrowed her eyes at me. "Yeah, I don't really think they should let psychos just enroll in classes here."

Hey, serial killers have a right to an education too, said the snark. A little of its edge crept into my voice, despite my best efforts. "Lucky for you, I've never been diagnosed as a psychopath. Just a regular girl who had an unfortunate episode a long time ago. Now if you'll excuse me—"

I tried to dodge around the crowd, and at the same moment, Ansel's arm shot out. He might have been trying to grab my elbow—or he might have purposefully knocked his hand into the wrist of that willowy girl next to him, sending her cup flying. Streams of coffee soared through the air and splattered all over the front of my blouse.

I yelped and jumped back a step, but it was too late. Hot liquid plastered the thin, baby-blue fabric to my chest with a brown splotch that was clearly going to stain. I swallowed a string of curses and held on to my cool as tightly as I could.

"My coffee," the girl muttered, her face falling, as if the biggest problem here was the loss of her beverage.

Ansel chuckled. "Let's see if the crazy comes out now."

As I tugged my shirt away from the outline of my bra, I imagined his mini-croc gnawing on his ear. "I'd better get this washed off," I said, stiffly now, and hustled away with determined strides.

This time, his fun apparently finished for the moment, Ansel let me go. More laughter followed me.

And that, according to some expert, was "normal." Standing around mocking a former classmate about something he didn't know anything about.

Of course, the fact that he didn't know might have made the comments harder to take. Because the truth was, *I* didn't know anything about it either. I had no idea what the "episode" that'd sent me to the hospital was. It'd short-circuited my brain, wiping all memory of what'd happened between walking up to my house one day and waking up in the ward the next.

Whatever had happened, it hadn't been *good*—that much was obvious. I was pretty sure doctors didn't keep you under supervision for seven years and refuse to talk to you about the specifics of your case unless you'd done something very bad.

Bad enough that my mom hadn't reached out once in all those years. Bad enough that my little sister...

I shoved those thoughts aside and sped up to a jog. Inside the building I'd been headed toward, I found a restroom halfway down the hall to my class. I ducked inside and splashed water on my blouse until I'd rinsed out the stain enough to take it from dark brown to medium tan. I still had a light blue shirt with a big brown stain all over the front, only now it was even more wet. Wonderful.

I held the fabric out under the blow dryer for as long as I could while keeping an eye on the time. When I had exactly one minute left before class started, I gave the shirt one last blast, grimaced at it, and hurried to the door.

Unfortunately, a gaggle of other girls burst in right then, so I had to dodge around them getting back to the hall. By the time I made it all the way to the lecture room at the far end, the clock inside was just ticking over to one minute past the hour.

I wouldn't have thought one minute would be that big a deal. The lecturers at the community college usually took at least five minutes just to rev up to anything resembling teaching. But the man by the projector screen at the front of the room—looking young-ish for a professor, maybe in his early 30s—was already in mid-sentence, tapping a pointer stick against the class syllabus displayed on the screen.

At my entrance, his body snapped toward the door, his eyes narrowing over high, sharp cheekbones. He shook his head disapprovingly, forcefully enough that a few tufts of his close-cropped brown hair stirred along his forehead. I darted toward the nearest seat at the end of the first tiered row, but he wasn't content to leave it at that.

"Who would you be, Miss…?"

I stopped a few feet from the desks and looked back at him. "Strom. Lily Strom."

His gaze flicked to a folder on his lectern and then back to me. Somehow his eyes managed to narrow even more. It was a wonder I could even make out the irises still. "Miss Strom. I did note your name in my enrollment list. Thank you for making it so easy to identify you."

Mr. Grimes turned to the rest of the students, some two dozen of them. "Class, it seems we have an exemplar of the subject of our course right here among us, and not just the delinquency of tardiness. In her juvenile years, this young lady was involved in an incident that required her to be removed from her home by the police followed by several years of rehabilitation."

Was he seriously going to make a production out of my past in front of all my peers? Well, yes—the answer was obviously yes.

My cheeks flamed, and my body burned with the conflicting urges to flee for the door and throw the textbook I'd already started getting out of my bag at his head.

But either of those behaviors would pretty much prove his point. I forced myself to breathe steadily, picturing a parakeet hopping around on the dickwad's head and pecking at those neatly combed strands. "I'm sorry I was late. It won't happen again. I just—"

"And perhaps next time you can manage to show up in more study-appropriate attire as well," Mr. Grimes interrupted in an icy tone, lifting his chin toward my wet blouse.

I crossed my arms in front of my chest instinctively, hugging the textbook to me. Did he think I'd *wanted* to get splattered in coffee? But from his sneer, he'd already made up his mind about me.

Think about what you're doing this for, Lily. Who you're doing this for. This asshat doesn't matter. If you do the work, he'll have to give you the grades you deserve. You'll prove him wrong too.

The little pep talk gave me the resolve to walk the rest of the way to my seat without a word. I got out my notebook and spent the rest of the class dutifully jotting down everything Mr. Grimes mentioned, no matter how unimportant-sounding. If I was going to be an exemp-anything, it was an exemplary student.

That didn't stop the professor from singling me out a few more times with pointed asides like, "Have you made note of that, Miss Strom?" I tuned out those remarks and kept my grip loose on my pen. And visualized the parakeet making explosive diarrhea all down the back of Mr. Grimes's head.

When class finished, I gathered up my things as quickly as I could and hustled to the door. Whispers followed me. "That girl…" "I heard about…"

There weren't *that* many locals here, but anyone in the room who hadn't already known the basics of my history did now. Mr. Grimes must have already been teaching at the college and living in Lovell Rise way back then, so he'd heard about it when it happened. Shit.

How many other professors were going to look at me the same way? With both a professor and Mr. Popular harassing me, how long would it take before the murmurs spread across the whole campus?

I couldn't think about that. I literally couldn't think about anything other than getting off the campus so I could breathe. Someone had turned the air into soup, which really wasn't very considerate of them, because you could drown in that stuff.

I strode right out to the far end of the parking lot where I'd had to park my junker of a car, the cheapest thing that still drove that I'd been able to track down. As soon as I reached it, I dropped into the driver's seat, jammed the key into the ignition, and gunned it out of there.

The engine coughed several times as if it wanted to remind me how lucky I was that it was still running. "Keep it together, Fred," I told it. "If I can get through this catastrophe of a day, so can you."

My grandfather had always named his cars, but he'd given them women's names, with a gag-worthy comment about women's duty to carry the load. I'd vowed to always name mine as men, because if I was going to ride anything, it'd be a dude.

And yeah, I talked to inanimate objects. It's the sort of habit you'd get into too if your main friends during your formative years were imaginary. At least the car actually existed.

Fred hung in there as I drove around town and took a turn toward the marshlands. Toward the place that'd been my home for the first thirteen years of my life. My hands tightened on the wheel, but I took the far lane that wouldn't bring me in view of Mom and Wade's house.

Even without seeing the building, my last conversation with Mom—through the screen door, with her hand braced against the frame as if she thought I'd try to ram it down—rose up in my head.

I just want to say "Happy birthday!" It's her sweet sixteen. She's my sister. Please.

How are we supposed to be sure that you're really well now? They kept you in treatment for so long. I don't think it's worth the risk, Lily.

They'd see. I'd show them. I hadn't hurt anyone, hadn't done anything wrong…

Except whatever I'd done seven years ago that'd sent me to St. Elspeth's Psychiatric Center in the first place.

When I reached the end of the lane near the marsh, I got out and told Fred, "Thank you," because it never hurt to be polite, even to a car. Then I walked down to where the ground got squishy under my feet.

The cattails rattled against each other in the damp breeze. This end of the lake was choked with vegetation for almost a mile out before you got to the open water, which was exactly how a six-year-old girl could end up wandering out into the middle of the marsh from clump to clump before suddenly setting a foot wrong and going under. I shied away from the distant memory of the cold, dark wetness closing over me.

I didn't know what I was looking for out here. I'd spent so much time by the marsh over the years when I'd hardly felt welcome in my own house with Wade lurking around scowling at me and Marisol. I'd played down here by myself and with my sister when she was old enough that I wasn't scared of her tumbling in. I'd make up songs for her to go with the warbling of the wind in the reeds.

A dull ache came into my throat. There wasn't anyone to sing for now.

The rasp of the jostling leaves formed a sound almost like someone else's voice. For a second, staring out at them, I could have sworn I heard my name. Something almost like a plea to listen.

But that—that was *really* crazy.

No wonder I'd been able to imagine up four invisible protectors out of the marsh, though. All it took was a little moving air to make the place sound haunted.

For a long time, I'd believed I wasn't really by myself even when I came down here alone. I'd imagined I heard voices in the breeze and that I could see the barest outlines of figures standing around me. That I'd felt the faint impression of their hands when we'd played tag or they'd caught me at hide and seek—that when I'd sung for *them*, they'd swayed along and applauded. In my head, they'd given me their own private nicknames like "Waterlily" and "Minnow," "Lil" and plain old "kid." When Wade would drive up, they'd make rude gestures in his direction, because obviously my imagination was more comfortable expressing how I felt about him than I was out loud.

Every time I'd come down here, I'd known I'd find them waiting. Watching over me. That certainty had made everything else bearable.

But they weren't really here. Of course they weren't.

An itch tickled my inner arm just below the pit. I scratched the spot without looking, not needing to look to know it was where I'd discovered the nickel-sized blotch of a new birthmark days after I'd come back to my senses in the hospital. As if whatever had happened that day, it'd marked me inside and out.

Some things would always be true. Marisol needed me, and I wasn't going to let her down. I'd make things right for her and with her however I could.

That meant I had to get through whatever life threw at me from here forward—no matter how many assholes came with it.

The sense of my name being called swept over me with the wind again, distant and wavering: *Lily!* I shook off the impression and the pang that followed it, and turned to face the cold reality I actually had to work with.

two

Nox

I'd say I shouted Lily's name until my throat was hoarse, but I didn't really have a throat. Or a neck or a mouth, come to think of it.

Just one of the many ways that being dead was deeply fucked up.

"Lily!" I hollered again, standing right next to her, as much as I could stand when I also didn't currently have legs or feet or—you get the picture.

Her gaze twitched a little, those pale blue-green eyes like the sky reflecting off the marsh water turning pensive, but I could tell she still hadn't really heard anything. Not enough to realize that someone was actually speaking to her, let alone who.

It was still hard to wrap my head around the fact

that she was right here in front of me. Even after all this time, I'd recognized her instantly. I wasn't sure how exactly long it had been since she'd vanished from our afterlives, but even though she'd grown from a gawky barely-teenager to a fully-fledged woman, so much of her had stayed the same.

Those eyes. The hair that gleamed like goddamned sunbeams as it spilled over her slim shoulders. The rosy lips that were set at an angle that looked both determined and sad.

I hadn't seen her smile since she'd turned up back at the house a few days ago, but it wasn't hard to figure out why with the way her dishtowel of a mother had sent her off—and then those pricks at school had started tearing into her. That was a fucking travesty right there. How could the idiots at that stupid college not see this was a girl—a *woman*—who needed to be held up and cherished, not ground into the dirt?

We'd see who got ground into what next... if I only had some real way of accomplishing that.

I swiped the vague impression of where I should have had a hand over Lily's hair, and the wavy strands fluttered, but little enough that she could dismiss the motion as the breeze. With the same stoutly defiant poise she'd sported since she was a little kid, she turned and walked back to the clunker she'd been driving.

At least no one had managed to beat the spirit out of her yet.

I spun around. I couldn't exactly *see* my friends, what with them being also dead and bodiless, but they gave off their own vague impressions, concrete enough to me that I had a sense of where the three of them hovered around me and even what gestures they were making. Or maybe the second part was only because I'd spent so much time around them when we'd been alive.

"What the hell is wrong?" I demanded to the landscape at large. "Why can't she hear us anymore?"

Kai was probably pushing glasses that no longer existed up his nose that also no longer existed. "She's grown up. Her mind has matured—it must have become too closed off to accept the possibility of people she can't really see."

Ruin hummed to himself in his typically carefree way, ever the optimist. "She could always hear us before. She's got to get used to it again, right? We haven't had much time to get through to her."

"She was pretty young when we first started talking to her," Kai said. "And she kept getting practice on a regular basis. It's been… a long time since she probably thought we were real. I don't know if we'd be able to establish that kind of connection again."

Ruin chuckled. "She's Lily. Of course all we need to do is make the connection."

The guy had the habit of not hearing so well—he tended to take whatever you said and spin it in the most upbeat way possible. Sometimes it was kind of cute. Frequently it was fucking annoying. It was a good thing I liked plenty of other things about him.

Jett, who'd stayed silent so far like he often did, let

out an inarticulate grumble before saying, "What now? Those fuckers… We've got to do *something.*"

None of us needed to ask which fuckers he meant. The same ones that had rage searing all through my irritatingly ephemeral presence. From the moment Lily had made her first appearance in Lovell Rise since we'd last seen her however many years ago, we'd kept a close eye on her, following her to the apartment she'd rented and the school where a bunch of dorks with high degrees thought they could teach her something useful.

I'd stopped going to classes partway through eleventh grade, and I'd turned out just fine.

Okay, I'd turned out dead, but that'd been almost ten years later, and getting gunned down hadn't had anything to do with my lack of algebra skills.

It wasn't the *dorks* at the college I had a real problem with, obviously. It was the asshole bullies who thought they could tear a strip out of our Lily. As if her prick of a stepdad and pathetic mom hadn't been bad enough. As if she deserved anyone harassing her after… after whatever she'd been through while she'd been gone.

I had no idea what that even was.

Kai spoke up again, picking up on my train of thought without me saying anything at all, which was *his* special unnerving habit. "The professor mentioned the police. The dick who splashed her with coffee talked about an 'insane asylum.' Whatever took her away from here, it must have been awful. And they *enjoyed* belittling her over it." His voice got sharper rather than louder when he was pissed off, and right now it could have cut through a Range Rover.

"We'll take care of them," Ruin announced. "A stab here, a bullet there." He was probably gleefully cracking his knuckles at the thought.

"How the hell are we supposed to do that when we're all fucked up like this?" Jett burst out, with what was possibly the longest sentence he'd uttered in at least two decades.

My non-existent teeth gritted with my own frustration. Every particle of my soul was screaming with the need to charge across campus and rip through all the jerks who'd so much as looked sideways at Lily… but I couldn't do more than mimic a bit of breeze. A growl escaped me.

We'd never really been able to protect her from her shitty so-called parents either, only given her an escape and a sense that she had someone on her side. Which was something, but clearly not fucking enough, given how much shit had gone down next.

Those long stretches of numbing ghostly nothingness brought what really mattered into sharp relief. Lily shone like a star, and everyone else in this podunk town was sewage.

I had the blurry impression that maybe life had seemed slightly more complicated before, but I didn't have a life anymore, so what the hell did that matter?

"If I could raise my fucking skeleton out of the marsh for even five minutes, I'd gut them all with a rusty butcher knife," I muttered.

"Choke them with their own eyeballs," Jett added.

Ruin's grin shone through in his voice. "Cut off their feet and shove them up their asses."

Kai was unusually quiet for a moment. Usually it was hard to shut the guy up, he had so many ideas and observations just spilling out of his brain. I whirled toward him. "Don't you think we've got to take the bastards down?"

"Of course," he said, and I could picture the glitter of inspiration sparking into being behind the panes of his glasses. "There was something I was looking into, before Lily vanished. I'd almost forgotten. I shouldn't have."

I wasn't going to get on his case about that. I wasn't sure what'd happened to any of us during the years of her absence. The day she'd crashed into the marsh, she'd stirred our water-logged spirits back to some kind of life. Being with her had kept us going for years after that. But without her presence, we must have drifted back off into a muddled, monotonous limbo. That state wasn't really a great environment for brilliant brainstorms.

"Well, what is it?" I prodded Kai.

"I'm not sure about this yet. I still need to do some experiments to make sure it'll all come together. But the theory is sound."

"The theory for *what*?" Jett said impatiently.

Kai's intellectual delight came through in his voice. "We might be able to get bodies again. Permanently."

I felt the attention of all three of my men shift to

me. They *were* my men—I'd been the leader of the Skullbreakers, and they'd been my closest colleagues as we built the gang together. We were in all of this together, in life and death… but ultimately, I called the shots.

This one wasn't remotely hard to call, though.

My theoretical eyebrows had shot up as if propelled by the rush of exhilaration that'd surged through me at the thought. "Seriously? Hell, yes. Experiment your fucking heart out and let's get this done."

Ruin let out a little whoop. His soul was probably doing a shimmy of a happy-dance that I was glad I didn't have to see.

Kai must have been rubbing his non-existent hands together like the maniac genius he often was. "No problem. I'm looking forward to it. Just to be clear, we can't create forms out of nothing or grow flesh back on our old bones. For the final plan, we're going to need to commit a few murders so we have bodies to take over."

A grin stretched across the face I no longer had, and a dark laugh spilled out of me. "Perfect. I know at least a couple of people who'll totally deserve it."

three

Lily

As far as I knew, Lovell Rise College didn't have much of a sports program, but its one claim to fame in that area was its football team. According to the student handbook, anyway. I hadn't given athletics much thought until I was skirting the main practice field during what looked like a casual scrimmage, and the ball came spiraling through the air to thump on the ground outside the foul line just a few feet ahead of me.

A bunch of the jocks came barreling over, hassling the guy who'd apparently made the "lame" throw. When they caught sight of me, they drew up short.

My skin prickled with trepidation. After a few more

days on campus, I could recognize in a matter of seconds what was about to go down.

Word about my psycho status had spread faster than the speed of light. Scientists should come study the bending of natural laws. I was seriously considering cutting my hair off and dyeing what remained black so I looked like a different person, but that'd probably help me for all of a millisecond before the asswipes caught on. And then I'd just be a pariah with really bad hair.

"Oooh," one of the guys said in a ghostly tone. "It's the loony girl. Are you going to put a curse on the ball for almost hitting you?"

It took a massive feat of strength not to roll my eyes. "I think you're confusing 'psychopath' with 'psychic,'" I said evenly, and kept walking by.

"She's going to come with a butcher knife and kill us all in our sleep," one of the other guys said.

"Better start double-checking the locks."

"I wonder what it'd take for her to drop the normal act and let the freak flag fly?"

"Let's find out," yet another of the guys said, far enough away now that I didn't even glance backward. Then a hurtling force slammed into the middle of my back.

I stumbled forward as the football that'd smacked me bounced on the ground. "Nice one, Zach!" someone crowed.

Spinning around, I saw the bunch of guys snickering with each other while also watching me with avid curiosity, probably hoping I'd snap. As my pulse thumped hard, I narrowed my attention to the guy in the middle of the bunch who was grinning most broadly while others slapped him on the back.

He must have been the one who'd thrown the football. Like a typical football player, he was beefy, though not especially tall, with his light brown hair slicked back and grazing the tops of his ears. A tattoo so amateurish I couldn't tell whether it was a skull or a soap dish marked one of his bulging biceps.

Oh, what a tough guy, Zach—hurling projectiles at unarmed women, my inner voice said. *Tom Brady would be so proud of you.* I willed myself calm while picturing a rhino prancing around on the jerkwad's head, kicking up those gelled strands.

"I think you misplaced this," I said, and gave the football a light punt toward them. Then I hurried away from the field even faster, tuning out the chuckles that followed me. For a second—just a second—I wished I really was a murderous psychopath who wouldn't hesitate to carve them up. We'd see how long they kept laughing then.

But so far, no matter what I *had* done, as far as I knew I hadn't murdered anyone, and getting a lethal rap sheet was not going to help my case in convincing Mom to let me see Marisol. Lucky for those dickheads.

I just wanted to get away from campus with the whispers and the speculative glances, but the student affairs office had called me in for an appointment they hadn't really explained. I strode into the admin building and managed to reach the office on time despite getting lost in the maze of hallways twice on the way there. I was starting to think they'd set the building up that way specifically to challenge students' commitment to their schooling.

I came into the office to find a woman built like an ostrich—big hips, tiny shoulders, long neck, big eyes—talking to a tall, skinny guy with dirty blond hair that was carefully tucked behind his prominent ears.

"Of course, Ms. Baxter," he was saying in an emphatically eager voice. "Whatever I can do to help the school run smoothly. It's my pleasure to help."

"Well, here she is now," Ms. Baxter said with a harried-looking smile. She waved me over. "Miss Strom, I'm so sorry I didn't manage to get this support set up until a few days into your time here. So many new students each year." Her head bobbed a bit from side to side, adding to the ostrich impression. "This is Vincent Barnes. He'll be your peer advisor during the next month, ready to assist you with anything you need when it comes to transitioning into life at Lovell Rise College. He's one of our top performing students, so I'm sure he'll be a great help. Any questions you have, you can reach out to him."

Well, that was a lot better than the interrogation or expulsion I'd been half expecting after the rest of the reception I'd gotten here. I glanced at Vincent as he turned around.

He was smiling brightly when his focus shifted from the staff person to me. The second his gaze landed on my face, his own face started to fall. He caught it with a flick of his eyes toward Ms. Baxter as if worried she might have noticed, but it'd gotten noticeably stiffer.

Okay, maybe this wasn't much better after all.

Ms. Baxter didn't appear to have picked up on his reaction. Her hands fluttered in the air, all flightless bird. "We've found the peer advisor program is very helpful for both the new students and the established peers who get to take on a leadership role. It's one of the things that make Lovell Rise College so special and welcoming."

I almost choked on my spit. As words to describe this place went, I'd put "welcoming" down at the bottom of the list. And that included the guy currently attempting to incinerate me with his eyes.

"I try to pitch in around the college every way I can," Vincent said, with a more brittle-sounding enthusiasm than he'd shown before. "Why don't we get started?"

"Perfect!" Still oblivious, Ms. Baxter clapped her hands together and shooed us off.

I curled my fingers around the strap of my shoulder bag as I walked with Vincent into the narrow hallway. One of the florescent lights was sputtering with a tinny noise, like it had a mouse inside it drumming on the glass.

Vincent marched around a bend in the hall that took us out of hearing of the student affairs office and then stopped with his posture drawn up rigidly straight. He shoved a slip of paper at me.

"That's my email and the number where you can

text me," he spat out. "If you have any *legitimate* concerns, it's my duty to answer them. You can forget about trying to copy my work or getting you out of whatever trouble you get yourself into. You won't be leaching off my GPA."

I stared at him. "Um, this wasn't my idea. I didn't ask for a peer advisor. And I can do my own work just fine, thanks." Clearly *he* hadn't volunteered for the peer advisor role out of any desire to be welcoming, only for extra credit or to look good for his favorite professors.

He let out a huff as if he didn't believe that I could possibly have had any plans other than to take advantage of him. "I know who you are. *Everyone* knows who you are. I don't know why they'd have let you enroll in the first place—" He cut himself off with a brisk shake of his head. "Let's leave it at this: You'd better not screw anything up for me. I've worked too hard to earn the grades and the respect that comes with them around here."

My teeth set on edge. Which might have been a good thing, because in the few seconds it took me to unclamp them, I had time to swallow the several heated responses I'd have liked to make.

Who the hell did this twerp think he was? I'd never even seen him before, let alone spoken to him, and he was already treating me like some kind of demonic force. With all his supposed smarts, you'd think he'd have picked up on the fact that no one could actually say what I'd done—and that whatever it'd been, it'd happened years ago.

"You don't need to worry," I said tightly, crumpling the slip of paper in my hand. "I won't be bothering you at all." *Let's just hope that whatever prime job you're hoping to score right out of college, it doesn't require treating the people around you like human beings, since you'd obviously flunk any course on that subject.*

Vincent apparently needed to work on his hearing too. He continued as if I hadn't spoken. "Don't come up to me on campus either. You need anything, we hash it out digitally. I don't need people associating me with you."

He stalked off with an offended air as if I'd orchestrated this situation specifically to piss him off. My fingers curled into my palms, acting out the intense desire to strangle the douche-canoe.

Well, he was gone now, and his contact info was going in the garbage. I had exactly zero interest in finding out what kind of "assistance" Vincent Barnes could offer.

Thankfully, his departure meant I was free to get the hell away from this school for the day. I wove through the halls and made it to the front door after only getting lost once this time. From there it was only a short trot across the lawn and the parking lot to the desolate spot at the far end that I'd picked to avoid notice.

It appeared my strategy hadn't worked out so well. As I came up on my junkpile of a car, my stomach clenched.

It looked even more junky than usual—because one of the back tires had sagged totally flat.

Swearing under my breath, I sped up to a jog. As soon as I knelt by the tire, it was obvious the flat was no accident. Someone had jabbed a hole into the rubber.

I stood up again and glanced around as if the offender might have stuck around to watch my reaction to his—or her—work. The lot around me was empty other than a few students just ambling over to cars closer to the buildings. No sign of the pissbrain responsible.

A surge of hopelessness washed over me. I'd been here almost a week, I hadn't lifted a finger against anyone, and still people were taking their emotional issues out on me. I had to get to my job—this was going to make me late for my shift. If I lost the job, I'd lose my apartment…

I dragged in one breath and another, shoving those despairing thoughts away. I was stronger than this. I was stronger than *them*.

They'd made one very major miscalculation: they'd only stabbed *one* tire.

Gathering my resolve, I opened up the trunk and tugged out my kit of car tools and the spare I'd made sure to have on hand specifically because I hadn't been sure how much life any of Fred's tires still had in them.

Thank God for the life skills course that'd been offered as part of St. Elspeth's rehabilitation program. Shove the jack in here, crank the lever. The faint, rhythmic squeaking formed a defiant melody in my head.

"I'm sorry you took the beating for my crimes," I

informed the old tire in a whisper of a voice. "I promise to get justice for you if I can manage it without looking even more psycho than everyone already thinks I am."

Which meant I should probably stop talking to random hunks of rubber too.

I loosened the nuts, unable to stop myself from thinking about a whole lot of *other* kinds of nuts I wouldn't have minded detaching from the slimeballs around this school. Then I pumped the crank some more. I hoped the asshat who'd done this *was* watching so they could see that they hadn't fucked me over half as much as they'd intended to.

I might be a psycho, but I was a psycho who knew her way around a tire.

"There we go," I couldn't help murmuring to the new tire as I slid it into place and finished attaching it. "Good hunk of rubber. Make Fred proud."

The tire didn't say anything back, but I liked to think the ridges formed a bit of a smile.

I tossed the punctured tire in the trunk just in case I needed it as evidence… of the fact that this was a school full of massive scumbuckets? There wasn't anywhere to throw it out anyway. Then I wiped the grease off my hands as well as I could with a tissue and checked the time. If the car held in there for me otherwise, I might be able to hoof it to the grocery store *just* in time to start shoving cans onto shelves by the assigned schedule.

"All right, Fred," I muttered as I dropped into the driver's seat. "Let's do this thing."

I grabbed the door to yank it shut, and my gaze

veered across the dashboard at the same moment. My fingers froze around the handle.

I'd grabbed fast food from a drive-through for a hasty lunch before my afternoon classes. The salt packets I'd carelessly tossed up on the dash had ruptured, spilling little white grains all over the dark plastic. But that wasn't what made me pause.

The grains had spilled in a very precise pattern. Into wavery lines that I'd swear spelled out *words*. It looked like they said… *We're coming*.

We're coming?

The next second, a gust of wind blew past the open door, and all the salt scattered. Now it was just tiny white polka dots all over the dash, the passenger seat, and the floor, spelling out nothing at all.

I slammed the door closed and sat there with my pulse thudding hard enough to drown out the chatter of a couple sauntering by arm-in-arm outside. My mouth had gone dry.

I'd just imagined that, right? With the way I kept getting harassed, maybe it wasn't surprising that I'd see ominous messages in random condiments.

I definitely wasn't hallucinating or anything. Because then I really would be crazy.

Nausea wrapped around my gut. I stared at the dash for a minute longer, trying to make sense of what I'd seen. Then I shook my head and turned the key to spark the ignition.

Crazy or not, I still had a job to do. Those grocery store shelves weren't going to stock themselves.

four

Kai

The room *had* to be perfect. We were only going to get one shot at this.

And I'd told the guys my strategy would work—I didn't plan on getting heckled by them for the rest of our eternal afterlives for getting their hopes up.

"Yes," I said before Ruin even needed to ask the question from where he'd glanced my way. He'd just finished nudging the jug of bleach Nox had painstakingly opened to the edge of the shelf. "Get it all the way to where you can feel it *just* about to tip. We need to have it ready to spill the second they're all inside."

"Fucking tiring," Jett muttered, as if he'd been doing anything other than lurking in a corner of the janitor's storage room and being his usual brooding self for the past half an hour. I guessed I'd give him a little credit for managing to spread the chemicals we'd dragged together in a narrow puddle along the concrete floor just below the shelf with the bleach.

I could only pick up scents vaguely in my current state, but I felt pretty confident in saying that this place smelled… unusual. I waved into being some semblance of an air current to try to keep the odor to the far side of the room.

"Not going to do us much good if they turn around the second they get a whiff of this place," Nox pointed out. I sensed his grin. "We'll have to give them a good shove."

"If we have the energy left," Jett grumbled.

"We're going to have *so* much energy and everything else," Ruin pipped up in typical chipper fashion. "We're going to have *bodies* again! All the pricks in this town had better watch out." He whirled around us so fast I had the impression of my hair rippling.

"We'll need to take things slow at first," I reminded him. "We don't know what effect the possession is going to have on our connection to the bodies. It might take a while for us to be fully coordinated." A grin of my own sprang to my ghostly lips. "But it's only a matter of time until we make all those assholes regret every jab they made at our girl."

"It shouldn't have taken us this long," Jett muttered.

"She'll know we're coming," Nox said. "We left that message in her car."

Ruin spun again. "Right. Help is on the way! And we deal with four of the worst assholes at the same time." He cackled to himself. "She's going to be so happy when she realizes we're back with her."

Yes. As much as I reveled in the thought of taking a whole lot of jerks around this place down several pegs, I enjoyed my vision of how Lily's face would light up even more. I'd never been the most popular guy around, alive or dead. People tended to be put off by the fact that, frankly, I knew a hell of a lot more than the vast majority of them did. They could have benefitted from my smarts, but instead they'd rather sneer at or shun me.

Well, their loss. Sometimes quite literally, considering all the objects and body parts I'd removed from their owners in my time.

But Lily... even when she'd only been a little kid without much sense of social graces, she'd never shied away from me. She'd laughed with delight when I could predict what she was thinking, ask me all kinds of questions to ferret out the knowledge I'd accumulated about one thing or another, as well as I could convey those facts through our ghostly channels of communication. Even my closest associates around me now had never been *that* enthusiastic.

I mentally rubbed my hands together in anticipation and took a final circuit of the room. Everything was in place. Nox had practiced turning the deadbolt in the door several times to make sure he could do it quickly. Our toxic cocktail was ready to tango.

And I'd chosen the brief messages we'd imposed into ink on notepaper insightfully tailored to our targets' horrible personalities.

Nox turned with a hint of a huff he probably didn't even realize betrayed his impatience. He was going to ask me how much longer we had to wait, so I answered him before he had to speak the words.

"Ten more minutes. I wanted to leave us plenty of time in case we had trouble with the set-up."

He shook his head. "It's still creepy the way you do that."

"Don't be so easy to read and I won't be able to read you," I retorted lightly, and a sudden thought struck me like a bolt of lightning. How could I have left that one variable unconsidered? Death had clearly muddled my mind.

"We need to be clear on who's taking which body," I said quickly. "We want to dive in fast, and we can't have two of us colliding in the same one." That'd be a recipe for disaster… or else multiple personality disorder, but I wasn't keen on testing out the possibilities.

Even as I said the words, the gears in my head were already spinning through what I knew about my friends and our soon-to-be puppets. I could make a solid guess about who'd want who, but they did *occasionally* surprise me.

Nox spoke up first, which was fair since he was the man in charge. "The teacher's mine. Let's see how the idiots around here like it when they've got a real authority figure." He chuckled.

"I'll take the one with all the friends who follow him around listening to what he says," Ruin announced. "Lots of people to 'play' with. And I've got tons of better things to tell them about Lily."

"I can go with the grades-obsessed guy who just wanted to be left alone," Jett said. "Works for me." He turned his attention my way. "Or were you hoping to take the nerd, Kai?"

I snorted. "It wouldn't work in my favor very well if I picked the one with the same strengths I already have. I'm happy to take the football player. My brains and his brawn should be an unstoppable combination."

A ghostly sort-of adrenaline thrummed through me at the thought. I hadn't been a weakling before by any means—you didn't survive in our kind of life if you couldn't throw a punch and slash a knife when you needed to—but I'd admit physical combat hadn't been my strongest skillset. Death was giving me the opportunity for an upgrade.

At the sound of voices in the distance, my senses went on the alert. No one came down into this dim hallway of the college unless they had to—or they'd been given a very good reason to think it'd be worth their while.

I snapped my fingers at Ruin. "Get ready by the bleach. The second you hear the lock slam into place behind them, give it a shove."

"On it!" Ruin flew to the high shelf, practically vibrating with excitement. I wouldn't have entrusted that part of the assignment to him if I hadn't thought all that energy would help give his push the heft it needed. Besides, I needed to oversee all the other variables, and Nox packed the most punch of the power we needed to lock the door.

Jett, well… There was always a risk with him that he'd get distracted ruminating about the paint he wanted to smear all over something and miss his cue. He didn't even bother to stir from his corner, not caring about the details of the plan until he got his chance to nab a body.

Nox followed me through the wall into the hallway, where three of our unlucky four were walking toward us.

"…some kind of special assignment," the golden boy said, not looking so special now that he didn't have an army of minions in tow. "He said it was important that he get exactly the right people for the job." He glanced at the others as if he was having trouble imagining how either of *them* could have qualified as "special."

"I just know he said the team would get new equipment if I pitched in," the jock replied. "And they'll all know it's thanks to me. Sweet."

The geeky guy had folded his arms over his chest as if to reduce the chances that he might brush against one of the other two and catch slacker cooties. "He mentioned extra credit," he said stiffly. "I wouldn't have bothered otherwise."

The golden boy smiled the same way he had when

he'd been tearing down Lily. "There's something in it for all of us then."

Oh, there'd be something in him, all right. Unfortunately for him, there'd be something coming *out* too—specifically his soul.

They peered at the doors they passed, the nerd's nose wrinkling and the jock's forehead furrowing. "Are we sure this is the right place?" the beefy guy asked.

Golden Boy checked the plates over the doors and a piece of paper he dug out of his pocket. "It should be just down here... I don't know why he picked this spot, but I guess this project is something *really* off the radar."

My hearing caught footsteps farther in the distance, and apprehension prickled over me. If the professor caught up with this bunch before they disappeared into the room, they might consult each other before they entered, and then they'd never go in at all.

"Wait there!" I ordered Nox, hoping he wouldn't decapitate me as soon as I had a head to remove for bossing him around, and dashed toward the bend in the hall.

The professor who'd berated Lily on her first day—and who hadn't let up on her since—was striding toward me from the stairwell. I'd told him to come five minutes later than the others, but apparently he had a hard-on for over-punctuality. Shit.

I darted past him into a room he'd already passed where the door was slightly ajar. A shove was a lot easier than manipulating a lock with our ghostly energies. I could manage that much even with the power I'd already expended setting this plan in motion.

I hurled myself at the door from inside, picturing my ghostly shoulder solidifying against it, the energy propelling it forward. In my mind's eye, it slammed into the frame with a thunderous *thwack*.

In actuality, it clicked into place with a light thud and the faintest crackle of the supernatural electricity our energy condensed into. I tumbled the rest of the way through the door, back into the hall.

The noise was still enough for the professor to pause and glance behind him. He frowned and rubbed his jaw. Any second he was going to keep walking.

I darted inside and rammed myself with another imperceptible sizzle into the nearest free-standing object, which happened to be a mop. It tumbled over with a clatter.

Thankfully, this stickler also had a hard-on for telling off delinquent students. He marched over to the room and flung open the door with a triumphant expression.

His delight faltered when he took in the room currently uninhabited by anyone living. Taking a few steps inside, he scanned the shelves and even the bucket by the door, as if a freshman might be hiding in there. Then, with a sigh, he strode back out.

As he left, I caught the click of the other door closing around the bend. I'd bought us enough time. Now to see the final part of this plan through.

Back in the janitor's room, Ruin was jittering

behind the bleach bottle like a kitten that'd bit a live wire. Our first three doofuses were inspecting the room around them with growing confusion.

"Why would Mr. Grimes want to meet us *here*?" the nerd said.

"With professors, you've really just got to go along with what they say," the jock said with an air of pathetic certainty. "That's what makes them happy."

"Fuck, it smells weird in here," the golden boy said, waving his hand under his nose. He took a step toward the puddle of chemicals on the floor. "Maybe this is some kind of test. He wants to see if we're really up to the challenge of the assignment."

That's right, I thought at him. *It's a big elaborate test designed to give you every opportunity to prove what a spectacular human being you are—oh, sorry, I mean what a pretentious prick you are. Congratulations, you're a winner!*

"I don't know about this," the nerd said, edging back toward the door, and I thought I might have to pull out a few more stops. But right then, the professor barged into the room.

He stopped just inside, the door swinging shut behind him, and stared at the collection of imbeciles we'd brought together. I'd bet he didn't recognize that he was the biggest one of all. His eyebrows drew together as he tried to figure out how this could possibly be the result of the note I'd sent supposedly from a female student hoping to get a little "extra help" away from prying eyes.

"What are—?" he started.

In the same instant, I called out to Nox. "Lock it!"

Our fearless leader slammed the full force of his energy into the deadbolt. It rasped over with an audible *thunk*. Ruin sucked in a giddy breath and hurled himself at the bleach bottle.

The dolts had whipped around at the sound of the lock. They whipped back when the bleach bottle careened off the shelf with a splatter of noxious liquid spilling from its mouth as it fell. The stuff hissed into the chemicals we'd sloshed on the floor, and the waft of stink shifted from weird to deadly.

Our dupes gagged and sputtered. I'd kind of wanted to watch them staggering around in agony for a little while, but we must have dosed them hard enough that the toxic gasses didn't take long overwhelming them. One and then another toppled to the floor like dominos. The professor, closest to the door, rattled the knob like his life depended on it— which, to be fair, it did—and then keeled over flat on his face.

I whisked from one to the next, grazing my spirit over them just long enough to confirm that their hearts had stopped beating. Their deathly silence was the most beautiful sound I'd ever heard. Anticipation hummed through me.

We were so close. Was this really going to work? Had I pulled off the ultimate gambit?

Only one way to find out.

"Open the door!" I hollered. "Get the fan going!" It

wouldn't do us any good to resurrect ourselves only to die all over again.

Nox smacked the lock open and threw wide the door. Jett got off his ephemeral ass long enough to light a spark in the circuitry of the industrial fan next to his corner. A blast of air washed the worst of the poisonous perfume out of the room.

"Now?" Ruin asked, hopping up and down as much as a being without legs could.

"Now!" I declared, and dove into the jock.

I'd told the others to go straight for the heart. Pummel right into it like one giant shock paddle, as if our entire spirits would fit in that four-chambered organ. Let our supernatural energies jumpstart the currents that would set it pumping again. Rev it like a Harley and settle in for the ride. And that's exactly what I did.

A shrieking darkness closed around me. An electric jolt reverberated through my being into the space around me. Then something shuddered, and a pulse echoed through my spirit. It sounded erratic at first before settling into a steady thumping.

My sense of myself stretched as if I were being smeared through the body like peanut butter on toast, tingling with the awakening nerves, heaving with the air rushing into the lungs, blinking…

Blinking eyes that now belonged to me.

I pushed myself to my feet and swayed. I *had* feet. Halle-fucking-lujah. And legs and arms and a big brawny chest—more body than I'd had to begin with.

A laugh spilled from my mouth. *My* mouth, that could now make noises people who weren't dead could properly hear.

Fuck Christmas. We should christen a new holiday right now. Un-undead Day. All right, that didn't have the best ring to it, but I'd figure out something better when I was done losing my shit with joy.

Around me, the other bodies were heaving themselves upright. "Fuck, yeah!" Nox said through the professor's mouth, the voice lighter than his previous baritone but the attitude all Lennox Savage.

Jett just stared at his hands, turning them back to front, like they were a fucking miracle. Which they kind of were.

Ruin bounded right at me, throwing his almost-as-brawny arms around me. Right. I'd forgotten that when he *had* arms, he was a hugger.

"You did it! It's fucking fantastic," he crowed, and launched himself at Nox next. "We're back!"

"Hell yes, we are," Nox said, shooting me a wicked grin that no one could have believed belonged to his host. "Now let's get out there and teach these assholes the lessons they've been begging for."

five

Lily

I could tell something was up the second I reached the edge of campus. Gods be praised, this time it didn't appear to have anything to do with me.

A horde of students was swarming the field to the left of the admin building, chattering to each other with a buzz of anticipation. I'd swear there were more bodies on the lawn than were enrolled in the entire school. Resisting the urge to start accusing people that they didn't even go here, I eased closer to the crowd with my ears pricked. Maybe I could find out what the hell was going on without turning into a target.

"I wonder how many people they're actually looking to hire," one girl was saying to another. "Seems like a lot of competition."

Her friend bobbed eagerly on the balls of her feet, craning her neck as if searching for something amid the other students. "I heard they've been expanding a lot in the last decade, so they always need fresh blood. It'd be pretty amazing to get in with them right out of college. Sometimes they even take people on before they've graduated, starting them parttime until they're done with classes."

A third girl glanced back at them. "Aren't you majoring in biology? Would they even have positions for that?"

The second girl shrugged. "They're into all kinds of areas these days. It couldn't hurt to try. Everyone says they're one of the best companies to work for in the country."

I ventured farther along the fringes of the crowd, trying to figure out who this mysterious "they" was and why people seemed to think they'd be tossing out jobs like tees shot from a shirt cannon. I got a few wary looks as I brushed past my fellow students, but no one said anything, which made this a good day. They all appeared to be too distracted to worry about me going psycho on their butts.

I'd made it about halfway around the field when I spotted the billboard-like sign set up near a small temporary platform with a podium. *Thrivewell Enterprises Recruitment Event*, it said in big crimson letters, and lower down, in darker, more subdued type, *Established in Mayfield in 1912. You've got a hometown advantage!*

A shiver I couldn't explain ran over my skin as I took in the words. Mayfield was the nearest city to Lovell Rise, close enough that its suburbs rubbed up against the edges of town. I hesitated to call it *big*, since it wasn't exactly Manhattan, but it had about a hundred times our population. When urbanites drove out here to enjoy the apple orchards and corn fields or to take a paddle in the lake, a lot of them seemed to forget that this wasn't just an extension of their city.

But I guessed sometimes that worked in our favor, like when some hotshot business that'd been founded in Mayfield wanted to round up new employees. Recruitment campaigns and corporate expansion hadn't exactly been on my radar in middle school, so I wasn't super familiar with Thrivewell, but the name sent a jab of recognition through me, a certainty that I'd heard it before. And the jab came with another shiver, one that sent my skin outright crawling.

What had Thrivewell Enterprises ever done to me? I had no memory of being bitten as a child by a dog sporting the Thrivewell logo, having my Halloween candy stolen by a jerk shouting, "Long live Thrivewell!", or anything else that could have resulted in deep, unresolved trauma. Maybe there wasn't anything all that deep about it, and it was just that I found the name pompously repetitive—was it possible to thrive *badly*?— to the point that even my body rejected it.

Several company reps in red-and-gray uniforms were handing out flyers and forms. A couple of them ushered students selected by uncertain criteria into little tent-like cubicles, I assumed to conduct impromptu interviews with the chosen few. As far as I could tell, everyone at Lovell Rise College was looking to get hired by these people.

Well, everyone except me. For now, I'd happily stick to my grocery-store stock-girl career where no one scrutinized my past all that closely, thank you.

I swiveled to head to class, wondering if I'd be the only one there—I thought I'd spotted a few professors in the crowd too, so even the teacher wasn't a guarantee —and a joyful-sounding *whoop* pealed out behind me. It was so unlike any sound I'd heard directed at me since I'd returned to town that I had no idea it was meant for me until the same voice called out, "Lily! There you are!"

The voice was... unnervingly familiar, and not least because wherever I was familiar with it from, I'd never heard it take on that cheerful tone before. And who the heck around here would be *happy* to see me?

With my nerves prickling on high alert, braced for whatever fresh hell the student body intended to rain down on me for simply existing, I turned around. Even if I couldn't avoid that hell, it was better to know what was coming so I could at least prepare.

When my gaze latched on to the figure pushing through the horde to reach me, my jaw dropped. It took me a second before I recovered enough to reel it back in.

Ansel Hunter was jostling past his peers to reach me. His eyes had lit up with an almost manically delighted gleam, and he was beaming from ear to ear. Not his typical broad but polished grin. This expression was so wildly gleeful I'd have believed he was genuinely ecstatic to see me... if he hadn't been *him*.

My first instinct was to turn tail and run like a rabbit in the sights of a fox. My dignity went halfsies with my sense of self-preservation, and I hurried away at a brisk walk.

Unfortunately, Ansel walked brisker. Actually, he ran me down like he'd been waiting his whole life just to have this conversation.

"Lily!" he exclaimed again, grabbing my arm as he caught up with me. He waved a half-eaten croissant with his other. "Have you had one of these here? They're fucking amazing. I swear I've never eaten anything this good in my life. Of course, it has been a while... You want a bite?"

He hadn't squeezed my arm hard, but my pulse lurched before he'd gotten through his second sentence. I wrenched myself away automatically, whirling around. "What? No. What do you want?" I asked, my voice firm but as even as I could keep it. What the hell had gotten into the guy?

Ansel blinked at me, still smiling away, no hint of animosity in his expression. Without his usual perpetual haughtiness and the cruel glint in his hazel eyes, which were shining now like autumn sunlight, he almost looked like a different person. I found myself studying him to confirm that it really was my former classmate and not just his evil twin… or, well, I guessed his *good* twin in this particular case.

"We've been looking for you," he said, with no indication of who 'we' was or why they'd have wanted to see me. He gulped down the rest of the croissant and spread his arms with a gesture toward himself. "Isn't this amazing? It'll be even better than old times."

Had Ansel taken a hard blow to the head? Or been snorting something he really shouldn't have? Because the only "old times" I had any memory of involved him smirking with his middle-school friends after calling me a weirdo. I'd agree that his current attitude was better than that, but it was a pretty low bar. I'd rather have chewed on nail clippings than go back to eighth grade.

"I don't know what you're talking about," I said. "Anyway, I have to get to class."

"But wait!" He sprang after me again, giving a very solid impression of an overgrown—and overenthusiastic—puppy. I had the impression he would have wrapped those well-muscled arms right around me if I hadn't dodged at the last second, leaving him simply holding them out beseechingly. "You don't understand. It's *me*. From the marsh. From before. I know you have to remember."

I definitely didn't remember ever seeing Ansel down by the marsh. He and his crowd had used to make fun of me for supposedly smelling like "swamp water."

"Look," I said, an edge I couldn't suppress creeping into my voice, "I don't know what kind of bizarro game you're playing here, but right now *you're* acting way more psycho than I ever have. Like I said, I'm going to class."

And maybe you should consider getting *a little class,* my inner snark added, just barely stifled.

I whirled away from him again, too bewildered to be paying full attention to where I was going, and my elbow smacked a guy who'd been walking past me with his gaze on the recruitment tables.

"Sorry," I said quickly, meaning to continue my getaway, but the second the guy laid eyes on me, those eyes narrowed.

"Eight years in a mental hospital, and they still didn't manage to teach you to keep your hands to yourself, you crazy cunt?" he snapped, patting himself down as if checking to see if I'd somehow picked his pockets with my elbow. Which would have made me some kind of genius thief more than a psychopath, but whatever, not worth mentioning.

I also restrained myself from correcting him that it was *seven* years, opening my mouth to instead repeat my hollow apology, but I didn't get the chance to do even that.

"What the fuck did you call her?" Ansel snarled, switching from exuberant puppy to rabid pitbull in an instant. He slammed his hand into the guy's throat and somehow lifted him right off his feet so the guy's sneakers dangled inches off the ground.

The guy gurgled and flailed, unable to answer the question, not that I expected he wanted to admit to what he'd said right now. People in the crowd near us turned to see what the commotion was, with a chorus of gasps and squeals of horror—and, let's be real, maybe a little excitement. I'd lost my breath and my voice entirely, my jaw hanging open so far you could have stuffed a bowling ball in there.

"That's what I thought," Ansel said, still in that feral tone, and tossed the guy aside like he was an inflatable dummy rather than an actual human being. The crowd parted, none of them wanting to face a collision, and he thumped to the ground in their midst, right on his sorry ass. And oh boy, did he look sorry.

A couple of bystanders, now that they were no longer in danger of being battered by his careening body, knelt by the groaning guy with murmurs of concern. Ansel's fingers had left angry red marks all across the guy's neck.

Ansel considered him with a huff and turned back to me, his smile springing back into place as if it and his fierce expression were opposite ends of a yoyo. "No one's ever going to talk to you like that again while we're around," he promised.

Again with this "we." Again with the acting like he had some kind of commitment to me instead of being a stuck-up bully. I couldn't wrap my head around any of this. It took all the effort I had in me just to collect my jaw again.

"I—I—" I stammered, and then I spotted two of the professors from the crowd weaving our way. Panic spiked through my veins.

If they saw me here in the middle of this, if people

started talking—dollars to donuts, it'd be spun into being all my fault, even though all I'd done was try to walk away. For fuck's sake, even Ansel being "nice" to me was getting me into trouble I didn't want.

"I'm sorry," I said quickly to the onlookers. "I had no idea he'd do that." Then I whirled on Ansel. "I don't know what's gotten into you or why you hurt that guy, but I never asked you to. All I want is for you to leave me alone."

"Yes," he said as if he hadn't heard me at all. "We should go off alone, away from these assholes."

What was it going to take to drive the point home?

I shook my head vehemently. "I want *you* to leave me alone. Stop talking to me, stop following me. Just… stop!"

The beaming grin faltered. Ansel started at me with such bewilderment that a twinge of guilt ran through my stomach despite myself. But I couldn't stay and find out what this craziness was all about. Not while I was trying so hard to convince everyone else that I *wasn't* crazy.

"But, Lily…" he said.

"No," I interrupted before he could figure out what else he was going to say. "Stay away from me." Then I marched off as quickly as my feet could carry me, wondering if there was any pill in the world that could take away the headache of confusion that'd started to pound in my temples.

six

Lily

My Sociology of the Family class went by totally normally, other than only half of the seats being filled. It was *so* normal that I almost convinced myself that the incident with Ansel had been a hallucination that I'd hopefully never repeat.

By the time I'd finished my second class of the day, my nerves had settled completely. I walked along the paved paths toward the main parking lot, the rasp of my shoes over the asphalt blending with the rattling of nearby tree branches in the wind into a subtle melody. I'd have been tempted to let myself sing with it if there hadn't been other people around.

I was just beginning to think I'd make it through

the rest of the day unscathed when I glanced across the parking lot and spotted Ansel staked out next to my car.

And not just Ansel. Like the worst kind of bad dream, standing next to him were the three other men who'd been competing for a top spot in my Worst Dickbrains at Lovell Rise College list: Mr. Grimes, my Juvenile Delinquency professor; Vincent Barnes, my peer advisor so reluctant you could have called him a peer adversary; and Zach something-or-other, who'd decided to step up the harassment from throwing words at me to hurling footballs.

I stopped in my tracks halfway across the lot with a good hundred feet still between me and them. Unfortunately, they'd already noticed me. All their heads turned my way from where they'd been clustered together as if in intense conversation. Although what this odd combination of people would have had to talk about for long, I couldn't imagine.

No, that wasn't true. Clearly they'd been talking about *me*—and whatever horrible plan they'd somehow decided to collaborate on to continue my massive unwelcoming party.

I blinked a few times as if I might have somehow been seeing things wrong. The four men were still standing there by my car, watching me. Ansel waved me over with the same apparent eagerness he'd shown at the recruitment rally. Zach cocked his head at a contemplative angle that didn't fit what I'd seen of the musclehead before at all.

There was no way this situation wasn't bad news.

54

The trouble was, I didn't have any good options. They were standing between me and my one way off of campus. Lovell Rise didn't have any public bus service. I guessed I could have walked the ten miles from the sprawling campus grounds to the other end of town, but I was hardly going to make it to my shift at the grocery store in less than an hour that way. Unless I grew wings on my feet, I'd get there just as I was supposed to be clocking out.

And that was assuming this bunch didn't come after me if I tried to make a hasty escape.

I wavered on my feet for several seconds longer, taking stock of my surroundings. There were a few other students drifting in and out of the parking lot. I was within screaming distance of the admin building. Surely if these asswipes decided to try to outright *murder* me, someone would step in on my behalf?

It was a little sad that I couldn't answer that question with any certainty, but I would put more faith in my fellow human beings than they'd shown me. Besides, that car might be a piece of junk, but it was *my* junker, and no bullies were going to take it away from me.

As I walked closer, my gaze flicked between the four men and the car behind them, scanning Fred for any signs of damage. As far as I could tell, all the tires were intact today. No cracks marked the windows or scratches marred the patchy finish—at least, no scratches big enough to stand out amid the marks and rust already dappling the frame.

They were cutting me off from my car, but they hadn't disabled it.

I halted again when I was about ten feet away, which felt like a safe-ish distance. By that point, Ansel was grinning his head off. Mr. Grimes was smiling too, in a self-assured way that felt weirdly warmer than his usual expressions—but then, I didn't think I'd ever seen him really smile before. Zach still had an unexpectedly incisive look on his face, as if he were a mad scientist eagerly analyzing me for some unknown purpose.

Vincent was the only one who didn't give off any enthusiasm at all, but even that felt out of character. He stood with his previously rigid posture a bit slouched, his hands slung carelessly in the pockets of his pressed slacks.

Every inch of my skin prickled with the sense that something was *very* wrong here. I mean, I'd pretty much figured that out when Ansel had gone into his buddy-buddy routine before, but I hadn't realized whatever disease he'd come down with was contagious.

Mr. Grimes stepped forward first, his gaze sweeping over me, avid and almost... heated? In a way that instantly made me twice as uncomfortable. "Fuck, it's good to be able to actually see you like this," he said in a cocky voice that didn't sound like the professor at all. "Properly, I mean—with *eyes*."

Who with the what now? I was starting to think Ansel really had caught and spread some kind of deadly illness, maybe of the brain-eating parasite variety. Even my inner voice couldn't come up with an appropriate snarky remark. It just gaped like I was holding myself back from doing on the outside.

"Of course this is confusing," Zach spoke up in a calmly matter-of-fact tone that would have fit the professor a lot better than the jock. "I promise you'll get used to it. It was the only way we could come back—it's pretty much a miracle we managed even this." He looked down at his body with a sharp little smile, as if awed by himself.

Picturing animals on their heads or throwing snark at them in *my* head wasn't going to make this scenario any more tolerable. "I have no idea what either of you are talking about," I said. "I don't know if this is a very convoluted joke or if you've actually gone off the deep end, but I'd rather not be a part of it either way. I just want to get to my car and go to work."

Ansel let out a huff that managed to sound cheerful and turned to the others. "We can't let her keep working at that drudge of a job. She deserves better. We've all got some money, don't we? I mean, *they* did, and now it's ours." His grin widened. "Which means it should be Lily's too."

"Definitely," Mr. Grimes said without a hint of irony. He swiveled around to consider Fred. "And a new car. We can do *way* better than this. Some of these new models... I'd like to give this baby a ride." He ambled a little farther to skim his fingers over the hood of a Mazda that was nice enough but didn't look all that special to me. Then his gaze settled on a motorcycle parked in the next aisle. "And I'm going to get the best bike they've dreamed up while we were gone."

I opened my mouth and closed it again, grappling for the right words to respond. Now they were planning out my life, even offering to buy me a car if I was understanding properly? My head was spinning so hard it was a wonder it didn't fly right off my neck.

"I'm fine with both my car and my job," I said firmly. "They let me get done what I need to get done. And I sure as hell wouldn't come to any of you asking for handouts."

Mr. Grimes turned back toward me. "You don't have to ask. This is why we're here. All the jackasses around here are pissing on you, so you'd better believe we're going to do whatever we can to make up for that... and make them pay." His smirk after that statement was downright evil.

My inner voice finally woke from its stunned stupor enough to sputter, *But... you all were some of the biggest jackasses of them all! Maybe deal with yourselves first?*

"Please," I said out loud, holding up my hands. "Don't go after anyone on my behalf. Like I said, I don't want anything to do with this. Why can't you leave me alone so I can just live my life?"

"Don't you see?" Ansel said, bounding over to me like he had on the field. He swung his arms as if to grab me in a hug but dropped them when I jerked out of the way. Instead, he motioned to the other guys. "It's *us*. We came to take care of you."

Vincent finally spoke up, in a flat but unshakeable

voice. "It took longer than it should have. We wanted to be here sooner."

"I don't know what went down when you left town," Mr. Grimes put in, "but all these assholes trying to tear you down can go eat shit. Literally, if I have anything to say about it. You're our Lily, and no one's going to get away with beating up on you."

"I'm not 'your' fucking *anything*!" I burst out, unable to contain my frustration.

Mr. Grimes raised his eyebrows. Ansel looked so startled I wanted to smack the surprise off his normally smug face.

Zach cleared his throat and raised his hands. "Guys, guys," he said in that same authoritative, almost condescending tone. "We've hardly even explained. We can't expect her to understand right off the bat."

He met my eyes, his bright gray-green irises strangely penetrating. "We're not who we look like. We dispatched the pricks who used to own these bodies and took them over for ourselves. I don't know if we ever managed to get across our names to you, but I'm Malachi—stick with Kai, thanks. Mr. Happy over here is Ruin, the sullen silent one is Jett, and of course this is our fearless leader, Lennox."

"Nox," Mr. Grimes corrected with a brief glower. He nodded to me. "Maybe you couldn't hear us anymore, but you've got to remember. We dragged you out of the marsh. We hung out with you for *years* until you went away. Did a hell of a lot better job of looking after you than that shithead stepdad of yours and your weakling mom just going along with whatever he said."

I hadn't thought my mind could whirl any more than it already was, but suddenly I was so dizzy I thought I might puke. How the hell did my professor know anything about my family life? And what did he mean about dragging me out of the marsh? This all sounded insane.

I pressed my hands over my ears as if I could block out everything they were saying. It wasn't the most dignified move ever, but it was either that or scream hysterically, so at least this route would draw fewer onlookers.

"Stop it," I said, my own words oddly muffled inside my skull. "I don't want to hear any more. This is crazy, and I'm not crazy. Please, just stop and let me go to my shift at the grocery store. I never did anything to any of you."

By the end of that little speech, my voice had gone ragged. Tears burned in the backs of my eyes.

The men looked at each other with expressions of utter bewilderment—and what I'd have sworn was concern. Ansel backed away, a hopeful light managing to shine through the misery on his face even now. "It'll be okay," he said. "We'll get it all sorted out, and it'll be just like before, only better."

"We're here for you, Lily," Vincent said, like it wasn't the total opposite of what he'd been telling me the last time I'd seen him.

Zach waved the others to the side. "I think she

needs some time to absorb it all. *We* could use some time to really get settled in and figure out what we've got to work with."

"But—" Mr. Grimes let out a sound like a growl of frustration and gave me an insistent look, as if he could make me react the way he wanted if he stared hard enough. When I didn't budge, he eased to the side with the others. "We aren't leaving you alone again. You'll see that."

The words should have sounded ominous, but something in his expression took away any trace of a threat. And they'd cleared the way to my car.

I hustled past them, fumbling for my keys. Naturally, a frog had chosen this moment to perch on the roof right by the windshield. I shooed it off as quickly as I could so it wouldn't get flying lessons when I drove off and threw myself into the driver's seat.

I half-expected the men to change their minds and move to stop me. Instead, they hung off to the side, just watching me go. I didn't give them any more chance to rethink their stance. Hitting the gas, I steered Fred toward the exit as fast as the stuttering engine would take me.

"What the fuck do you make of that, old boy?" I asked the car, disbelief and confusion still tangled up inside me.

Fred answered with only a gargling sound.

"No kidding," I muttered, and tried to breathe evenly through the rapid thudding of my heart.

I'd left them behind. I was okay. Whatever wacko stuff they'd been saying, it didn't matter now.

Other than the fact that they'd all but promised that this reprieve was only temporary. And I had no idea when or how I'd find myself dealing with them next.

SEVEN

Ruin

I wouldn't have thought anything could get me down now that Lily was back with us. I hadn't counted on how awful it'd be to have her more than ever before but not really have her at all.

"She was right here," I said, making a grabby motion in the space where she'd been standing in the parking lot. "Right in front of us. But she still didn't know us."

I felt as if I'd have known her anywhere, no matter what face she'd had on. But I guessed she'd never seen us wearing any face at all.

I spun toward the others with a rush of hope. "It'll just take a little while, right? When she understands who we are, she'll be ecstatic."

Kai rubbed his eyes. It was weird seeing him without his glasses, even though the guy he was currently inhabiting hadn't worn them. Glasses just went with Kai the same way paint went with Jett. He squinted for a second before focusing on me, as if the lack of glass panes bothered him too.

"I may have miscalculated slightly about how easily she'd recognize us in our new forms," he said. "She was obviously incredibly confused. I'm not sure… It's not as if we ever told her anything about who we were before. We just went along with her games and whatever she needed."

Nox's mouth tensed. "She's never seen us before. It's been years since she even heard us—and then it wasn't even clearly. What if she *has* forgotten all about us? Fuck!" He kicked at the tire of the Mazda he'd been admiring earlier.

"She couldn't have forgotten," I said with total certainty. "We just have to figure out a way to convince her that we're us."

Jett let out a low cough. "Not just that. She might not even believe we're *real*."

I furrowed my forehead. I was about to ask him what that was supposed to mean when Kai jumped in, always quick with the answers.

"As far as she knows, we were just whispers in the breeze, vague impressions of friends…" he said. "It *is* possible she never knew we were really there. She might think she made us up. Holy shit." He blinked and squeezed the bridge of his nose.

The thought of Lily not even knowing I existed—never having known it—made my stomach ache in a way I didn't like at all. I groped in my pockets and found the beef jerky someone had been handing out samples of. The first piece had been so satisfying I'd gone back for more.

I bit into it now, my senses sparking at the flood of spicy flavor. A lot of the students I'd seen chomping on the samples had started coughing and chugging whatever drinks they had within reach, but I grinned through the burn on my tongue. Anything that got my nerves singing was awesome in my book.

And I'd been extra hungry ever since I'd gotten into this dude's body, which maybe made sense since technically I hadn't eaten anything in about twenty years.

Nox scowled. The teacher he'd taken over didn't look all that much like his former self, but I could already see bits and pieces of the real him showing through. That squaring of his shoulders like he was about to go into battle, and the way his eyes flared with brutal determination. I'd follow our captain to the ends of the earth, because he got things done.

"We'll make her see. Whatever it is she needs to see, we'll get it straight for her." He shook his head. "It isn't her fault she's freaking out over this. After the way the pricks around here have been treating her because we didn't get here fast enough to stop them…" His lips pulled back from his clenched teeth with a growl.

"We're not letting any of *that* happen ever again," I

said, and grinned wider at the memory of the asshole I'd tossed out of her way on the field this afternoon. "That part is going to be fun."

Jett rolled his eyes, a gesture that made the narrow face he'd taken on look a little more like him. "They'll regret messing with her—that's for sure," he muttered, and glanced at the piece of jerky I was just popping into my mouth. "You got any more of that stuff? I'm starving."

"Sure!" I fished another piece out of my pocket and handed it over. I might have cleared out the rest of the sample container when the woman handing them out had been distracted. It'd seemed only fair when I'd gone without for two decades.

Kai chuckled. "You'd better be careful with that. Knowing Ruin's tastes, it'll ruin your tongue."

Jett wrinkled his nose. "I know what he's like. Some things don't change." He took a bit of the jerky and shuddered but kept chewing.

As usual, Kai answered the question we hadn't asked yet before it'd even totally formed in my head. "It's to be expected that our metabolism will be all over the place for at least the first little while. Ghostly energies mingling with the systems of a living body... The transition must take a certain amount of fuel... We should be prepared for unpredictable fluctuations in all bodily functions."

"Fucking fantastic," Jett grumbled, popping the rest of the strip into his mouth.

Nox stalked back and forth in the parking space

where Lily's car had been. "How long will we be dealing with that effect?"

Kai shrugged. "I don't know. It isn't as if *anyone* has ever done this before and written up a report about it. I'm just giving you my best speculation. Our physical manifestation might become more even-keel over time as we adjust to the new situation, or we might have minor oddities crop up for the rest of our, well, lives." A thin smile curved his lips.

Nox grunted. His gaze skimmed over the parking lot, occasionally resting covetously on the motorcycle he'd noticed. I had the feeling that if the owner turned up while we were here, they weren't going to own that bike for much longer. Nox was very good at making things his.

If he thought we could get through to Lily, then I'd assume he was right. He'd always led us well before. We weren't going to let her down ever again.

The idea that we'd let her down already by fading out of her life and taking too long to get back into it brought back my stomachache. I started gnawing on another piece of jerky to douse the discomfort.

Kai's head swiveled around. "Looks like we have company. Those are some of the idiots who were hanging around your boy, weren't they, Ruin?"

I followed his gaze, my spirits rising at the thought of more company. There was a certain energy in a crowd of people that I hadn't gotten to experience to full effect in as long as it'd been since I last had a square meal.

Even when the people in that crowd were mostly jackasses, I was all for it.

Three guys and a couple of girls were sauntering toward us. They did look familiar, although I'd seen so many new faces in the past week—and I hadn't really been focusing on any of them except Lily's and the biggest jerks'—that I couldn't have said for sure who these ones were. They definitely appeared to know *me*, or at least the guy who'd used to inhabit this body. They looked from me to the company I was keeping with puzzled frowns, and one of the guys motioned me over to them.

"Hey, Ansel," another called out.

Right, that was who they saw. What were they up to?

I ambled over to find out. Ansel's friends kept eyeing the guys behind me as if they were trying to read something on their foreheads that they couldn't quite make out. What was so fascinating about them?

"Hey," I said, smiling at them the way you do with friends. Ansel's buddies weren't necessarily all bad. He'd set an awfully bad example, which wasn't their fault.

"Ansel," one of the girls said in a simpering voice, and tilted her head coyly to one side so her thick brown hair swished over her shoulder. "We've been looking all over for you."

"Why are you hanging out with *them*?" one of the guys asked, peering at my bros again like I'd been consorting with green Martians or something.

"Nothing wrong with making new friends, right?" I

said, flashing a brighter grin as I laughed inwardly. I'd been friends with the guys behind me before this bunch were even born.

"Right…" another guy said in a skeptical tone. "I've been trying to text you for the last couple of hours. Peyton was too." He motioned to the girl with the swishy brown hair.

Oh! I touched my pocket where I could feel the sleek rectangle that was apparently Ansel's phone. It didn't look anything like the clunky plastic devices we'd used to shoot quick messages to each other in our lives before. I'd jabbed at it a little and then forgotten about it.

"Sorry," I said. "Didn't realize. What's going on?"

"We were just going to grab some burgers at Philmore's. You said this morning that you were dying for one."

That'd been another man who wasn't me, but I had the feeling it wouldn't go over well to tell them that. I was supposed to be covert and undercover here, using my new identity to my—and Lily's—advantage. I nodded as if I remembered, my mouth watering and my stomach grumbling at the thought of a thick, juicy burger.

I wouldn't *die* for one—been there, done that, not interested in repeating—but I'd happily live through that meal.

Of course, I had other responsibilities. But we could make a larger group outing of it, right? Maybe Kai could do some kind of research on these students that'd help us somehow.

"Right," I said. "Absolutely. I'll just see if the other guys want to come along—"

I started to motion to my bros, and all the faces in front of me stiffened. "What are you talking about?" the third guy said. "I mean, Zach's kind of okay, I guess, for a freshman, but that dweeb what's his name? And why the hell would you invite a professor along? Have you gone mental?"

"I think he must have," the second girl piped up. "I saw him talking with psycho girl at the recruitment rally. He seemed like he was trying to get cozy with her."

The brunette—Peyton—went even more rigid. The first guy sputtered a laugh. "Hey, don't have fun with her on your own. I bet she's got plenty of wildness to go around, if you know what I mean."

"Oh, yeah," the second guy said with a leering grin, and made a pumping gesture with his arms and hips. "They say don't put your dick in crazy, but I bet it's a real thrill while it lasts. You just don't stick around too long. Gotta use trash like that for the little bit she's worth—"

My vision hazed red. Every shred of jauntiness I'd been feeling seared away beneath a surge of rage.

It was Lily they were talking about. Our Lily—*my* Lily.

I didn't think, but that wasn't my strong point anyway. I just moved. My hand shot out like it had when the guy had cursed her out at the rally, but this time it closed into a fist and socked the last guy who'd spoken in the nose. Bone crunched; blood gushed over his chin and shirt like one of Jett's warped paintings.

The guy yelped and staggered backward, but I was already closing in on him. The whip of my other fist threw his head to the side. I stomped on his foot, kicked the other leg out from under him when he wobbled, and caught him in the gut with the toe of my sneakers as he tumbled to the ground. Then I slammed my heel down on one of the arms that'd formed his crude demonstration of what he wanted to do to my woman hard enough that another bone snapped.

He wasn't going to be pumping into anyone for a while.

I stood over him as he moaned and made a mess of the pavement, my lips pulled back in a fierce grin.

"What the *fuck*?" sputtered the other guy who'd joined in the taunting.

I swung around to face him, the rush of getting to put this new body to use washing through me like the best kind of high. Oh, I'd missed this. Stretching my muscles—and other people's—to their limits. Destroying anyone who fucked around where they shouldn't have fucking tried it.

"You want a taste too?" I jeered, my grin widening, daring him to try me.

The guy blanched. They were all staring at me like *I* was the alien now. Then they helped the bleeding guy onto his feet and scuttled away with him in a flurry of nervous murmurs.

I swiped the back of my hand across my mouth, triumph thumping through my veins. One step closer to crushing every one of Lily's enemies.

When I walked back to the others, Nox tipped his head to me approvingly. "They're all going to get what's coming to them. But we need to sort out ourselves and Lily first."

Yes, it didn't do Lily much good for us to fight for her if she thought we were still trying to mess with her. I shook out my limbs, adrenaline jangling through me followed by a roar of hunger. "I'm starving again."

"I could eat a fucking moose," Nox agreed. "Okay. You've all got at least a little money on you, right? Let's go out into town, get what we need to feel more like ourselves again, and chow down on some fuel. We meet up outside the hardware store at eight." He pulled his own phone, which looked like a slightly older version of mine, out of his back pocket and turned it around. "These things still show the time along with the million ways they're hardly phones anymore, don't they?"

"I think they can send messages too," Jett said. "If you can turn it all the way on." He shook his and jabbed at the screen, scowling at it.

I peered at mine, turning it upside down and then waving it back and forth. It felt way too light to hold half the things I'd heard people saying they were doing with theirs. Then I tapped the round button with my left thumb. The screen just jittered.

Kai let out a cry of victory and gestured to me. "Try your other thumb."

Ansel must have been right-handed, because pressing the button with that thumb did the trick. I found myself staring at a screen of a gazillion little icons laid over a bikini babe with duck lips shoving her tits toward my face. If that was the kind of girl Ansel was into, no wonder he couldn't appreciate Lily.

"Let's all get each other's phone numbers," Nox ordered. "We need a way to stay in touch. If... If you can figure out what your number even is. Who the hell thought these were an improvement over our old phones anyway? And they think Lily's the crazy one."

He blew out his breath. "We're going to get these working, and we're going to get Lily to see who we are. That's all there is to it."

eight

Lily

My car might have been a junker, but at least I'd coordinated it with the rest of my life. If there'd been such a thing as junker apartments, the one I was living in definitely qualified.

It was in a basement set so low in the ground that the few windows were more like peepholes. In September, it was already chilly down there, so I could just imagine how many blankets I needed to stock up on for the winter.

The "kitchen" consisted of a fridge that'd probably worked well in the '80s, a sink with a thick ring of rust around the drain, and a hot plate. I'd tried adding a microwave to the mix, but it'd blown a fuse every time I ran it for more than five seconds, which didn't let me heat up anything. So now I also had a way-too-expensive paperweight sitting on the floor next to the fridge.

I hadn't had the money to buy much in the way of furnishings yet, so other than the kitchen area, the only things in the boxy room that played a triple threat of living room and dining room as well were a wobbly glass dining table with a crack running down the middle that'd come with the place, a couple of splintery crates I was using as end tables, and a futon couch that sagged so bad in the middle you could feel the bumps in the cement floor through the cushions.

I did have the luxury of a separate bedroom, although it was only just big enough for a twin bed and the narrowest, tallest dresser I'd been able to find, which I'd swear was going to topple over and kill me in my sleep someday.

It was a place that was all *mine*, though, which I'd never had before, and that made it pretty special no matter how awful it was. It worked just fine for me, and I didn't plan on inviting company over.

Unfortunately, company decided to invite themselves.

I'd just finished a gourmet dinner of canned stew heated on the hot plate and eaten right out of the can when someone rapped on the door. It could have been my landlord stopping by, but after the day I'd had, my nerves jumped. I tramped over, wishing the door had an actual peephole on it.

"Who's there?" I asked, feeling like I'd entered a

knock-knock joke and hoping it turned out to be one that was actually funny.

"That's what we'd like to explain," said a voice it was hard to identify after it'd traveled through the door. "I promise you, we're only here to help."

That sounded an awful lot like the kinds of things four guys I definitely didn't want to talk to anymore had been saying just a few hours ago. "If it's the same bunch of you who swarmed me in the parking lot, I think you've said everything you could say."

"No, we haven't," a firmer voice replied. "You need to listen to this, Lily. It's a matter of life and death."

Not even that claim budged me, but then a third voice said, "It's a pretty pathetic lock. I could pick it in a few seconds."

"Are you serious?" I demanded.

"Give us a chance, and it'll make a lot more sense once you've heard the whole thing," the second guy, who I thought was Mr. Grimes, said.

How had they even found my address? I guessed in a town this small it wouldn't have been too hard to find someone who'd seen me heading home. I gritted my teeth, but under my trepidation, a tiny part of me itched with curiosity.

What the hell *was* going on with them? They hadn't tried to hurt me at all before—they hadn't even insulted me. What was the worst that could happen if I let them talk a little more? It might be more interesting than anything on TV.

"Okay, but you'd better explain fast," I said. I eased

open the door, planning on making them stand where they were while they told their story.

I hadn't counted on the momentum of four eager male bodies. The second the door swung aside, all four of them—Mr. Grimes, Ansel, Vincent, and Zach—barged right past me into the apartment.

I didn't protest, because I was too busy staring at them to form words.

It *was* the same four as this afternoon in the parking lot, but they'd all gotten makeovers. Mr. Grimes had styled his short hair up in little spikes, dyed black with crimson at the tips. Somehow his presence felt bigger, bulkier, than it had just a few hours ago.

The others had dyed their hair too. Ansel had gone for a vibrant fox-red. Vincent had turned his blond locks a deep plum and cut them so they flopped across his dark eyes instead of tucking behind his ears. Zach had only darkened his brown hair to a richer shade, but he was also sporting a pair of rectangular glasses that looked unexpectedly natural on his face. Maybe because that face seemed somehow leaner than before, just like Mr. Grimes had expanded.

Mr. Grimes was prowling around the room, frowning at everything he set eyes on. "*This* is how you're having to live? Hell, no."

I'd have said that he was welcome to offer me someplace better if I hadn't been afraid he'd take me up on that suggestion after the way they'd talked about my car and my job earlier.

"It's the best I could manage," I said stiffly. "I couldn't go home."

"Of course not. That fucking prick."

Wade, I guessed he meant after his comment about my stepdad before.

My attention was diverted by Vincent in his new weird combination of geek and goth. He was chugging from a can of cola in one hand and using the other to re-arrange the random assortment of objects on my tiny kitchen counter: saltshaker, pen, rubber band, scraps of paper, a bill I hadn't opened yet. When the elastic was dangling over the side of the shaker and the scraps were arranged in a triangle around the pen, he stepped back with a satisfied hum, as if he'd created a grand piece of art.

Oh-kay, then.

"I think it's kind of cozy," Ansel declared in his new role as The Most Optimistic Guy Alive. I was starting to think if I offered him a glass with only a dribble of water in the bottom, he'd still say it was half full. "And it's great that you have your own space."

That much was true, but it wasn't what I wanted to be discussing with these dudes anyway. I opened my mouth, and Zach jumped in with that new disturbing way he had of knowing what was running through my head.

"You want us to get on with explaining, obviously," he said.

I guessed that wasn't so hard to figure out. "Yeah," I said. "And not in here. I didn't say you could come in, in case you didn't notice. How about you start by getting out of my apartment?"

Mr. Grimes gave me an incredulous look, which I returned automatically, because it was so bizarre seeing my professor with this new punk hairdo. "We're not going anywhere. This isn't stuff for anyone else's ears anyway."

In a show of bravado, I pulled out my phone and waved it at them. "You can get out *now*, or I'll call the police. Trespassing is against the law, you know."

I wasn't sure if I really would have followed through on that threat. I had no idea if the police would arrest these guys or assume I was delusional in thinking I hadn't invited them in, since the local cops probably knew who I was too. Apparently some of the officers had been part of that horrible blank in my past. But I wanted the men to know that I wasn't going to just sit here and accept them stomping all over my boundaries.

In theory. In practice, Mr. Grimes snatched the phone out of my hand without missing a beat and shoved it into his own pocket. "No need to be calling anyone, least of all those idiots. Why don't you sit down?"

I set my hands on my hips. "Now you're stealing my property?"

He folded his arms over his chest. "I'll give it back when we're done here. You *need* to hear this, for your own good. So, are you going to sit on your own, or am I going to have to pick you up and put you on your ass myself?"

"Nox," Ansel said in a breezily chiding voice, and hustled over to slip his arm around me as if to guide me over more gently. I slipped his grasp with a flinch, but I sank onto one end of the futon.

Mr. Grimes had sounded like he'd meant his sort-of threat. I'd rather not test it out.

"Talk already," I said.

The guys gathered in a semi-circle in front of me. "Let's get one thing straight from the start," Mr. Grimes said. "We're *not* the guys who treated you like shit. They're gone. We kicked them to Kingdom Come and confiscated their bodies to put to better use." He grinned.

Yeah, this didn't sound any saner than the things they'd said before had. "What does that even mean? You're not making any sense."

Zach let out a breath with a rasp of frustration and pushed his new glasses up his nose. "We should start at the beginning. I assume you remember falling into the marsh at the end of your yard and nearly drowning when you were a little kid?"

I glowered at him, willing myself not to shudder as the memory rolled over me like the water had, shutting out the light and the warmth. "That's the kind of thing it'd be hard to forget. How exactly do *you* know about it?"

I'd never told anyone—hadn't even mentioned it to Mom when I'd gone in later that day. I hadn't figured she'd care. Marisol had only been two, so she would hardly have understood why I'd been shaken by the incident.

No, wait, it wasn't totally true that I'd never told anyone. It'd come up in therapy a few times at St. Elspeth's.

As I worked that out in my head, Zach nodded. "We know about it because we were there too. You *almost* drowned, but you didn't. Because you got a push toward shore. We encouraged you, told you to cough up the water, reassured you afterward."

Ansel dropped onto the futon on the other side of the dip, his face lit with hope. "You remember *that*, right?"

I did… but not the way they were talking about it. I eyed each of them one after the other. "I pulled myself out of the marsh—I made up voices in my head talking me through it." I hesitated, a hint of a blush coloring my cheeks at the fact that I was going to admit it, but clearly they already knew about my childhood pretend play. "I created imaginary friends who'd protect me. It's not that strange for a six-year-old."

It was a heck of a lot more strange that I'd still talked to those imaginary friends when I was thirteen, but my circumstances hadn't exactly been normal.

Ansel laughed. "You didn't create us. We were *there*. We heard you splashing and it woke us up, and after we helped you we wanted to stick around. Because you're special." He shot me a bright little smile that made my stomach wobble in an unexpected way.

I rubbed my forehead. "You're not making any

sense. No one was there. No one else ever saw those 'friends.'"

"Because we weren't properly visible. That's why we needed bodies." Mr. Grimes gestured to himself. "How else would we know about all this?"

I fixed my gaze on him. "Maybe you got into my files from the hospital somehow? Or someone overheard me talking with my imaginary friends when I was a kid and spread that info around now that I'm back in town with a target painted on my back? There are ways. Ways that make a lot more sense than *you* having been some invisible being."

"We were ghosts," Zach said matter-of-factly. "In some ways, we still are, just possessing new bodies."

"Ghosts," I repeated. My head was starting to ache again.

"We were dead," Vincent said shortly. "Some fuckers shot us down."

"And dumped us in the marsh," Mr. Grimes said, picking up the story. "A few years before you took your tumble. I guess we would have faded away completely if it wasn't for that. We wanted payback, but there hadn't been any coming. Kai hadn't come up with this fantastic strategy yet." He tapped his chest.

I leaned back on the futon. "Let me get this straight. You're telling me that you're ghosts. Someone killed you, and then you haunted me for most of my childhood. And now you've decided to take over new bodies so you can... hang out with me again?" Did they seriously expect me to believe that load of bull?

Apparently so. "Exactly!" Ansel said brightly, oblivious to the skepticism in my tone. He beamed at me. "Now you understand."

"Except we didn't come back just to 'hang out,'" Mr. Grimes said. "You *needed* us. All the shitheads around here were beating up on you, and we weren't going to stand back and let them get away with it."

Zach—who was also Kai?—clapped his hands together. "Exactly. We'll be protecting you from now on. Helping you however you need it."

They sounded earnest. I couldn't deny that. Whatever the hell was going on, I couldn't shake the sense that *they* bought into this shared delusion. But it was impossible, wasn't it?

No matter what was really going on with these guys, their approach to "helping" me had nearly screwed me over at least once already. The last thing I needed if I was going to prove I was on the straight and narrow was four crazy dudes following me around laying down their own violent kind of justice.

"Attacking people who are being assholes isn't going to help me," I said in the steeliest voice I could summon. "I came back because my sister needs *me*. My mom and stepdad won't let me see her. I have to prove that I've gotten better from… from what happened before, and that means I can't get into even a tiny shred of trouble. Why do you think I've been putting up with the crap everyone's been putting me through instead of snapping back at them?"

A puzzled hush fell over the group. Ansel cocked his head. "But they shouldn't be able to get away with it."

"I don't care! All I care about is getting to be a sister again, and that's not going to happen if you get me into trouble because everyone thinks I'm asking you to beat people up for me. The best thing you can do is back off and let me handle this my way."

Mr. Grimes's eyes had narrowed. "What *did* happen 'before'? Where have you been? What made them send you away?"

My pulse stuttered. I was weirdly both grateful and disappointed that they didn't know either. Admitting that I had no clue felt like a risky move. Even thinking about that fact made my gut twist.

"It doesn't matter," I said, standing up. "Shit went down, and now I have to deal with it. Now will you give me my phone back and leave? I heard you out. I got your story. It doesn't change anything. I still need you to leave me alone."

"Lily," Ansel said pleadingly.

I pointed to the door. "Out. Now. I'm tired, and this has been the craziest day in my entire life. And you still look a hell of a lot like four jerks who were pretty awful to me, whoever you really are. You wanted to help. I'm telling you how. Give me a break and let me show that I'm *not* some crazy, dangerous girl who hangs out with crazy, dangerous people."

The four of them exchanged a glance. Vincent threw back the rest of his cola and crushed the can in his fist. Mr. Grimes grimaced, but he nodded to me.

"We're going to do right by you," he said. "If that's what you want right now, then that's what we'll give you. But we *are* going to be here when you need more than that, and I don't think it's going to be very long before you do."

He handed my phone back to me and motioned to the others. They stalked out as quickly as they'd barreled in.

I shut the door behind them and shoved the deadbolt over, exhaling in a rush. They were gone, and they'd taken their delusions with them. I could pretend everything was normal again.

The apartment definitely didn't suddenly feel twice as lonely as it ever had before.

nine

Jett

It took a few tries before I found myself at the room that went with the key I'd found in the nerd's bag. The two small residence buildings looked like identical dreary blocks of brick, and each of their floors showed the same puke-green walls with a line of smog-gray doors. The only difference was how many steps I had to walk up. And for some reason they'd started with 0 on the first floor, so 2-14 was actually on the third floor, not the second.

I was going to guess that whoever had built this place wasn't great with design *or* math.

The room itself was even more depressing than Lily's apartment, which was saying a lot. The smog-gray extended over the interior walls, like I'd stepped into an exhaust pipe, and a faint whiff of BO hung in the air. The room was laid out with a twin bed and narrow desk crammed next to each other on either side with the sliding door to a closet just beyond the headboard. It only gave about five feet of space between the two sides. You could have been lying on one bed and given a high five to a guy on the other without getting off.

It suited me just fine that there *was* no other guy in the room at the moment. I shoved the neatly stacked piles of binders and textbooks off the desk I could tell was the nerd's with one sweep of my arm, not caring how they tumbled onto the bed for now, and grabbed one of the pieces of blank paper he had sitting in a tiered tray toward the back. One tier for lined, one for unlined, another for various writing instruments.

I'd have laughed at him for being such a dork if I hadn't appreciated his organization skills in this particular way. Making art on lined paper was like cutting cheese with a chainsaw.

Of course the doofus didn't have any paint—or pastels, or markers other than highlighters, or anything remotely decent for getting color and texture on the page. I grimaced at the offerings, wishing I'd tracked down an art store after I'd fixed my hair as well as I could and lifted a shirt that didn't make me feel like a total dweeb. But the itch to create jabbed at my gut too insistently for me to put it off.

Putting forms to paper had always been how I worked through the mess of ideas and emotions that so often cluttered my head. And I had a hell of a mess now, after our conversation with Lily.

Talking wasn't my thing, but Nox could usually make any order he gave stick, no matter who he was giving it to. Kai could talk circles around anyone arguing with him, and Ruin's perpetual good mood might be irritating, but it also tended to disarm people... sometimes with perfect timing for him to hit them where it hurt. But somehow none of them had been able to get through to her—to make her want us around the way she always had before.

Maybe there were other answers. Maybe there was something I just wasn't seeing. The best way to find it was to spill my guts and my brains onto the paper and take a look at what I ended up with.

I cracked open another can of cola and took a long chug, wishing I had some actual coke to lace it with. The sugar and caffeine combo sent a hum through my nerves, but I craved a stronger buzz. After so long without any real bodily sensations, I wanted to soak in every bit of sensation I could get. Even the pinch of hunger that kept rising up to gnaw at my stomach no matter how much I ate was a fucking miracle.

Then I got to work.

I snapped the nibs off three of the nerd's—now my —pens: one blue, one black, one red. Let me never again mock a brownnoser for his thoroughness. There were plenty of other things to mock anyway.

Dribbling ink from each on the paper, I smeared it with my other hand, letting instinct and the thrum of emotion whirling through me guide my fingers. I never *thought* about what I was making or how it'd look to anyone else. Art was pure feeling, and anyone who didn't get that could suck my balls.

Just as I started rubbing some of the blue and red together in a purplish haze, another key clicked in the dorm room door. A guy I assumed was the nerd's—now my, *shit*—roommate strolled in. From the corner of my eye, I saw him do a doubletake as he took in me, the paper I was working over, and the jumble of books on the bed.

"Vince?" he said in an incredulous tone. "What the hell are you *doing*? What's going on?"

I debated not answering since my name wasn't Vince anymore, but it was going to be hard to keep that up with this idiot standing two feet away from me spewing peanut breath all over me. I didn't know what he'd been eating, but he could have sent someone allergic to the hospital just by exhaling in their general vicinity.

I finished the last line of color that'd called to me and glanced up at the guy. He was a collection of shapes and colors: a tan circle topped with cinnamon brown hair, skinny blue body—okay, the blue was his shirt and jeans, not his skin—with brown lumps of loafers at the bottom.

My mind had always been in the habit of breaking people down into an impressionistic version of themselves, like they were walking Monet paintings, but since my death, I'd been veering all the way from impressionist to abstract. Roomie here looked more like a Picasso. If my brain kept heading in the same direction, it was only a matter of time before the whole world was a blur of Rothko rectangles.

Except my crew and Lily. I saw them, even the guys in their not-quite-right bodies, exactly as they were. They were the only ones who mattered.

"I'm painting," I said, since the dimwit apparently couldn't figure that out for himself.

The guy's eyes bugged out even more. You'd have thought he'd have heard of the concept back in kindergarten. "Painting?" he said in disbelief, and then shook his head. "And you dyed your hair? What's gotten into you, man? Don't tell me the stress is cracking you up."

"No stress," I said. Other than the effort it was taking not to jam one of these broken pens into his eyeball so he'd shut up. Actually, he'd probably get louder then, unless I shoved it in far enough that I'd then need to figure out hiding a body. I didn't have time for that right now. "Just wanted a change."

My roomie flopped onto his bed, still staring at me. "Well, whatever. Stop 'painting' so we can get to work on that proposal. We need to get it turned in by tomorrow."

"Proposal?" I asked, not that I cared. This prick was dampening my buzz. I brought the can of cola to my lips, but only a dribble seeped out. Maybe if I shoved it down his throat, he'd shut up?

Very soon, the dolt's eyes were going to pop right

out of their sockets. "The proposal!" he shouted. "For Thrivewell. Don't jerk me around like this. I know you want it just as bad as I do. If we get it right, the Gauntts might even look at it. They run the whole show—if we impress them, we have it made."

Most of that went in one of my ears and out the other, jumbling into little more than a bunch of hysterical jabbering. I shrugged and turned back to my painting. "I don't care about that anymore. Do whatever you want with it."

"*What?*" For a few seconds, the guy only sputtered incoherently. "We were in this together. I need your accounting expertise to get the numbers all lined up. You're joking, right?"

"Nope."

I narrowed my eyes at the picture. It wasn't speaking to me yet. The smears and smudges needed something more to bring them together.

Or maybe the chaos in me was just too much to ever make anything quite right.

I shoved that flicker of panic down and reached for one of the broken pens. There was one surefire way to spill enough on the page to bring it to life—and that was literally spilling some of my life there. Or what had been Vince's life, but he wasn't around to care about that now.

The broken plastic edge sliced through my skin with a stabbing pain. I closed my eyes, taking in the sensation and the flares of red and violet that shot with it through my nerves.

A fucking miracle, all right.

Then I brought my bleeding thumb to the paper. A streak here, a dabble there…

As the deeper scarlet brought the other colors into sharper relief, I was so fixated on the image in front of me that I didn't register my roommate's reaction. The next thing I knew, he'd sprung off the bed and grabbed my shoulder.

"What the fuck is up with you? Have you gone totally insane? Snap out of it, man!"

I swatted him off me, my teeth gritting at the interruption. "Who the hell asked you?"

"We've been working on this proposal all week! And now you're slicing up your hand and making freaky pictures and— You're having some kind of breakdown. You can't do this to me!"

"Write your own fucking proposal," I snapped at him, and brought my thumb back to the picture.

"You promised we were going in on it together, as a team. Look, I've got all the texts. You can't deny that. It's in writing—that's practically a contract."

He fished out his phone and tapped at the screen, which somehow activated the circuitry within those bizarre devices. What ever happened to buttons?

Then he thrust the shiny thing at me, its screen showing a bunch of blue and gray blobs, as if that was going to mean anything to me. "Look. Right here. Those are your words. You can't fucking—"

I'd show him what I could fucking or not fucking do. My blood-smeared hand shot out. I snatched the phone out of his waving hand and rammed it into the edge of my desk. Once, twice, three times.

The screen sputtered black. The glass had splintered into a spiderweb of shards. I admired the erratic pattern for a moment before tossing the thing back at the idiot. "Now it doesn't show anything."

"What the hell!? Vince, you totally broke it. I can't believe—"

"Believe it," I interrupted, losing my last bit of patience. "And also believe that if you don't shut up and leave me alone, it isn't the only thing that'll get broken."

I shot a glance over my shoulder, fixing my gaze on the blobs of vague color that were the nitwit's eyes. His jaw swung up and down for a few iterations without any sound coming out. The color drained from his face, taking it from tan to an ashy beige. A noise like a strangled groan finally worked its way out of him. Then he fled out into the hall.

Mission accomplished. Maybe next time he'd get the message faster. I licked my thumb to start the blood seeping again and added a few more streaks to the image on the paper before me.

A tingling of satisfaction crept up over me. Crossing my arms on the desk and leaning on my elbows, I peered down at the warped jumble of colors.

Yes. I could see it now. There was Lily, a fragile form in the middle of a swirling storm. She'd said she wanted to stay out of trouble, but there was so much of it blustering around her, trying to suck her down into it. How could she avoid getting pulled under?

She didn't want us with her right now? Fine. We could keep our distance *and* make sure everyone else who wanted a piece of her did too. And once she'd gotten the peace she needed, maybe she'd welcome us back with open arms.

The only question was, which of the assholes circling around her did we dispose of first?

ten

Lily

"Should they even let her in this class?" a girl seated behind me faux-whispered to her friend. "I mean, 'Deviance in the Modern World'? What if it sets her off on the crazy train again or something?"

"Maybe next time we shouldn't sit so close," her friend muttered back. "I heard she murdered half her family."

"*I* heard she ate someone's brains for breakfast."

I grimaced to myself and tuned out their voices as well as I could. Even if I had no idea what I'd actually done that'd gotten me shipped off to St. Elspeth's, I was one hundred percent sure it was neither of those things. For one, I had visual confirmation that all of my existing family members were fully in the world of the living. And I'd never had the slightest urge to chow on anyone's brain.

But the gossip mill ran best on the juiciest—and bloodiest—material it could get, so it was no surprise that those were the sorts of stories making the rounds. I doubted my classmates believed them either, or they wouldn't have sat within stabbing range to begin with.

I couldn't see them, but that didn't stop me from imagining a possum hopping from one of their heads to the other, making their hair increasingly messy as it went. One more crappy day, a few more idiotic comments. Eventually they had to get bored when I didn't fly into a psychotic rage, and then they'd find something else to blather about, right?

Unfortunately, some of my fellow students weren't content to stick to talking. I seemed to have gathered a small but adamant group of "fans" who were dedicated to making me crack whatever way they could… either because they were convinced I was going to go batshit sometime and they'd rather it was on their terms, or because they thought it'd be funny to see. Maybe it was a little of both. It was hard to tell.

But that was probably why I walked out of the lecture hall at the end of the class into a sudden deluge. A plastic fast-food cup bonked me in the head; chilly liquid laced with ice cubes splashed my face and trickled down my shirt. The culprits snickered somewhere to my left.

I swiped my hand across my eyes and mouth,

getting an unwilling taste—Mountain Dew, *ugh*—and didn't even glance backward. Why give them the satisfaction?

Good job putting that beverage out of its misery, my inner voice snarked as I strode onward. It was my last class of the day, so I could go right home and change. Whatever.

I'd just turned a corner in the path to veer around the admin building when my ears caught a distant yelp. It shouldn't have meant anything to me. The more social students were hollering or cackling or whooping about one thing or another all the time. But there was a distinct edge of pain to this sound even hearing it so faintly, and my experiences from the past few days had me immediately on red alert.

Reluctantly, I swiveled on my heel and marched back the way I'd come. I didn't see anything unusual near the doorway, but another noise of protest, this one mostly muffled, carried from around the side of the building. Crossing my arms over my damp shirt, I stalked around it—and found Vincent and Zach in the middle of some kind of bizarre game.

Zach was holding a guy I didn't recognize upside down by his ankles, swinging him back and forth. Vincent was whacking him from his hips down to his head with a large stick, like the guy was some kind of living pinata. From the force of his strikes, he might literally have been hoping to burst him right open.

The thumping of the smacks and the grunts emanating from the guy fused together in a bizarre harmony that made me start to sway instinctively. Then I caught myself and stiffened my posture, because I *wasn't* some kind of maniac.

The guy's cries were muffled because of the fast-food wrapper stuffed in his mouth. A fast-food wrapper with a logo I could just barely make out, the same one that'd been on the cup hurled at my head. Suddenly I didn't need any other explanation.

Zach chuckled and said, "Come on, you should be able to break a rib or two. Then we can work on his skull."

Vincent made a grumbling sound. "Can't I just stab him right through?"

My heart had sunk, but I forced myself to quickly clear my throat. "Let him go."

The two guys—the ones on their feet, not dangling in mid-air—jerked their heads around with vaguely guilty expressions. Although not guilty like they thought they shouldn't have been doing what they were doing, only like they'd screwed up by getting caught at it.

Zach raised his eyebrows at me, his glasses having slid down his nose during their game. "We're just dealing out some justice. You asked us to stay away from you, and we did."

Obeying the fucking letter of the law but not much else. And breaking who knew how many other laws in the process.

I waved at them haphazardly. "I don't want this

either. No justice on my behalf. Nothing for me at all. I thought I was pretty clear about that."

Vincent shrugged and looked down at his stick. "What if we just think it's fun?"

I glowered at him. "Then pick on someone who has nothing to do with me, please."

"Fine, fine," Zach muttered, and tossed their victim feet over head against the wall. As the guy lay there groaning, the—former?—jock shoved his glasses back up. "It's a good outlet for us too," he informed me in his matter-of-fact tone. "Our transition has left us with a lot of erratic energies."

Oh, right, their supposed transition from being dead to uninvited bodily hitchhikers. I shot him a skeptical look and gave my inner voice free rein. "Tell me you didn't just try to justify attempted murder on the basis that you needed a good workout."

Vincent had been pretty dour most of the time I'd seen him, but now a hint of a smile touched his lips. "If it's accurate…"

I let out my breath in a huff. My hair was still dripping Mountain Dew, and my shirt was getting sticky against my skin. I didn't have the bandwidth to deal with this extra brand of craziness on top of everything else.

"Whatever," I said. "Just find a new hobby that doesn't involve me in any way."

I hurried back toward the parking lot before I had to hear any more of their insanity. And before anyone else could stumble on the scene and think I'd had something to do with it instead of doing my best to prevent it.

When I reached my car, I flopped into the driver's seat and tipped over to rest my forehead against the steering wheel. My insides felt as if they'd bunched into one big knot.

This was all so ridiculous. Everything—the guys claiming to be who they said they were, the way half the student body was harassing me and the other half avoiding me like I really did eat brains for breakfast, me trying to keep a calm front in the face of all that...

Was it even worth it? Why didn't I just drive the fuck out of here and start a new life somewhere I'd never even been to before, like Timbuktu or Finland?

But even as I asked the question, my whole body resonated with the answer: Marisol. My little sister was the reason I'd come back, and so far I hadn't even gotten a glimpse of her except briefly from afar as she'd gotten into Wade's car. And even stealing that peek had been risky—I'd just needed to be sure she was really here and okay.

Of course, I wasn't actually sure about the second part of that statement yet. Just because she could walk around didn't mean she was *okay*.

Maybe I'd been playing it too safe, following Wade's rules when he was nothing to Marisol and me except the jerk Mom had married, letting my fears of what I didn't know I'd done stop me from reaching out to her directly.

I'd looked after Marisol her whole life—while I'd

been around. Until she was nine. What kind of sister was I if I couldn't look her in the face and ask her what I'd done wrong... and how I could make up for it?

Resolve congealed in my chest. It was time to try, if for no other reason than because I wasn't sure how much longer I could keep going the way things were without at least letting her know I was fighting for her.

Showing up drenched in sticky soda wasn't going to make the right impression, so I took a detour for a quick shower and change before I drove out to the high school that served the teens of Lovell Rise as well as a couple of neighboring small towns.

I had a half hour before classes got out, so I sat in Fred a few blocks away and rehearsed what I wanted to say in my head. The practice didn't help much, because I had no idea how Marisol was going to react to seeing me. She might fling herself at me in one of those epic hugs I'd used to savor. Or she might run in the other direction screaming. And there were a whole lot of other possibilities on the broad range in between those extremes.

By the time the final bell rang, my palms were sweaty. I got out of my car and nearly tripped over a frog that was hopping its slow and steady way along the sidewalk in the opposite direction.

"Where are you going?" I asked it. "Hot date?"

I'd swear it let out a faint croak in answer before hopping on.

I approached the high school on the opposite side of the street, both to be a little stealthy and so I could scan the kids emerging from the wide front doors more easily. I'd barely seen my sister in seven years, but I recognized her the instant she stepped outside.

The sun caught on her wavy blond hair, which had always been a richer golden shade than my pale flax. She had sections of it woven into narrow braids that swung amid the loose strands. She hustled down the front walk amid her peers with her head low and her hands gripped around the straps of her backpack, not making eye contact with anyone. No waving good-bye to friends, no shooting flirty glances at a crush.

My stomach knotted. She didn't look all that okay right now. She looked… a lot like I'd probably looked back in middle school. Except I'd at least had a few casual acquaintances I might have nodded to on my way out.

Marisol had always been more mellow and affable than I'd been, even when she was little. What had changed?

Had *I* done this to her?

That question stalled me in my tracks for long enough that I almost lost her. Rather than heading in my general direction to make the two-mile trek home, she veered left and then around the corner out of sight. I gave myself a shove forward and hurried after her.

I'd been counting on approaching her on one of the quiet residential streets between the school and our house. Instead, she was heading toward the small shopping strip a couple of blocks away. Hanging half a block back and still on the opposite side of the road, I debated my best course of action.

Maybe somewhere more public would be better? She could feel safer knowing that there were more people around if she felt like she needed to call for help... to save her from me.

The thought twisted me up even more inside, but I put on a fresh burst of speed to pull ahead of my sister. Then I crossed the street and doubled back, slowing my pace so that I didn't barge right into her.

Marisol still had her head low, but that didn't mean she wasn't taking in her surroundings. When she was a couple of storefronts away from me, her chin jerked up and her gaze caught mine. She froze in place, her eyes widening.

"Mare," I said. My voice came out in a croak like one of those damned frogs had taken up residence in my throat. I cleared it and tried again. "Hey. I just—I wanted to see you. I didn't know if Mom and Wade even told you I was back in town."

I tried to keep my posture as non-threatening as possible, although it was hard to decide how to do that when I'd never felt particularly threatening in the first place. Marisol didn't move an inch. I couldn't tell if she was even breathing.

"Lily?" she whispered.

I guessed I must have looked at least a little different than I had the last time she'd seen me. And it'd been a long time.

I nodded slowly, pushing my mouth into a careful

smile. "I'm home. I mean, kind of. Mom won't let me stay at the house." *Not that I'd have wanted to shack up with her and the dipshit again anyway*, my inner voice added. "She and Wade didn't want me to see you, but… you're my sister. You're the whole reason I came back here. I came as soon as the hospital would let me."

The mention of where I'd been for the last seven years made my chest clench up. I added quickly, "I don't —I can't remember what happened when they took me away. People have made it sound like you were there— like maybe I did something that hurt you. I know I'd never have meant to do that. I hope you know that too. Whatever happened, you can tell me, and I'll do whatever I can to prove it's never going to happen again."

A tiny crease had formed in Marisol's forehead, more like she was confused than nervous. But then her gaze darted from side to side, her shoulders tensing as she took in the pedestrians ambling by and the figures behind the store windows. She took a step back, still watching them rather than me.

My own forehead furrowed. She did seem scared, but… not of me. More like she was scared about who else might see her. See us?

Had Mom or Wade threatened her because she'd wanted to see me and they didn't agree? My hands clenched at my sides, and I forced them to relax before she could notice. The birthmark-like blotch on my arm started itching, as if it had secrets to spill. Too bad it couldn't speak.

"Please, just talk to me, Mare," I said quietly. "You know you could always count on me."

My sister drew in a shaky breath and yanked her gaze back to me. "You're all right? You're not, like, sick or something?"

Was that what they'd told her? I frowned. "No, I was never sick. The doctors just took a long time deciding that I had my head on straight. I've been totally cleared. One hundred percent sane." Although they might have revised that decision if they'd heard about the strange company I'd been inadvertently keeping lately.

"Oh." Marisol seemed to draw in on herself a little more with another flick of her eyes along the street.

"Who are you looking for?" I asked.

A little shudder ran through her. "I—no one. I just —I should go." She started to turn.

A bolt of panic shot through me. "No!" I forced my voice to soften. "Marisol, I just need to know what happened so I can make it right. *Were* you there? What did I do?"

She paused just long enough to catch my eye once more. The words tumbled out so fast they bled into each other. "You didn't hurt me. You didn't—I'm sorry."

She darted across the street and around another bend. My legs ached to run after her, but at the same moment, a police car cruised by along the street. My stance went rigid until it'd passed.

Marisol had said I hadn't hurt her. But I'd done something back then, something awful enough to get me locked away. If I chased her down, tried to force her to talk to me, that wouldn't make me look like any kind of model of stability.

I hadn't hurt her. But I couldn't help thinking after seeing her reaction that someone sure as hell had. Why had everyone talked as if I'd traumatized her somehow?

Suddenly I was sure of two things. The stories I'd been told weren't totally right... and my sister needed me in her life even more than I'd imagined. She needed my help.

I just had no idea with what or how to give it.

ELEVEN

Lily

Ultimately, talking with Marisol didn't really change anything about what I needed to do. It only made me ten times as determined to actually do it.

I had to be the most stable, sane, upstanding citizen Lovell Rise had ever seen, and when people stopped seeing me as a psycho, I could get some real answers. I could force Mom and Wade to let me have a proper conversation with my sister.

I just had to be sure they wouldn't have the slightest excuse to call the cops or the loony doctors to pick me up again.

I thought I'd get a break at work from the craziness

that'd been following me around. Mart's Supermarket was the one big grocery store in Lovell Rise, off on the outskirts of town where people ventured when the mom'n'pop corner stores wouldn't quite do the trick. The place felt as big as a football stadium and as sterile as a doctor's office, all off-white walls and polished steel shelving. The air was always a bit too chilly, people always talked in hushed voices because the high ceiling tended to echo, and everything that happened there was utterly mundane.

At least, that's how it'd used to be. When I arrived for my late afternoon shift an hour after I'd seen Marisol, Burt Bower—the manager—was waiting near the row of cash registers.

He beckoned to me with one of his fat fingers. "Lily, a quick word?"

Even as I followed him over to the cramped office next to the stock rooms at the back, I assumed he wanted to talk to me about some normal job consideration. He needed me to work an extra shift next week or to cut my hours a little. I was packing the cereal boxes too tightly or stacking the cans too high. Something like that.

Instead, the second we stepped into the office, he turned and said, "What's this I'm hearing about some trouble between you and the police?"

A finger of ice traced down my back. Who'd he been hearing about that *from*? It wouldn't look good if I asked that instead of answering his question, though.

"That was a long time ago," I said quickly, deciding

it was better not to mention that I didn't actually remember what the cops had done or why they'd been called in the first place. "I was only a kid—I had a bit of a breakdown. I didn't get in any legal trouble. I don't have a record." The job application hadn't required that I disclose mental health treatments or hospitalizations. I'd been able to put down the online high school degree I'd gotten while I was at St. Elspeth's, as well as my year in community college and summer internship, so I guessed my history had looked pretty normal.

The hospital hadn't *wanted* to give people an excuse to shun me when I'd returned to regular society. The only reason I'd run into problems at school was because of former classmates like Ansel spreading rumors. It hadn't seemed like anyone else in town cared all that much—if they even recalled—what'd happened seven years ago to some random teenager barely any of them had interacted with anyway.

But then, I didn't remember Burt being around back then. Maybe I just hadn't noticed him with typical teenage myopia, or maybe he was new to the area, so he couldn't have remembered anyway.

He was frowning, his doughy face dour. "I know there's no record. I called the police department to confirm. But it does raise some concerns. I hope I don't have to worry about you finding yourself in a questionable situation again."

I'd be able to guarantee that more easily if I had any fucking clue what the first "questionable situation" was, I muttered inwardly. Outside, I gave him my best placating smile. "I'm sure it won't be a problem. If there are any ways I can improve my work, just let me know."

Burt still looked uneasy, but he had to admit, "So far you've been doing just fine. Well, get on with your shift. It started five minutes ago."

Like it was my fault he'd dragged me over here for this conversation before I could get started. I managed not to roll my eyes at him and tried to lift my spirits by picturing a cat washing its ass on the rounded dome of his head. But as I hustled over to the stock room to pick up my first load, my stomach stayed knotted.

Who would have bothered to mention my past to the manager of the grocery store? I guessed it could have been anyone who'd found out at school and then noticed me working here. Trying to get me in trouble at my job was a huge step above harassing me at the college, though. Who had it in for me so much that they'd want to totally screw me over?

I'd have suspected Ansel, but he'd been the opposite of hostile since his sudden personality transplant. Unless that transplant had included a dose of multiple personality disorder? How the hell should I know what to think when he and his buddies were claiming to literally be ghosts possessing some of the biggest jerks at school?

It didn't matter. As long as I kept doing my job and keeping my nose clean, Burt and everyone else would have nothing real to complain about.

"That's right," I murmured to the jars of pickles I was adding to the shelf. "All in a nice row, pretty and shiny." Then I snapped my mouth shut. Getting caught talking to the merchandise wasn't going to win me any sanity points, even if it was a satisfying way of staving off boredom.

I focused on the clink and thunk of the bottles, cans, and boxes sliding into place. There was a beat to it when I got a rhythm going, something that could have gone well with a twang of country lyrics. Those lyrics had started composing themselves in the back of my head when the last voice I wanted to hear, no matter how cheerful it was, rang out from the other end of the aisle.

"Lily! You can help me with my shopping."

My head jerked up, my heart already sinking. Ansel was standing by the canned vegetables—if it was still Ansel behind that pretty boy face with his hair dyed red and his features somehow softer-looking every time I saw him.

I couldn't exactly run away from him now without abandoning my shift. Gritting my teeth, I shuffled closer to shove cans of diced tomatoes onto the shelf near him.

"What are you doing here?" I muttered under my breath. "I told you guys to stay away from me."

As usual, the new Ansel seemed totally oblivious to my trepidation. "I had no idea you'd be here," he said, as if my presence was the best surprise he'd ever gotten across all his birthdays and Christmases. "I'm just looking to stock up. Got quite the appetite these days. What've you got around here that's really spicy? Or sour, that might work too. Mmm." He licked his lips. Which were annoyingly delectable lips, now that he'd drawn my attention to them.

It didn't look like there'd be any budging him before he'd gotten what he was looking for, so I figured my best bet was fulfilling his demands ASAP. I glanced at the shelf of veggies. "I don't think you're going to find much here… unless you want to chug pickled jalapenos."

I'd meant that as a clear non-starter, but Ansel brightened up like a kid who'd been offered a trip to the ice cream store and snatched several jars off the shelf, chucking them into the plastic basket he'd slung over his arm. The last one, he popped open and took a swig of chopped peppers and pickle juice right there in the aisle.

My jaw went slack. At this rate, it was going to fall off its hinges permanently around these weirdos.

I half-expected smoke to start billowing out of Ansel's ears like in an old cartoon, but he just grinned even wider as he screwed the lid back on. "Perfect. What else have you got in here like that?"

"You know, you're supposed to *pay* for things before you start eating them," I grumbled, motioning him farther down the aisle.

"We make a point of paying for as little as possible," he replied in the same cheery voice. "The Man's already got enough money."

I stopped in my tracks. "If you shop and dash on

me, *I'm* the one who's going to get the blame, you know."

Ansel froze, his upbeat demeanor vanishing for just an instant. "I won't let that happen. I can cover these. Of course I wouldn't get you in trouble." His expression flashed back to a brilliant smile an instant later. "You never have to worry at all when we're around."

Past experience would indicate otherwise, my inner voice retorted.

I pointed him to the salsa jars, where he grabbed the ones labeled *Extra Hot*, and then the rows of various barbeque sauces. He popped open one with a ghost pepper warning and threw back a third of the bottle in one go. His eyes went briefly wide, and I'd swear a hint of a flame sputtered from his mouth along with his gleeful laugh. He did at least put the lid back on and stick it in his basket with the rest of his intended purchases.

"Why do you need my help finding stuff?" I asked quietly as I ushered him to the candy aisle. "How long ago did you supposedly die anyway? Didn't they have groceries back then?"

Ansel chuckled again. "It's only been about twenty years. Not that we could tell while we were in limbo, but now that we've been able to check the date, we know. A lot of the brands are different—there's tons of new products they didn't use to sell. I figure you can get me to the good stuff faster than I'll find it on my own. And so far that was right on the money." He beamed at me.

I sighed. "So glad to be of service."

My sarcasm went right over his head. "Then we're both happy," he said, and strode ahead of me with a bounce in his step to consider the rows of chip bags.

I still wasn't buying this whole undead thing, but it was possible that packaging and flavors had changed a fair bit in the past twenty years. It wasn't like I remembered what'd been on offer the year I was born. I motioned to the spicy nacho-flavored corn chips and salt-and-vinegar flavor potato chips, since he'd mentioned sour too. Ansel tossed in several bags of sour gummies, apparently unfazed by how heavy his basket must have been getting. Then I glanced over at the produce section.

"I mean, there's lemons," I said doubtfully.

"Right!" Ansel gave me a thumbs up and dashed over to scoop up a few handfuls of those.

Was he going to eat them on their own, like they were oranges or something? A shudder ran through me at the thought, but I guessed he could put whatever the hell he wanted in his mouth.

Feeling I'd completed my mission, I went back to the stock room to grab another cart. I'd just emerged when Ansel popped up seemingly out of nowhere, springing in front of me so abruptly a squeak slipped from my lips before I clamped them shut.

My glower had no effect on his good cheer. "I just wanted to say that I'm really happy we could spend a little time together like this," he said with that unshakeable smile. "You're getting used to us being back —that's fantastic."

I wouldn't have put it that way, but somehow I couldn't bring myself to go any farther to dampen his mood. "Well, go pay for that stuff," I said. "I've got to get back to my real job."

"Of course, of course." He gave me a joyful little wave and ambled off. To my relief, I saw him approach one of the cash registers. I wasn't going to get written up for aiding and abetting a shoplifter, at least.

And maybe Ansel's presence hadn't been so bad this once. He'd distracted me from my unsettling conversation with Burt. It might even have been comforting—just slightly—to have someone around for a little while who acted happy to be with me instead of like I was a loose cannon one spark away from exploding.

So I ended the shift in a little better mood than I started it off in. As I crossed the parking lot to my car in the far corner, where it was less likely to be noticed by the kinds of idiots who liked to write *Garbage bin* and *Tow this!* on it, I swung the frozen lasagna I'd bought for my dinner at my side and might even have smiled a tiny bit myself.

Then a convertible sped by on the street next to the parking lot, and the prick I barely had a chance to glance at in the passenger seat hollered, "Go back to the psycho ward, crazy cunt!" A mostly eaten carton of fries flew from his hand to smack into my chest, splattering my shirt—which I actually *liked*—with ketchup and grease.

Something in my mind went icily blank. I looked down at myself, not quite processing the mess plastered all over me.

The carton thumped to the ground. The convertible roared off. Footsteps pounded across the asphalt behind me.

"That fucker," Ansel snarled in a voice so different from the buoyant one he'd given me earlier that I did a double-take to make sure I hadn't mistaken someone else for him. But no, there was no mixing up that stark red hair and well-built body. Those didn't come in value packs.

He was glaring after the convertible, his hands clenched at his sides. He moved forward as if he was going to try to chase the damn thing down, but then his gaze darted to me, and his stance tensed even more. He looked me over.

"Did that asshole hurt you?" he demanded, his pale eyes flashing with searing fury.

A giggle that sounded hysterical even to my own ears tumbled out of me. "No. Not really. I'm just starting to wonder if I've somehow become a magnet that specifically attracts fast food, since I can't seem to go a day without getting some flung at me."

My chest was clenching up. As the humorless laugh died in my throat, the burn of tears abruptly seared in my eyes. I turned around and braced my hands against the side of the car, holding myself together as hard as I could.

I wasn't going to cry. It was just one more asshat being an asshat, someone who didn't know me at all. That jerkwad's opinion mattered less than a flea's fart. I wasn't going to let him or anyone else in this stupid town break me.

But it felt as if a crack were opening up inside me right now.

"Lily." I'd never heard my name said so tenderly. The next instant, Ansel was there beside me. He wrapped his muscular arms around me like he'd been trying to do since our encounter at the recruitment rally, and this time I didn't have the wherewithal to dodge. He hugged me gently but steadily, not minding that I didn't budge from the spot where I'd been standing.

"We're not going to let *anyone* hurt you," he said in a fierce whisper. "Not in any way. If I see that prick again—"

"No," I said through the lump in my throat. "I don't want *you* hurting anyone either."

"He fucking deserves it. First all those jackasses at the college, and now here where you work—they won't get away with this."

His words sunk in, and I realized that was the problem. Before, the harassment had all been at the college. Ansel—the old Ansel—and maybe a few of his friends had spread the word around about my supposed psychotic tendencies, but I'd been able to escape the jeers whenever I'd left campus.

What had just happened, both the convertible driver and Burt pulling me aside, meant the plague was spreading. People were starting to talk about me all through Lovell Rise.

No matter where I went, they'd be watching me, judging me. Evaluating whether every word I said and every move I made showed that I was on the edge of fracturing into insanity again.

And none of them had any more clue what I'd actually done than I did. The one person who definitely knew wouldn't talk to me about it. I was fucked to the moon and back.

A wave of despair rolled over me, threatening to pull me down into its hopeless undertow, and I clung to the one solid thing I had: Ansel. Or whoever he claimed to be. He was *here*, holding me close, murmuring reassurances by my car that I'd stopped really listening to.

I turned toward him, pressing my face into his chest, and his arms tightened around me. He stroked one hand over my hair.

"We've got you," he said. "We would have been there for you all along if we'd known where you were. Now that we're here with you properly, we're never letting anyone beat you down again."

My body gradually relaxed into his. As the wrenching emotions that'd threatened to overwhelm me dwindled in the warmth of his embrace, I became increasingly aware of the solid planes of muscle beneath the thin fabric of the shirt I was clutching. Of the way his bright, emphatic tenor hummed through my ears into my nerves, settling them.

And had Ansel always smelled this good? I didn't know if I'd ever gotten close enough to him to tell before. He was all sunny amber with a whiff of musk.

Something stirred inside me with a hitch of my pulse and a spike of heat that shot through my belly. When Ansel ran his fingers over my hair again, a tingle spread through my skin in their wake. My heart thumped a little harder, with a weird mix of anticipation and fear.

What was I thinking? What was I *feeling*? How could any part of me—?

I knew sexual attraction when it came over me. After all, I'd spent my teen years in a hospital, not a nunnery. I'd gotten away with makeout sessions and a brief hookup with a guy who'd done a quick stint at St. Elspeth's a couple of years ago, and had a short relationship with a classmate in the community college that'd been more friends-with-benefits than anything else... and not so much with the friends part.

I just hadn't expected to feel it now—with this guy —like this...

Another flare of longing rippled through me, hotter than I could ever remember experiencing before, at least not with someone who'd barely done more than hug me. Some part of me wanted to meld right into Ansel's body this very second.

And it seemed like it wasn't just me. Ansel swallowed audibly and eased back just a few inches so he could meet my gaze. A hungry light danced in his hazel eyes, tempered by a hint of confusion. His hand slipped over my hair to my cheek and rested there, his thumb teasing over my cheekbone in a way that made my pulse skip another beat. Then a new smile stretched his lips, this one softer and so sweet it made me ache to see it.

Deep down, I knew it was just for me. I wanted to fall right into the look on his face. I'd never thought he was so amazingly good-looking before, but like this...

"I forgot," he murmured in a tone full of awed exhilaration. "I forgot what it's like to have a woman in my arms. And you *are* a woman now, aren't you, Lily? I can't forget *that*."

I didn't want him to forget it—and at the same time, his words terrified me.

What the hell was I doing? This maniac had been going around thrashing anyone who said a harsh word to me and talking about coming back from the dead, and I was an inch away from mashing lips with him.

Now who was the insane one?

A flood of cold washed away the heat that had kindled in me. I jerked away from Ansel, a tremor running through my body that was desire and panic colliding.

"I have—I have to go home," I babbled, and scrambled for my keys.

Ansel didn't try to stop me as I dove into the driver's

seat. He just stood there and watched, close enough that I had to veer to the side to avoid running him over as I pulled out of the parking spot. I'd swear I felt his gaze on me even after I'd rounded the bend and left him and the lot behind.

I squirmed in my seat, trying and failing not to notice how damp my panties had gotten. These guys might be dangerous in ways I'd never even considered.

twelve

Nox

The worst part of being an official authority figure was that people expected you to actually go and be officially authoritative about things. To other people. On subjects you probably didn't care about, because you weren't really the guy they thought you were anyway.

It was a heavy burden, and I wasn't enjoying bearing it.

I'd shown up for today's lecture that Mr. Grimes was supposed to be giving because a secretary of something or other had called me specifically to remind me, and I'd been in such a low mood that I'd thought bossing around some dorks might improve my spirits. I was in a low mood because I'd just gotten back from visiting Gram's grave.

I hadn't even known she was in a grave until this morning.

Gram had been both mom and dad to me when my actual Mom and Dad had flaked out on us to run around getting stoned and funding their habit with petty crimes. She'd *always* been there, even though she barely had enough for herself. I'd sworn that I was going to set her up with a better life as soon as I really built a name for myself with the Skullbreakers: a new, nicer house, a fancy car like she'd always admired, takeout every day of the week…

But before I'd gotten a chance to do much of that, those fuckers who'd stormed our clubhouse had pumped me full of bullets and dumped me in the marsh. And while I'd been gone, Gram had passed on without me.

I hadn't been there for her, and now I wasn't being there for Lily either. I couldn't even get her to *let* me look after her.

This whole rising from the dead thing wasn't opening anywhere near as many doors as I'd been counting on. I'd have to chew Kai out about that the next time I saw him.

But for now, I was lecturing the dorks who were taking Mr. Grimes's class. Fine. If they wanted to learn something, I'd teach them a thing or ten. I'd bet I knew a billion times more about actual juvenile delinquency than the nitwit I'd possessed had anyway.

When the forty or so students had filtered into the room and taken their seats, I clambered onto the chair and then onto the desk, where I had the best vantage point of the entire room. Several eyebrows shot up, but everyone fell totally silent.

Ha. I was already better at commanding their attention than their former professor.

Lily wasn't here. I had the vague memory that it'd been a morning class when she'd had to deal with Mr. Grimes. This must be another section of the same course. Maybe another year? It could even have been another subject—I hadn't exactly committed the prof's schedule to memory. I didn't see how it really mattered.

I was nursing a ginger beer in one hand and chowing down on an apple fritter from the campus bakery with the other. If I didn't keep fueling myself every hour or so, it felt like little lightning bolts were going off inside my stomach. Before I'd experienced it, I might have thought that eating lightning would be cool, but I could now say it was very definitely not.

I popped the rest of the fritter into my mouth, chewed hard, chased the swallow with a swig of ginger beer, and peered over the rows of seats. "So. Juvenile delinquency. Why don't we switch things up? I've associated with all kinds of juvenile delinquents. I was a pretty awesome one myself. Ask me what you want to know, and I can tell you all kinds of shit that doorstop of a textbook won't cover."

A girl in the second row raised her hand tentatively. She was going to need to learn to buck up if she didn't want to get trampled in this world. I waved at her, and she said, even more timidly, "Sir... are you all right?"

I narrowed my eyes at her. "I'm completely fine. Better than ever. Do you have a problem with creative teaching strategies?"

She paled. "Um, no, not at all, I just wanted to make sure."

I glowered around the room. "Anyone else have a problem with me teaching this class however the hell I want to teach it? Speak up, and I'll demonstrate some juvenile delinquency on your asses right now."

Everyone stayed totally silent and rigid in their seats. Another score for me.

I paced from one side of the desk to the other, shoving back the taunting image of Gram's plain gravestone when it rose up in the back of my mind. "Doesn't anyone have anything to ask about the actual topic of the course? This is a rare opportunity for you to learn something real around here. But I guess you all prefer the neat and pretty version on paper, huh?"

A guy in the front row cleared his throat. "Well... what did you mean when you said you *were* a juvenile delinquent?"

I chuckled darkly. "I wouldn't have called myself that. But the cops sure would have. It's a dog-eat-dog world, right? And you've got to be the top dog if you want things to turn out in your favor. I took what I wanted when I wanted it, crushed anyone who got in my way, raised up the guys who'd have my back, and we had it made. Just about."

My mood abruptly soured even more. Those fucking pricks who'd blasted up our clubhouse and screwed up all our plans… I wasn't even sure which rival gang they'd belonged to. They hadn't bothered with introductions before they'd opened fire.

A girl at the back raised her hand and started talking before I'd even called on her. "Like… what kind of crimes are we talking about?"

I let out a snort. "Whatever did the trick. Robbery, extortion, gambling, blah, blah, blah. You want a list?"

"Is this some kind of joke?" a guy off to the side demanded.

I fixed my gaze on him. "Do I look like I'm joking?"

I hopped off the desk and strode right over to him. This body had felt too small when I'd first inhabited it, but with every passing hour, my spirit expanded its limits. Mr. Grimes had never packed this much muscle, that was for sure.

The idiot who'd shot off his mouth cowered in his seat. I swatted him across the head anyway. "Does that *feel* like a joke?"

"N-no, sir," he mumbled. I hoped he'd brought a change of pants, because he looked ready to wet the ones he had on.

"You can't go pushing us around!" another guy protested.

I spun around and stalked over to the twerp. Grabbed him by the front of his shirt and yanked him right out of his desk. Oh, yes, just a few workouts in my soul's new home, and all my old brawn was coming back.

I cocked my head and aimed a jagged smile at the guy. "Funny, it seems like I can." Then I shoved him back into his seat. He landed there with his mouth agape, looking like a total goon.

All at once, I was fed up. What was the point in trying to teach these idiots anything when they cared more about keeping their existence all nice and peaceful than finding out how the world really worked?

I marched back to the desk and swung my arm toward the door. "Okay, we're done for the day. I hope the next time I see you, you're ready to stop whining like a bunch of asslickers."

A few *very* hushed murmurs passed between the students as they hustled out, but no one dared to even look at me after my demonstration of who was boss. I set my hands on my hips, wishing I could feel happier about my success, and waited until the last of them had filed out. You didn't want to turn your back on anyone who might have it in for you, even if they were asslickers.

When I strode out of the lecture hall a minute later, two very stern and stodgy men were standing just outside. They both took a small step back in the wake of my exit, their postures stiffening as if they thought I might take a swing at them. Good. I would if they gave me a hard time.

"Leon," one of them said in a hesitant voice a lot like the girl who'd first spoken up in class. More twerps.

"We've had some… concerning reports about your recent behavior in class."

Had one of the dorks gone running off to the dean that quickly? Or maybe during class someone had been twitting or tick-tocking or whatever the hell it was kids did now on those tiny computer-cameras they still called "phones" for some ungodly reason. I hadn't seen anyone actually talking into one my entire time on campus.

Either way, my response was the same. I shrugged. "I'm trying out some new teaching methods. More of a hands-on approach. If they can't handle it, they probably shouldn't be gearing up to work with criminals, huh?"

The second man grimaced. His gaze lingered on my hair. The hairdresser I'd gone to had matched my old style almost perfectly, but this dude didn't look suitably impressed.

"Well, I suppose you might have a bit of a point there," he said. "But we do have policies about student and staff behavior, which include expectations of language and physical aggression… I'm sure you can understand that there are lines we need to draw, or the legal ramifications could be immense."

I felt like he could have said all that in half as many smaller words and he'd have sounded a lot less pompous. But from the looks of him, pompous was probably what he was going for.

I spread my arms. "You hired me to teach because of

my expertise or whatever. I'm teaching. Or at least trying to, if the kids get their heads out of their asses."

The first man coughed. "See that right there—throwing around that sort of inflammatory language—"

I rolled my eyes. "Are you serious? *Asses*? We've all got them, and a shitload of people around here *are* them, so I'm going to say it."

They both winced, possibly at "shitload." I'd better not pull out "motherfucker" or "cuntbugger," or they might have a joint heart attack.

Actually, maybe we'd all be better off if they did.

Before I could test that theory, the second man rubbed his mouth and said, "Yes, I see the problem is as severe as reported. I'm going to recommend that you take a leave of absence and talk to your doctor, perhaps about a referral to a psychologist?"

"Are you calling me fucking nuts?" I demanded, fixing him with a glare and stepping forward to loom on him.

"Uh, no, not exactly—only you seem like you could use a break from the stresses of your course load," he babbled. "We could discuss the details later. It'd be paid leave at least to start, I'm sure—"

The full meaning of what he was offering sank in. A grin spread across my face. "You're saying I'd get paid to *not* teach classes."

"Well, er, yes. Essentially. While you get some help."

I wasn't here to get help but to give it, but it'd be a heck a lot easier to look after Lily if I didn't have these academic twits breathing down my neck. I slapped the man on the shoulder. "You should have said so from the start. I'm in. Or out, I guess. Looking forward to not seeing you around!"

I set off down the hall with a bit more of a spring in my step, glad to have at least that one problem off my plate. It wasn't as if I could have kept on being Mr. Grimes the professor forever anyway. As soon as we got all the assholes off Lily's back, the Skullbreakers were going to have a grand reunion. I looked forward to seeing the whole town piss themselves then.

I'd just come outside when furtive voices caught my attention. A small cluster of students was standing off to the side, gesturing to each other like they'd been electrocuted with excitement.

"…stuffed her right in the trunk," one of them was saying.

I drew up short and sidled a little closer without glancing at them openly. My senses were already jangling, and for good reason, because the next thing I heard was, "She's *really* going to go psycho on them now."

"I think that's the idea. They're saying she's screwed with their friend's head, and maybe some other people too. Gotten them wrapped around her finger somehow. The one guy broke someone's *arm*. So they're going to prove how loony she really is."

My jaw clenched so hard I practically cracked my teeth. I barged over to the cluster and grabbed the guy who'd said the last bit by the shoulder. With one sharp heave, I sent him stumbling into the side of the building, barreling after him so I could pin him there the second his back hit the bricks.

"You're talking about Lily?" I growled.

The guy stared at me, his mouth gaping. "I—the girl they're saying is psycho. I don't remember her name."

"What the hell are you doing?" one of his friends barked, and I swung around just long enough to clock that guy in the face. He doubled over, clutching his bruised cheek. I didn't bother to tell him he'd look better with some color in it.

"Where did they take her?" I said, turning back to the guy at the wall. "*Who* took her?"

"I—I'm not sure—I—"

Fuck that stammering. I snatched one of his hands and squeezed his little finger between my forefinger and thumb. Some guys like to go for the big pain all the time, but if you have half a brain, you figure out that a whole bunch of little pains often gets the job done better. There's time to anticipate in between. Time to realize it's only getting worse and worse. And it saved me having to work any harder than a quick twist of my hand…

Snap. The bones in the guy's finger fractured. He yelped, all the color draining from his face. When he tried to jerk away from me, I slammed him back into the wall with my other hand on his chest. "You're staying right there until you tell me who has Lily and where they took her. Get talking!"

"I think—it was that guy named Adam or Aaron or

something—his friends are the ones who got pissed off. They didn't tell me anything about it."

Ansel. The fucking king of campus who'd started this whole mess. As if Ruin's revision to his personality hadn't been a stunning improvement.

I grasped the guy's ring finger and broke it with another swift flick. He hissed through his teeth, his eyes squeezing shut.

"They didn't tell you, but you heard anyway," I said. "Where. Did. They. Go?"

"They mentioned something about the docks," he spat out in a strangled voice. "That's all I know. I swear."

I believed him, but he'd also pissed me off taking so long to get to the point. So I broke his middle finger for good measure before I pushed away from him. I glared at him and the friends standing dumbstruck around him.

"No one touches or insults or even *thinks* anything about Lily Strom again," I informed them. "Or I can break a whole lot more than that. Any questions?"

Like good little students, they quickly shook their heads. My mouth pulled into a grim smirk. "Class dismissed."

As they dashed off, converging around their injured friend, I strode toward the staff parking lot where I'd left Mr. Grimes's car. I fished his phone out of my pocket at the same time, but it took almost the whole journey there before I found the right icon out of the million or so on the screen to get into the address book and find my crew's numbers.

"Kai," I snapped, getting ahold of him first. "Get the others. We're going out to the docks. Someone's got Lily."

"How the fuck— On it," Kai replied without hesitation.

In a just world, I'd have had a sweet bike to hop onto and roar down the street on. Instead, I was stuck with the professor's decade-old Nissan, which looked like a box on wheels, and not even a pretty box. I scowled at it as I unlocked it, swearing to myself that I'd trade it in for a proper ride the first chance I got. Then I was gunning the engine, nothing on my mind except for getting to the docks ASAP.

And oh boy, were the fuckers out there *not* going to be happy to see me.

thirteen

Lily

The car jerked to a halt, throwing me against the back of the trunk. I winced, grateful that I'd wrapped my arm around my head to cushion it. I'd tried banging and yelling for the first five minutes of the drive, but all I'd gotten was sore hands and an aching throat. Since then, I'd gone into defensive mode.

It wasn't the car's fault I'd been shoved in here anyway. I had nothing against it. If anyone was going to end up sore, I'd rather it was the dipshits who'd tossed me in here.

Assault. Abduction. Hopefully not too many more a-words to come. And they called *me* crazy?

A tiny bit of air filtered into the dark space of the

trunk, with enough of a marshy scent to tip me off that we were near the lake even before the lead dipshit swung the top open.

He glowered down at me with a hard-edged grin, two of his companions flanking him. I recognized them from Ansel's usual gaggle of friends. Or maybe it was more like a cult, given the lengths they were going to on his behalf.

At least, I assumed this had to do with Mr. Popular and his sudden personality transplant. I couldn't see them acting without his guidance otherwise.

Does your mother know you're offering up human sacrifices? my inner voice snarked, but my mouth stayed tightly shut. I didn't know how to play this situation yet —and as much as I was trying not to let it show, I was pretty freaked out. My heart was thudding double-time, and a cold sweat had broken out down my back. I couldn't even bring myself to imagine bizarre beasts frolicking on their heads.

These goons had literally tossed me in the trunk of their car and driven me to the outskirts of town with evil intentions in mind. I had no idea what to expect from them next. They were worried about me going on some kind of manic rampage while they were already in the middle of one.

The hypocrisy was intense around here.

"Out you come," the leader announced, and yanked me up by the arm so hard my shoulder banged the rim of the trunk. I stumbled out onto the gravel road, my legs wobbly after being cramped in that tight space for so long. His friends, including the fourth who'd just gotten out of the car, spun me around and pushed me toward the scene waiting up ahead.

They'd brought me to the docks. The sagging wooden structures arced along the shoreline and jutted over the murky water at the spot where the marshy coastline gave way to stony beach and open water.

Apparently, several decades ago, some mayor had built up this spot figuring it'd make for lovely family picnics and fishing excursions. But then acid rain had killed all the decent-sized fish and it'd turned out docks were easier to build than to maintain, so the whole project had turned into a decrepit mess that no one bothered with except bored teenagers and asshats like the guys around me.

And maybe the smell had something to do with it too. I kind of like the marshland scents in the marsh proper, all wild and seaweedy. Out here, I got the less pleasant notes of rotten fish—from the old fisherman's shack at the base of the dock area—and gasoline—from the boats that occasionally cruised by from farther down the lake. No watercraft hung around here except an old rowboat that had taken on so much water only an inch of the bow still protruded above the waterline like one last, plaintive cry for help.

There was no one *I* could call out to for help. The lake was still, no boats out on the water on this hazy fall day, no teenagers doing cannonballs into depths that really weren't deep enough for it or jumping across the gaps where boards had outright splintered away. Just me and the four stooges who'd dragged me here.

"You know, this is technically kidnapping," I found myself babbling as they prodded me toward the longest dock. "I'm not sure you've totally thought this through. If you figure I'm so dangerous, shouldn't you be staying away from me, not forcing me to hang out with you? I'm sure there are lots of other people who'd volunteer to keep you company if you're so lonely."

"Shut up," the leader snapped, and got out his phone. So did one of his friends. They held them up in a way that told me they'd started recording me. "You've already fucked up Ansel. We're staying here until you admit what you did to him or let loose all the crazy you've been pretending you're over. We know *something's* rotten in that head of yours."

Um, no, that would be the ancient fish guts over there, I thought but managed not to say out loud. Provoking them was seeming like less and less a good idea by the second.

I looked for a way to dash past them, but they kept in a close semi-circle, herding me up the dock. They all had at least fifty pounds and a several inches on me. Even if I managed to dodge around one of them, they'd tackle me in two seconds flat.

Could I make up some story about Ansel? Tell them he'd been bullying me so intently he'd tripped over his shoelaces and hit his head, so it was brain damage and really not my fault after all?

Somehow I didn't think they were going to buy

that.

The boards creaked under my feet. I had to tear my eyes away from my harassers to make sure I didn't step through one of the gaps or a crumbling plank on the verge of becoming one. Our march was starting to turn into a demented game of hopscotch.

One of the guys scooped a rusted can off the ground and hurled it at me. It glanced off my shoulder. Another snatched up a long stick and jabbed me with it.

I bit my tongue to keep the acidic remark I wanted to make inside. *You know what they say about guys who carry around big sticks. Overcompensating much?*

The guys kept herding me on until I was just a couple of steps from the end of the dock. The water lapped gently at the aged supports. It might have been a peaceful setting if not for the douche-nozzles penning me in.

"Come on," the leader said, waving his phone as his friend swung the stick at me again. "Are you going to dance for us, psycho girl? You're really just going to stand there and take it? We can dunk you right in the lake if that's what it takes to set you off."

I stared firmly at the cameras. "There's nothing to set off. There's nothing wrong with me, and I had nothing to do with whatever's going on with Ansel."

"Oh, yeah?" another guy said. "He's sure been hanging around you a lot lately. Talking about you. Attacking people over you. Breaking the *bones* of people who used to be his friends over you. Doesn't sound like that has nothing to do with you."

"Peyton says she saw you hanging all over him, getting him riled up," the third guy added.

I didn't have any idea who "Peyton" even was or why she was making up lies about me, but I was sure of one thing.

"I don't have any control over what he says or does," I retorted. "I thought you were all saying I'm crazy, not that I'm some kind of voodoo sorceress."

"But somehow this all started when you came into town, and now he's totally fixated on you," the leader shot back. "You've done *something*. Everything started going crazy the moment you got back into Lovell Rise. You don't belong at the college, and we want you out of here."

You're not really giving me much opportunity to leave, my inner voice said. I glanced down at the greenish water.

At the same moment, a frog leapt right out of it onto the edge of the dock. I looked at it, and it looked at me as if to say, *Where do we go from here?*

As if I knew.

An itch prickled from the mark on the underside of my arm. My chest started to constrict around an uncomfortable hum that spread up through my lungs. I dragged in a breath, trying to steady myself. I couldn't let these asswipes break me down.

What if I simply jumped into the water and swam away from them? I could paddle off into the reeds where they wouldn't be able to see me, wait them out until they got tired and went home. Of course, that could mean hours crouching in the muck and the wet in the autumn chill, probably getting hypothermia, and then walking all the way home as an ice cube in the dark.

Understandably, I hesitated.

Staying on the dock was seeming like a worse option by the second. The guy with the stick rammed it at my thigh. The other one who wasn't recording spat at me. He missed, the glob of his spit dropping to the boards by the toe of my sneakers, but I couldn't call that much of a win. The hum inside me expanded, my hands shaking.

Then a rumble sounded in the distance and quickly rose into a roar. Three cars came tearing up the gravel road, spewing pebbles and grit everywhere.

My tormenters' heads whipped around. The cars slammed to a halt around theirs, and four figures sprang out.

Mr. Grimes. Vincent. Zach. And my kidnappers' good buddy Ansel.

Relief and horror smacked into me together, choking me up. I couldn't tell whether I was happy to see them or twice as terrified as before. But I didn't have much time to debate the issue with myself.

My four self-proclaimed protectors didn't waste time hashing things out with words. They lunged at Ansel's friends with a whoop of a battle cry and a feral snarl. And then things really went crazy.

Vincent—scrawny, nerdy Vincent, who'd somehow gotten significantly less scrawny in the past few days—

slammed into the guy who'd spat at me with a one-two-three flurry of punches that left the guy's lip split and his eye swollen shut like he'd just gone through a four-hour torture session.

The guy wheeled around like he was thinking of escaping by jumping into the lake like I'd been considering a moment ago, and Vincent helped him along with a kick in the ass. He hit the water in a clumsy belly flop.

As that guy thrashed around in the water like a half-beached fish, groaning and muttering, Mr. Grimes let out a roar and slashed at the leader of the bunch with a handful of little barbed whips—old fishing lines he must have grabbed from near the fishing shack, I realized. The tiny rusty hooks caught on the guy's nose, forehead, and chin, and he shrieked like a little kid.

"Look what I caught," Mr. Grimes said with a broad grin. He took the opportunity to snatch the guy's phone, crack it over his knee, and shove it into its owner's mouth so far the guy gagged. Then he pushed him into the lake after his friend.

Beefy Zach had slimmed down since the football incident, but he still barreled into the other amateur documentarian without breaking a sweat. He heaved the guy right over his shoulder and snickered as he swung his opponent around so his head smacked into one of the dock posts. Grabbing the back of the stooge's jeans, he yanked them up so high the guy hissed through his teeth and folded them over the pointed top of the post to hang him there in an endless wedgie.

And Ansel, dear ol' Ansel who my kidnappers had been supposedly defending, let out a sound somewhere between a cackle and a growl as he bounded into the fray. He yanked the stick from the last guy's hands to ram it against the guy's throat. While the prick sputtered, Ansel kneed him in the back so hard his knees buckled. With a triumphant whoop, he brought the stick down on the guy's head hard enough to split it in half. Then he held the pieces as if considering stabbing them into his opponent's temples to turn him into some kind of grotesque reindeer.

I'd stood frozen at the end of the dock during that entire barrage of action. Abruptly, my voice broke from my throat. "No! Don't—don't *kill* them." I found I couldn't quite bring myself to care about anything that fell short of literal murder. But somewhere in the back of my mind, images of cop cars and the guys in handcuffs were flashing like a siren, and I... didn't want that.

Ansel glanced at me and hesitated.

"It'll just make everything worse," I added. "For *you*, not just for them."

Next to him, Zach sighed and sneered at the guy squirming on the post. He picked up the phone the dipshit had dropped, snapped a picture, and tapped the screen until there was the sound of the image soaring off. "I hope everyone on your Contacts list enjoys that," he said, tossing the device beneath the guy's feet.

Ansel settled for rapping the sticks on the guy's head

like he was performing a drum solo, only stopping when his former friend groaned.

"Got a headache?" he asked, smiling fiercely as he tossed the sticks aside. "You only have a *head* still because she asked. You'd better remember to show her nothing but gratitude for that from now on."

Mr. Grimes whistled and whirled a few more hooked lines in a circle by his hand, watching the asshats in the lake. "Should I see if I can hook some bully fish and hang them out to dry? We don't have to kill them ourselves. We can leave them on the verge and let nature take its course."

I didn't have any sympathy for my tormentors, but my stomach turned at the thought of ordering their deaths. "No. Just tell them to get out of here. You've hurt them plenty already."

One of the guys whimpered as if in agreement. Mr. Grimes gave a huff and glowered down at them. "If you're gone from my sight in ten seconds, I won't decide I'd rather listen to my gut than hers."

They splashed and staggered out of the water, bleeding and swaying. As they dashed for their car, the one sprawled on the dock lurched to his wedgied-companion. He hauled the guy down so abruptly they tumbled over together in a tangle of limbs that flailed like an overturned spider before they managed to scramble for dry land. Vincent gave one a boot to the butt to hurry him on his way.

The stooges were in such a hurry they collided with each other and tumbled over each other trying to dive into their vehicle like clowns into a car that shouldn't hold them. Then they were racing away with a cough of the exhaust.

A smile sprang across Ansel's face. He bobbed on his feet with a whoop of victory. "That felt *good*. Laying down the real law with those fuckers." He made a few hasty punches at the air.

Mr. Grimes's smile was grimmer but still satisfied. "They shouldn't have gotten their hands on Lily in the first place." He caught my gaze. "We're not leaving you alone like that again. I don't care what you have to say about it."

My legs trembled under me. I swiped my hand over my face, my throat so tight it took a moment for me to speak. "Is this really better? You think they're going to be *nicer* to me after you went to town on their asses?"

His eyebrows shot up. "You'd rather we let them keep thrashing you?"

My hand dropped to the spot where the stick had jabbed me the hardest. I was going to have a bruise. But all the same...

"They were looking for an excuse to say I'm trouble. Now they have one, don't they? They were upset in the first place because Ansel's been acting so weird. I... I'm glad they're gone, but when word gets around tomorrow..."

Oh, God, what was I going to be dealing with then? Would anyone believe me that I hadn't put these guys up to this fight somehow?

Mr. Grimes shook his head. "We're not backing

down. No way, no how. If they come at you again, then we make them pay even more. That's how it goes from now on."

"But—"

"No arguments. We tried your way, and they made you walk the fucking plank. Not one of those pricks is getting his hands on you ever again."

I inhaled, and the trembling spread through my whole body. I wanted to just get out of here, but the four of them were standing between me and the foot of the dock.

Mr. Grimes stepped up to me, and I was struck by how he'd changed too. He seemed taller now, and broader, and his chin seemed to have filled out into more of a square than a point. Between that and the spiky crimson-tipped hair, he barely passed for my professor at all.

He rested his hand on my shoulder, renewed fury burning in his dark blue eyes as he looked me over. "They did a number on you, but you're okay now. We're going to make sure you're okay. We're here for real, and no one's getting through us. I'm going to keep telling you that until you believe me."

I hugged myself. "I just want—I just wanted things to be normal."

He chuckled dryly and rubbed his hand up and down my arm. "You've never been normal. Normal's for losers. You're with us, Minnow, just like you're meant to be, and we can show you ten times better than any fucking *normal*."

Minnow. The nickname sank into my brain with a spike of adrenaline.

I stared at him. My voice came out in a whisper. "What did you just call me?"

Mr. Grimes—or the man who wasn't really Mr. Grimes anymore—grinned. "Minnow. Like old times, when you were a little thing splashing around in the marsh like you were going to learn to breathe water. Are you going to complain about *that* now? I guess I can come up with a more fitting one since you're not so little anymore."

No. It couldn't be.

I gaped at him. He... He knew. In therapy, I'd talked a little about the imaginary friends who'd occupied so much of my free time, but I'd never gotten into that much detail. I'd never told anyone—and it'd always been him talking to me when he called me that name, not the other way around, so no one could have overheard—*no one* could have known about that...

Except the guy who'd coined the nickname in the first place.

Swallowing hard, I studied every plane of his face, every angle of his body, as if I'd be able to recognize the hazy impressions of those ephemeral presences in this new manifestation. "It's... *How* did you know that?"

He squeezed my shoulder. "How could I forget? Technically we rose from the dead last week with Kai's little trick, but really *you* brought us back to life ages before that. If it wasn't for you, we'd have faded away into that numb nothingness. Fuck that."

"We all remember, Waterlily," Ansel said, taking a step closer. At the second familiar nickname, my heart stuttered.

Zach shrugged. "We've been trying to tell you all along, kid."

Vincent shot him a look. "She's not a kid anymore. But that doesn't mean she doesn't need us. She's our Lily." He shot me a hesitant smile. "Or maybe Lil when the mood is right."

My head was spinning. How could their crazy story be true? How could they be the formless figures who'd romped through my childhood games? How could my imaginary friends actually be the ghosts of a bunch of murdered guys? How could those ghosts have stolen totally new lives?

But either I'd hallucinated most of the past week… or any other explanation I could come up with was just as impossible.

They were here. My protectors, my friends, my voices in the dark. And however that'd happened, they'd made it more than clear that I wasn't getting rid of them. I wasn't even sure I'd want to anymore.

I couldn't run away from this insanity anymore.

I drew my spine up straighter and looked each of them in the face. "I think you'd better come back to my apartment, and I'll let you really explain this time."

What was the worst that could happen?

No, wait, after the day I'd just had, I didn't really want the answer to that.

fourteen

Lily

I f I'd thought having the guys around would somehow feel less weird now that I'd started to believe they were who they said they were—and not who they continued to kind of look like—I'd been wrong. It was still absolutely fucking bizarre.

They burst into the apartment like a storm of clashing air currents. Ansel bounded through the space, back to his now-typical cheerful energy, and stopped with a smile in front of the old boombox that I'd found in the apartment when I moved in. He flicked through the radio stations, evaluating one after another and shaking his head.

Vincent moved in his more languid way toward the futon. He sank into it on one side of the deadly dip and leaned forward to nudge the items I'd left on the crate that served as an end table next to him. For whatever reason, he seemed to think the novel I'd been reading belonged on top of my empty juice glass, and that the sociology textbook next to them should be tilted at a forty-five degree angle.

Mr. Grimes barreled through the kitchen-living-dining room like a human-shaped tank, his gaze sweeping this way and that as if he thought there might be more tormentors lurking under the table or behind the fridge. He even checked inside the microwave. I guessed I should be grateful he didn't comment on the bits of food splattered on the inside.

I was going to clean it, really! In all the free time I'd have approximately never from now.

Zach only took a few steps inside before stopping with a contemplative air that was starting to seem almost normal behind those new glasses. He narrowed his eyes, making a similar if less active scan of the room to what Mr. Grimes had.

"You haven't had anyone over since we were here," he said—an observation, not a question.

I gave him a baleful glance. "I don't exactly have a thrilling social life, in case you haven't noticed. I didn't even mean to have *you* guys over the first time."

"Fair," he said with a vaguely approving nod, as if I'd passed a test I hadn't known I was taking.

Ansel settled on a hard rock station spewing screeching guitars and thunderous drums into the room. At a hard look from Mr. Grimes, who I was gathering was the boss of the bunch just like he would have been if the other guys had been his students, he nudged the volume down. Then he wandered over to my fridge. He swung the door wide and peered in, his tongue coming out to flick over his lips.

The gesture brought back the image of his face so close to mine yesterday, his arms around me, his warmth and scent enveloping me. An equally uninvited flare of heat tingled through my belly.

He straightened up abruptly with an abashed look. "We shouldn't eat any of Lily's food. It's for her."

Vincent waved toward the door. "There's all that stuff in your car."

"Right!"

Ansel all but skipped out of the apartment and returned in a flash with his arms laden with bags of the spicy chips I'd pointed out to him yesterday. He handed one to each of the guys and then produced a lemon he'd also grabbed. Before my horrified eyes, he dug into it with his teeth to break the peel and then squeezed sour juice all over the contents of his chip bag.

That right there was the scariest thing I'd seen all day.

I managed not to grimace as he popped the first few chips into his mouth and chewed with a blissful expression, but I almost sprained my face with the effort. To divert myself, I sank down onto the futon opposite Vincent and swiped my hands back over my hair.

"Okay," I said. "This is all still really confusing to

me. And impossible-sounding. So can you start from the beginning and explain to me—slowly—who you are and what you're doing here?"

Maybe I shouldn't have been surprised that Zach took the lead when it came to giving explanations rather than orders. He spun one of the chairs at the table to face me and dropped into it.

"We were dead," he said. "Someone mowed us down in our clubhouse and dumped our bodies in the marsh—weighted down so they wouldn't float and be found."

"Your clubhouse," I repeated. "What kind of club? Why would anyone want to murder you?"

"We had a gang," Mr. Grimes put in. "*My* gang. The Skullbreakers. It must have been rivals who wanted our territory."

A gang. These were gangsters.

Somehow that realization didn't surprise me. The extreme violence I'd already seen them commit might have had something to do with that.

I did remember, from the muddled blur our past conversations had become in my memory—"You have names. I mean, obviously you do. But you're not really… the guys you took over or however exactly that worked."

Zach gave me a pleased little smile that warmed me more than was optimal. "That's right. Zach Oberly kicked the bucket when I claimed this body. I'm Malachi Quinto. But everyone calls me Kai, so it's probably better if you do too."

"Kai." I studied him for a long moment, as if I could mold the name to this face in my memory. It wasn't just his dyed hair that was a darker brown than before but his skin too, deepened from peachy pink to a more tan shade even though he couldn't have spent all that much time in the sun in the past few days.

Then I turned to Vincent, who was plowing through his bag of chips with a pensive expression. "And you're not really Vincent."

The guy who looked like Vincent shook his head. "Jett," he said tersely. "Jett Vandamme."

"Doesn't pack quite as much of a punch as that name would make you believe," Kai said, his smile turning a bit teasing.

Jett glowered at him and popped another chip into his mouth. I thought that name would stick in my head easily enough. With his new goth appearance, he looked more like a "Jett" anyway.

"I'm Ruin," not-really-Ansel said with a little wave and another cheery smile. "Ruin Wolfrum. My parents had strange taste in names."

Mr. Grimes cuffed him on the shoulder. "The dire, foreboding vibe fits him so well, doesn't it?" he said with sarcastic amusement, and fixed his dark gaze on me. "My name's Lennox, but that sounds like a dork, so we'll stick with Nox. Nox Savage. It's good to finally —*properly*—meet you after all this time."

Kai, Jett, Ruin, and Nox. The names sank in slowly, but they were only one small piece of the puzzle. "So, you were murdered and dumped in the marsh," I prompted. "About twenty years ago?"

Kai picked up the thread again. "Twenty-one, to be exact. We hung in there as spirits… I'm not sure how far gone we'd gotten when you came along. Time turns pretty hazy. The whole situation messes with your mental state."

Yeah, I could imagine death would have a way of doing that. From what I'd seen, un-dying hadn't exactly restored their mental states to anything resembling normal. But then, who knew what they'd been like in their original lives? Maybe they'd always been this bonkers.

Ruin grinned. "It was all a big fog. But then you crashed in and woke us up."

"We sensed another life slipping away nearby," Nox said. "I don't know if all spirits are sensitive or what. But you were drowning, and you were just an innocent little kid—and we all just knew we had to try to stop you from ending up like we were."

My throat constricted, thinking back to the pressure of the water closing in around me and the darkness that'd started to consume my mind as I'd run out of air. It'd been *their* voices back then—these four men. Like a faint echo in the back of my mind. *You can do it. Kick those feet, they're coming free. Just reach—reach!* Tiny nudges against my limbs, prodding me forward.

"We could manipulate the physical world a little with a lot of effort in that state," Kai went on. "We managed to untangle your ankles from the weeds that'd wrapped around them, gave you a push toward solid ground."

Ruin nodded. "You did the rest. We couldn't have dragged you out on our own. You were so strong—you *are* so strong."

I didn't feel it. Even my bones wobbled reliving that moment, understanding it in a totally different, unnerving way.

Unnerving, but their story rang utterly true, right down to my soul.

"And then you stuck around," I said, my voice coming out in a rasp.

Nox made a careless gesture with his hand. "Like Ruin said, you woke us up. You were the first thing that really brought us to life in years. It was a good feeling. We liked it, and we liked being around you. All your games kept us entertained, and of course we had to make sure you steered clear of any other dangerous situations."

"You talked to us like we were really there," Jett added.

"Looking out for you gave us mental and emotional stimulation, as well as a sense of purpose," Kai said in his matter-of-fact tone. "You grounded us in this world, and we wanted to be here."

"And you needed us like we needed you." Ruin's smile softened. "So strong but with so many people trying to pick away at that strength."

I couldn't argue with that assessment. They'd been a bigger part of my life than I'd ever wanted to admit to anyone when I hadn't known they were actual people. When I'd thought I was just clinging on to figments of my imagination to keep myself sane. As if that wasn't kind of insane on its own.

But the only truly insane part of this was the fact that they were real.

Nox frowned. "Then you disappeared. One day you just never came out to any of the usual spots, and we couldn't find you around the house… Are you going to tell us what happened, Lily?"

Shame washed over me, leaving my skin tight and hot. I felt like a hotdog left too long on a barbeque. "I—I don't actually know."

Kai's eyebrows leapt up. "What?"

My gaze dropped to my hands on my lap. "Yeah. I went back to the house one day, and something happened… Mom and Wade have made it sound like I traumatized my sister, but they've refused to give any details, like they can't bear to talk about it… and they—and she—were the only ones there. I think. It's just a big blank in my memory. I can see myself walking up to the house, and the next thing is waking up in the hospital."

I raised my head. "I was in a psych ward for most of the last seven years. I never did anything crazy there, so whatever I was going through when I was admitted, it *must* have been bad, or how could they have held on to me for so long? When I turned eighteen, they only just started letting me transition out of in-patient care, but it was a long time before they agreed I was stable enough to live completely on my own. As soon as that happened, I came right back here. I have to— You know what my mom and stepdad were like. Marisol's still stuck with them."

Nothing I'd done to her could be as bad as living with them on her own. If I'd even done anything at all.

"Those fuckers," Nox growled. "We can go right over there and knock some sense into that stepdad of yours. It'll have been a long time coming."

Panic flashed through me. "No. You can't just go beating up whoever you're pissed off at. They'll stick *you* in the psych ward—or in jail."

Kai shrugged. "We managed to avoid getting arrested for years in our lives before."

I gave him a skeptical look. "Somehow I have to believe that back then you were *slightly* more discreet than playing pinata with students in broad daylight on campus."

He cocked his head. "Our inhibitions may have dwindled with death. But we can still keep ahead of the cops. If you don't care about the law, it can rarely touch you."

"And our way works." Nox folded his arms over his chest in an authoritarian pose that brought back dissonant echoes of the man he'd possessed. "We're putting the fear into people, and they're figuring out not to mess with you. It's only been a slow start because you kept telling us to back off."

"And you listened so well," I muttered, but part of me unraveled with a sense of resignation. What was the point in continuing to argue with them about it? Was I *really* bothered by what they'd done to the jerks who'd hauled me across town in their trunk?

As long as I didn't do anything crazy myself, it didn't matter what stunts the guys pulled, did it? If people got scared and backed off, then there'd be less chance of me slipping up because of their pranks and harassment.

I wasn't sure if that line of thinking really made sense or I only wanted to believe it, but I was going to go with it either way.

"Okay," I said. "But no attacking Wade—no one in my family. I need to be the one who tackles them. You don't know them like I do."

Nox's frown deepened, but after a moment, he dipped his head. "All right. For now. If they come at you, though—"

"It's not going to happen," I said wearily. "They want to keep as far away from me as they can."

"We'll get your answers," Kai promised, his gray-green eyes sparking even brighter. "Unravel the mystery. You've got all of us working with you now."

I exhaled in a rush and sagged back against the futon's lumpy cushions. Was it possible it really would be easier with these guys around? Would they find some way to help me figure out what'd gone down seven years ago?

A pretty big part of me suspected my life was only getting more complicated, not less, but it was nice to dream.

As if he'd picked up on that thought, Jett reached

across the futon and twirled a lock of my hair between his fingers before letting it go. "You don't sing anymore," he said abruptly. "You used to—every day. Making up songs, singing your favorites. Why'd you stop?"

All of the guys waited for my answer intently. My throat closed up all over again.

"I just... it was something I mostly did for Marisol," I said quietly. "I mean, I'd sing on my own—or with you—too, but it was always the best when I could use it to get her smiling or even singing along. When I can't be around her... when I maybe even hurt her... it's felt wrong somehow."

None of the guys told me that my reasoning sounded stupid or that I was making too big a deal of it. Jett simply nodded.

Ruin came over behind the futon and brushed his fingers over the top of my head in a reassuring gesture. "We'll fix that too," he said, firm but eager.

I didn't share his optimistic outlook, but I wasn't going to put a damper on it right now, not when he was being so hopeful on my behalf.

I looked around the room. "So... what now? How did you see this working after you got me to believe who you are?"

The guys exchanged a glance. Nox focused on me. "We're going to stick close by. Make sure no one gets in your face or takes any jabs at you. Deal with anyone who tries. I don't think it'll take very long—most of the kids at that college have never had to deal with a *real* threat in their lives." His face split with a vicious grin that shouldn't have thrilled me... but did.

Please tell me my panties didn't just get wet, I begged myself. Myself pleaded the fifth.

He was my professor—but he wasn't. He was a gang leader—but he wasn't. He was a guy who'd flung rusty fishhooks into another guy's face—yeah, that one was definitely true.

He was also, with his new imposing presence and dark demeanor, undeniably hot.

And damn it, he wasn't the only one. They were actually all pretty easy on the eyes now that they'd mostly obliterated my associations with the men they'd used to be. In ways I definitely hadn't noticed or even been thinking about when I'd been a kid and they'd barely been real.

"If there's anything else you need from us, you just let us know," Ruin said, his gentle touch stirring up more little sparks of heat.

Kai tapped his lips. "It would be easiest if we could stay nearby at night as well as during the day. Our current accommodations aren't exactly ideal. I've got a roommate who seems to think that talking is an Olympic sport he's training for, but somehow never has anything remotely interesting to say."

"Oh, Lord, don't get me started on roommates," Jett grumbled.

"I'm not totally sure where this guy used to stay," Ruin announced. "I've been parking out past the college and sleeping in his car."

He said it without a hint of concern, but the words tugged at my heart all the same. These guys had literally come back from the dead—and for *me*.

I opened my mouth, closed it again, and decided I owed them. If not for that, since I'd never asked them to resurrect themselves, then for making sure *I* had hung on to any life at all fourteen years ago.

"You can crash here as long as you want," I said quickly, before I could regret the offer. "It's not super comfy—I'm keeping the bed, just to be clear—but there's the futon. It folds down into a big enough bed for two, if you can stand sharing. And I guess if you got sleeping bags or something, or air mattresses…" I eyed the floor, trying to figure out how they'd all fit.

Nox clapped his hands together. "We'll figure it out. And we'll bring our own food. We're not going to have you starving either." He motioned to Ruin. "Come on, you bottomless pit. Let's go out for supplies."

Jett got up too. "I'm going to grab a few things from Vincent's room before that doofus of a roommate messes with them."

Kai stole Jett's spot on the sofa and picked up my textbook. "I'm perfectly happy staying right here, thank you. Bring me back something comfy and something tasty. But not both in the same item."

Nox snorted and headed out with the others. Kai started flipping through the textbook so fast he couldn't have spent more than a couple of seconds on each page. I watched him for a minute before venturing, "What are you doing?"

"This is how fast I read," he replied. "Speedreading is a very useful skill for absorbing as much information as possible. The more I know, the more I can get done."

I wasn't sure I wanted to ask what kinds of things he'd generally gotten done in this gang of theirs. *The Skullbreakers*. After today's performance, I could see how they could have come up with that name.

A trickle of dread ran through my gut. What if I'd just made the worst decision of my life?

But it had to be better keeping these guys mostly contained in my apartment than having them running around interacting with all kinds of other people, right? Maybe I couldn't cage the chaos, but I could rein it in a little.

I looked at the coffee table and then the still-screeching radio, both of which I might have made a few wry remarks to on any other day. But I didn't have to talk to random objects now. If I wanted to start a conversation, I had actual people—the people I'd always been talking to before, without fully realizing it—right here with me.

A feather of a smile touched my lips, dulling the edges of my apprehension. I'd never really been alone when I was in Lovell Rise, and I still wasn't.

Now I just had to make it so Marisol could say the same.

fifteen

Ruin

The thin beam of sunlight that came through the tiny basement window managed to hit right on my closed eyelids. It poked right through into my brain and jabbed me out of sleep.

But I didn't mind. Waking up early gave me even more time to revel in the fact that I was waking up *here*, in Lily's home. Just a few feet from her bedroom door. I could even make out the hushed rasp of her sleeping breath through the gap where that door had drifted ajar. The latch didn't appear to work right.

Her smell permeated the whole space, lightly sweet with an aquatic tang, like wildflowers that'd been drifting down a river. I wanted to roll around in it and slather it all over me like a cologne.

We were here. Really here with her, in every possible way, not just as the phantoms we'd been before.

Well, not quite in *every* way. There was still a wall between me and her right now.

I peeled off the sleeping bag and got up, careful not to disturb my friends. Kai and Jett had grudgingly agreed to share the futon, where they were currently stretched out at opposite ends with at least two feet of empty space in between them. Nox had insisted on taking the other air mattress, which he'd laid out right by the front door as if he thought he might need to defend Lily from middle-of-the-night intruders.

Of course, who knew if we might after all? The pricks around here had gone way too far already. We couldn't be too prepared.

But for now, all was peaceful in the apartment. It might have been cramped and dingy, but it was Lily's, and that made the whole space brighter all on its own.

I eased the bedroom door wider open and slipped inside. That room was even more cramped. My knees brushed the side of her bed. Lily sprawled on her side facing the wall, her face angelic in sleep, her pale hair fanned across the pillow.

A swell of affection filled my chest. She'd been through so much, but she'd hung in there. She'd grown up from that quirky, lonely kid into a woman who was maybe still quirky but also tough as steel and fiercely determined beneath the "normal" front she was trying to keep up.

And she didn't have to be lonely anymore.

I couldn't just stand there looking at her, not with all those joyful emotions whirling inside me. I sank down onto the edge of the mattress and tucked myself against her with the blanket between us, looping my arm loosely around her waist and nestling my face against her hair. Even through the covers, her figure was soft and warm against mine. Her smell flooded my lungs.

Maybe the four of us lost souls had never gotten there the usual way, but I'd finally made it to heaven right now.

Lily adjusted her position in her sleep. Her muscles twitched as she must have registered my presence. Her body went rigid with a sharp inhalation.

"It's just me," I murmured, and loosened my embrace even more, ready to roll away if she pushed. As much as she'd accepted my hug outside the grocery store two days ago, before that she'd shied away from physical affection. I wanted her to feel how much I adored her, but only if she was enjoying the demonstration.

She stayed tensed for several seconds, but she didn't pull away from me. Gradually, her body relaxed, sinking into the bed and my arms. "Are you always this cuddly first thing in the morning?" she muttered in her softly husky voice.

"Only with people I like!" I declared, and nuzzled the back of her neck—gently, still careful not to overstep my welcome.

Lily snorted. "Somehow I don't think you spoon the other guys in bed. And I assume you like them."

I cocked my head, considering. "I *would* if they wouldn't punch me in the face. The guys aren't much for PDAs. But they're like brothers to me. I'd die for them. Of course I'd *hug* them. If they wanted." Every now and then, they did give in. First thing in the morning was definitely not the best time to try it, though.

Lily grumbled something inarticulate and doubtful before burrowing her head back into the pillow. The tiny movements of her body against mine stirred another sensation, one that was more than affection. One I hadn't felt in decades, because spirits didn't have skin that heated or dicks that hardened at the feel of a pretty woman's curves.

A flicker of the same desire had teased through me when I'd held Lily in the parking lot, but it was nothing compared to the fire that licked over me now. I'd forgotten how overwhelming this kind of hunger could be. How torturous it was but thrilling at the same time.

I couldn't remember exactly what lust had felt like all those years ago, but I wasn't sure it'd ever hit me quite as hard as this back when I'd had my original physical form to get all hot and bothered.

But then, no one had ever affected me like Lily in any way. She was woven right into my soul. And she was so much more now than she'd already become when I'd last been around her. She *was* a woman now...

She must have hungers like this too.

If we'd already had that kind of relationship, I might have tugged her ass against my rising cock and dipped my hand right between her legs to wake her up in a very different way. But I wasn't going to assume that she'd be hungry for *me* that way.

Words lodged in the base of my throat—*I love you. I want you.*—but I swallowed them down. Not now. I might be overflowing with happiness at being around her, but I wasn't so dizzy with it that I couldn't tell she was still getting used to the situation.

I couldn't resist pressing the softest of kisses to the crook of her neck. Lily's breath caught, and something in her scent changed just slightly in a way I didn't think I'd ever have been able to notice before. Maybe it was another one of those strange effects Kai talked about, from our spirits mingling with these new forms.

I liked it. It made my dick even harder. I kissed her an inch higher on her neck, stroking my thumb over her belly through the blanket.

"What are you doing?" she asked, her voice gone a bit rough.

"Making you feel good," I said, watching my breath stir the wisps of hair behind her ear. "I hope."

"And do you do *that* with everyone you like?"

My entire body stiffened up. I'd fooled around with plenty of girls when I'd been alive before—if they were up for it and so was I, why not?—but the idea of so much as *thinking* of touching any other woman like I was Lily right now made every nerve in me pang in refusal.

I hadn't had Lily back then, and I did now. I couldn't imagine getting friendly with anyone other than my own hand if she didn't want me. There wasn't room for any other woman in the life I had now. I wouldn't have this life at all if it wasn't for her.

"No," I said with absolute certainty. "No one but you. There never will be anyone else from now on. And I don't mean just for enjoying ourselves. You've got my whole heart."

Lily shifted away from me, but only so that she could roll over toward me. She peered into my eyes, her face so close now that it took my breath away. Her pale blue-green irises shimmered like the water in the lake at dawn, as if she'd always been a part of the marsh, as if she'd been meant to crash into it and our afterlives from the moment she was born.

"Am I really that special?" she asked.

I had to scoff at the question. "Of course. Even when we knew you before, you were all kinds of special."

At the slight lift of her eyebrows, I felt the need to convince her. I reached back in my mind to all the things that'd made our existence alongside her wonderful.

"You could find things to celebrate everywhere you went—in the trees, in the grass," I said. "Everything was an adventure with you. You could make me laugh—the things you'd notice, the way you'd talk about them... And you came back. Even after everything that happened here, how awful your parents were, you came back because you care so much. There aren't many people like that, you know."

Lily swallowed audibly, still holding my gaze. Her tongue darted out to wet her lips. "This is totally insane. You know that, right?"

I grinned at her. "But it's pretty fucking amazing too, isn't it?"

"Yeah, maybe it kind of is." And then she nudged forward and brushed her lips to mine.

Oh, hell, if that'd been heaven before, then I didn't have the words to know what to call this bliss.

I kissed her back, stroking my fingers over her scalp and into her hair, and she let out a little gasp that fanned the fire inside me into a full-out blaze. Still kissing her, because you couldn't have dragged me away from this delight with a bullet train, I tugged down the blanket with my other hand to reveal the thin T-shirt she'd slept in.

At first I only trailed my fingers up and down her bare arm while I got familiar with the taste and texture of her lips. But as she scooted closer to me, melding her mouth even hotter against mine, I couldn't resist tracing them across her chest over the subtle swell of her breasts.

Lily kissed me harder, her fingers curling into the shaggy strands of my hair. When I flicked my thumb over the nub of one nipple, she tugged hard enough to kindle sparks in my scalp. Her chest hitched with a whimper, and I knew I had to work even more of those perfect sounds out of her.

"My waterlily," I murmured against her skin,

nibbling her jaw, kissing my way down her neck. "My angelfish."

A giggle tumbled out of Lily at the old nicknames, cut off with another gasp when I rolled her nipple between my fingers. "Ruin," she said, her voice thick as honey now. I wished I could engrave that tone into my name.

"That's right, precious," I said, sliding up her shirt to bare her chest. "I'm gonna take care of you. You just keep telling me how much you're liking it."

I slicked my tongue over the nipple I'd been playing with, lapping up her watery wildflower scent. A soft moan escaped her.

My dick was hard as granite now. Maybe I'd get the chance to show her where I could take her on *that*. I sucked the peak of her breast right into my mouth, nipping the sensitive nub between my teeth—

And the door creaked wider open, with the growl of my boss's unmistakable voice. "Ruin," Nox said. "Get your ass out here."

Lily flinched. I pulled back quickly, tugging her shirt back down to cover her and giving her one last quick kiss on the mouth to show her nothing was wrong before turning to face Nox. He *was* my boss, and my friend and practically my brother, but a faintly defiant air came over me. I wasn't going to apologize for this.

Nox simply glared at me without saying anything. His gaze softened as it shifted to Lily. "Everything okay?"

When I glanced back, she was blushing so hard her pale skin had gone nearly as red as my hair. Her lips looked delectably tender from all our kissing.

"Yes," she said, with a hint of her own defiance. "And it might have gotten even better if you hadn't interrupted."

Nox huffed and ushered me out of the room, yanking the door shut behind him. Kai and Jett were just stretching into alertness on the futon. The boss walked me right over to the other end of the apartment.

"What the fuck was that about?" he demanded, keeping his voice low.

I gazed steadily back at him, the pleasure of my interlude with Lily thrumming through my veins, and smiled. "We were enjoying ourselves. I didn't see why I couldn't look after her *that* way too."

Nox's jaw worked. "Our first priority is keeping her safe. And making sure those assholes don't pull any more crap on her."

"I'm not going to get distracted from that mission."

"You'd better not," he grumbled, and sighed. "It seems like she wanted it too. So fine. But that's not— You shouldn't— We have to be careful with her. She's been through too much crap already."

My heart lurched. "Of course I wouldn't do anything she didn't want. She's our girl. Our woman." My lips curved back into a smile at my self-correction. And then another reason Nox might have been upset occurred to me. "I'm not trying to make her all mine. We're all with her. However she wants any of us."

The thought of her kissing any of the other guys sent a twinge of jealousy through me that quickly faded. I'd messed around with however many girls had made me happy back before. Why shouldn't Lily have as many guys as made *her* happy, if she decided to?

As long as they were the right guys and not some random assholes who wouldn't understand how precious she was.

Nox gave me a glower. "Good. You'd better remember that. Now why don't you make yourself useful and grab us some breakfast. Something extra nice for Lily too. All she's got right now is one sad box of cereal."

I offered him a salute and gave myself a quick onceover to make sure sleep and the make-out session hadn't wrinkled my jeans and tee too horribly. Then I popped in the earphones I'd gotten during my last shoplifting spree and set the phone that was now mine blaring a raucous metal tune as I headed out.

The constant assault of auditory sensation kept my stomach's grumbling at bay. I found a bakery I'd visited before, bought enough muffins and cinnamon rolls to feed an army—or four very hungry, recently resurrected ghosts and their gal—and didn't even mind running the card that said *Ansel Hunter* on it through the machine. You burned bridges if you dashed without paying on little stores where people would actually recognize you if you came in again, and anyway, it wasn't even my money.

I was just ambling back down the street when a

silver SUV pulled up to the curb just ahead of me and idled there. I just strode on by, rocking on my feet with the roar of the music.

Apparently I'd missed some cue I wasn't aware of. Suddenly a guy was leaping out of the SUV's passenger side and striding over to cut me off.

The sun shone off his bald head, and his eyes got all squinty while he said something I couldn't hear over the music with very emphatic motions of his mouth. Total dork.

I laughed and popped out one of the earbuds. "What?"

The man scowled. He didn't look old enough to be bald from hair loss, his eyebrows still bushy and brown. "I said, where have you been? You haven't reported in at the expected times. What, did you have one long hair appointment?"

He eyed my newly dyed hair with obvious disdain. I'd only been returning it to its proper color. Not that I gave a flying fuck what this idiot thought of me anyway.

I blinked at him. Whatever he wanted, it must have had something to do with the prick I'd ousted from this body and not me at all.

"I'm done with all that," I said breezily, which was the same excuse I'd given when a couple of teachers had asked why I hadn't shown up in class and when Ansel's old friends had badgered him about hanging out with them. It was an excellent catch-all explanation. "Sorry."

The man coughed and blocked me again when I

tried to walk around him. "That's not how this works, kid. You made a commitment."

I raised my hands innocently. "I'm not very good at keeping those. You'll have to find someone else. Have a nice life!"

This time when I made to brush past him, he grabbed my elbow. Bad idea.

I whirled, careful of my load of baked goods, and yanked my arm away from him only to swing it right back and wallop him in the throat.

Baldie doubled over, sputtering, and I strode off at twice the pace I'd used before. The sun was still shining brightly, I still had a bulging bag of breakfast delicacies, and Lily was waiting for me back at her apartment. But a shadow had slipped over my mood.

What the fuck had Ansel Hunter gotten himself mixed up in anyway? And how many bones was I going to have to break before I got *myself* out of it?

Oh, well. Breaking bones was kind of fun, really. They'd just better not bring their grievances around my woman.

sixteen

Lily

I didn't know when Kai had managed to go to a library, but somehow he'd borrowed a stack of news magazines as tall as my supposed end tables —magazines he was now flipping through so fast the pages made a whirring sound.

I flopped down on the other end of the re-folded futon with one of the few leftover cinnamon rolls from breakfast clutched in my hand. If it looked like I was afraid someone might try to snatch it from me, I kind of was. The guys had plowed through the spread Ruin had brought back like they hadn't eaten in years.

Which, okay, was sort of true. I guessed they had a lot of meals to make up for. But it'd been hard not to watch them for signs of impending explosion.

"When you're Pope Somebody the 16th, you've really got to wonder if they should put more names in circulation," Kai muttered to himself, dropping one magazine and reaching for the next.

"You know, everything in those you can find on the internet," I told the former gangster with glasses, who still kind of looked like Zach.

He made a scoffing sound. "The world wide web is a *mess* these days. Everything is trying to sell you something, or else trying to sell you on selling things. This is a much more straightforward way to catch up on what we've missed in the last two decades. I'll deal with the internet when I'm up to current events."

He said all that while flipping away. Apparently Kai could talk and speed-read at the same time.

He might have had a point about the internet. If I could have inhaled a book in five minutes flat, maybe I'd have spent more time at the library than on my clunky secondhand laptop. And Google mustn't have been much of a thing back when these guys had last been in the realm of the living. I took my ability to filter out the bullshit for granted.

"Seems like those weapons of mass destruction were as AWOL as we were," Kai murmured, and read on without missing a beat.

He definitely had some catching up to do on recent history. I stretched out my legs on the nearest box and nestled myself into the futon's cushions while I savored the iced pastry with its cinnamon zing. It was my one rare day with only one class late in the afternoon and no shift at the grocery store. I'd finished all my reading, and I didn't have any assignments due for the next few days. I could chill out for a few hours.

Chill out, and observe my new roommates in their new habitat. As Kai whipped through magazines, Jett had stationed himself at my rickety table. He'd brought back a paint set after he'd gone out with the others yesterday, and he was smearing some of the colors across a broad sheet of thick paper with his hands. Somehow he made it look a lot more elegant than a toddler fingerpainting, even though the motions were technically the same. I wasn't about to question his technique.

Nox and Ruin had gone out a couple of hours ago after a muttered conversation with each other. Well, Nox had been muttering and Ruin had been responding in typical bright whispers, like he even spoke sunshine. They'd been cagey when I'd asked where they were going, which made me suspect I didn't really want to know. If I wasn't there and I had no idea what they intended, then nothing they got up to could be blamed on me, right?

Thinking of Ruin—his pale eyes and the sweep of his blazing hair, the brush of his hands and mouth over me this morning—sent a quiver of heat through my belly. It was hard to even imagine him having been Ansel before. He owned that body now, and he'd owned mine pretty damn skillfully too.

I hadn't meant to start anything with him, but he'd been right there, talking to me like I'd hung the moon, and he'd made it clear *he* was game… Maybe it was crazy, but I deserved a little craziness after how hard I'd been working at being a picture of perfect sanity.

I just hoped I could keep that craziness contained. Living in the same small space as the guy who gave out hugs as freely as he did smiles could be a lot of temptation. And that was without getting into the other guys who'd staked out my apartment.

The more they settled into the forms they'd taken over, the more the traces of the men they'd used to be faded away. All I could see when I looked at Kai now was the analytical set of his jaw and the intensity in his eyes beneath the fall of his dark brown hair, nothing that said *Zach*. Unless I really searched for it, no Vincent showed through Jett's deep purple tufts and the ropey muscle that was filling out his arms.

I didn't know exactly what the guys had looked like before they'd died, but their spirits were clearly shifting their new physical presences to match their most essential qualities.

Then there was Nox. Lennox Savage. Something about the name sent another quiver through me that was both giddy and unsettled. Every time I saw him, the professor guise had fallen away more, brawn taking over the formerly mediocre build, his square jaw getting stronger.

He ruled this crew like he had when they'd been the Skullbreakers, and I suspected he had twice as much brutality in him as the rest of them. So why wasn't I outright scared of him?

Because he looked at me like the world began and ended with me, and I didn't have the slightest concern that he'd ever aim his brutality my way. If I was going to be scared for anyone, it was the people who came near me... and I was having more and more trouble summoning much worry for those dicksicles.

It was still kind of hard to believe these guys were for real at all. Four fearsome spirits who'd saved my life and stuck around for years just to watch over me? Considering that even my own mother hadn't cared how many marshes I fell in, I wouldn't exactly have expected to inspire that level of devotion.

As if summoned by my thoughts, my phone rang. Mom's number appeared on the screen.

I stared at the phone for a few seconds, my heart thudding. Mom hadn't reached out to me since I was back in town—hell, since I'd been admitted to St. Elspeth's, really. This could either be really good or really bad. It was possible she'd decided Marisol should have her big sister back in her life after all my being on my best behavior, right?

Kai and Jett had paused in their respective work to focus on me. I raised the phone tentatively to my ear. "Hello?"

"Lily! I can't believe—after everything we've said—you tracked down Marisol at her school?"

She had that tone I hated, all wispy and yet scathing at the same time, like she didn't know whether to bawl or snarl. My shoulders came up instinctively. "It wasn't exactly *tracking down*. There's only one high school. Everyone knows where it is."

"We told you clearly that you need to leave her alone. You've already put her through enough!"

With the guys' gazes on me, a sudden spurt of defiance seared through me. I'd been playing by my parents' rules as well as I could, and where had that gotten me? I wasn't going to sit here and be berated.

"*She* didn't seem to mind seeing me," I retorted. "You've never told me what it is I supposedly did to her. What horrible crime did I commit that no one's ever been able to explain anyway?"

Mom let out a sound somewhere between a cough and an indignant sputter. She'd learned the second part from Wade. "You're in no position to question our judgment. What Wade saw—the way you acted—we can't trust you around here and certainly not around Marisol ever again."

"Maybe if you'd tell me what exactly I did, I could accept that," I protested.

"I don't want to have an argument about how bad or not it was," she replied. "Stay away from your sister. Stay away from us. If I find out you've been harassing her again, we'll notify the police."

She hung up, leaving the dead air in my ear. I lowered the phone, my stomach twisting.

I hadn't been *harassing* Marisol… but Mom and Wade could definitely spin it that way.

The way she'd talked, it'd sounded like nothing I did was going to be good enough. I could graduate at the top of Lovell Rise College with commendations from my manager under my belt, and she'd still talk to me like a psychotic mental patient.

My hands balled on my lap. I'd been angry at Ansel for spreading the story and the other students—and professors—for running with it, but the worst betrayal by far was my own mother. The words she'd just thrown at me stung ten times more than anything hurled at me before. I'd rather have been stabbed by a stick and shoved off the docks.

"What was that?" Jett demanded, shoving back the chair. Blue and purple paint mottled his hands like the deepest of bruises.

"My mom," I said quickly. "She found out I talked to Marisol—just for a couple of minutes… She and Wade are pissed. They said they'd call the cops on me if I go near her again."

Kai took in my clenched hands, and something in his gray-green eyes hardened. "Are you sure we can't simply get rid of them?" he asked in his usual even tone that nevertheless left no doubt about what he meant by *get rid of.* Especially after he added, "We can make sure the bodies aren't found."

He spoke with so much certainty I shivered. I still didn't want to order anyone's death, although I didn't think that was an excuse that'd hold much weight with these guys. But besides that— "Wouldn't that just make things worse? Child services would probably take Marisol away, and I'd lose her completely."

Jett sucked a breath through his teeth. "If it wasn't for that, I'd go take care of them right fucking now."

I held up my hands. "No. No taking care of or getting rid of. I'll—I'll deal with them somehow. I haven't had much time to make a case for myself yet."

Kai made a skeptical sound but turned back to his magazines. A moment later, he was shaking his head incredulously. "They gave *Ant-Man* a movie before the freaking Black Panther?"

Jett sank into his chair and glowered at his painting as if it'd offended him. I swallowed the last of my cinnamon roll, but the sugar tasted like dust in my mouth.

The gloom of my conversation with Mom trailed after me all the way to class. There were no snappy remarks I could imagine or goofy images I could conjure that'd erase what she'd said. Or how forcefully she'd said it.

What if I was still delusional—delusional to think she'd ever give me a second chance?

Jett had insisted on coming along to campus with me, but he stayed on the lawn outside after I persuaded him that it'd raise more questions than would be helpful if he kept hanging around near lecture halls he wasn't meant to be at. I didn't think anything too horrible could happen while I was in the building. So I headed down the hall alone.

I was so lost in my thoughts about Mom—and trying to avoid thinking them—that I didn't pay attention to the footsteps around me. I didn't realize how closely I was being followed until I stumbled backward to dodge a frog that'd hopped into the middle of the hall of all places. My unsteady feet sent me bumping into a body right behind me.

"Watch where you're going. Walk much, klutz?"

I spun around and found myself faced with three girls. They all looked vaguely familiar, but the only one I was sure of was the slim girl in the middle with the cascade of chestnut-brown hair. As she peered down her arched nose at me, a flash of memory rose up—her hanging so close by Ansel he'd splashed her coffee onto me. I'd seen her with him before too, hadn't I?

She was carrying a bottle of water today rather than a coffee cup. Both of the other girls were too, like they'd decided to go for matching accessories.

The other two gave me looks of bored hostility while Ansel's fan drew her lips back in a sneer. "Oh, it's psycho girl. I guess we can't expect her to know where to put her feet when she's barely got her head on straight."

The girl on the left snickered. "Good one, Peyton."

Ah, so *this* was the Peyton who'd been making up new rumors about me, as if the shit already being talked hadn't been smelly enough. I couldn't summon even a flicker of surprise.

The girls were acting like they hadn't known who I was until I'd turned around. I couldn't help thinking it was an awfully big coincidence that they'd been sauntering along so close behind me if they *hadn't* been hoping for an opportunity like this.

"Sorry," I said briskly. I didn't have much patience

left to put up with their crap, and I didn't think telling them that messing with me might put them on a bunch of undead gangsters' shit list would do anything but reinforce their ideas about my sanity or lack thereof. "I'll stay out of your way." I swept my arm in a motion for them to go ahead of me.

Instead, they stepped a little closer, backing me up toward the wall. My pulse hiccupped. I could have hollered for Jett, and I'd bet he'd stayed close enough to hear me and come running. But then I'd be making even more of a scene over a few girls who were just looking to flash their claws around. I could fight some kinds of battles on my own.

Peyton waved her bottle at me aggressively enough that a little water spurted from the mouth and splashed my shirt. "You'd better stay away from Ansel from now on."

I should have said, *I haven't been anywhere near him*, which was sort of true, even if the guy wearing his body had been all over me this morning. Instead, the snappy response I'd usually have kept in slipped out. "Why, does he belong to you or something?"

Something flickered in the girl's eyes, a hint of pain followed by a hardening of determination, and that was enough of an answer. He didn't, but she wanted him to. "He doesn't belong to anybody," she announced, "even if you're trying to warp his mind with your craziness."

My teeth set on edge. "I'm pretty sure he makes his own decisions. Why don't you go tell *him* to stay away from me? I'm sure that'll go really well."

"Bitch," Peyton snapped, and my last nerve frayed. The unsettling hum that'd risen up inside me yesterday on the docks reverberated through my chest again, potent enough that my ears started to ring. My breath snagged in my throat.

And the entire contents of Peyton's water bottle leapt from its opening and splatted into her face.

"What the— You—" she spluttered, swiping the drips from her cheeks and eyes. Her mascara was already running down her cheeks, her lipstick smudging, like she was a watercolor painting someone had hung up before the colors were dry.

A giggle bubbled up inside me. "I didn't do anything!" I said, suppressing it. "I didn't touch it."

"You did something," she snarled, and hustled off toward the nearest washroom with her lackeys in tow.

Any sense of amusement drained away with her last words. The hum had quieted, but now my nerves were jangling in a totally different way.

I hadn't done anything on purpose. Maybe I really hadn't done anything at all. But water didn't fling itself out of its container on a whim. Something must have propelled it out.

And I had no idea what.

Fear prickled over my skin. There were too many things I didn't know, too much I didn't understand. I didn't need more to add to the list.

Hugging myself, I hurried the rest of the way to class.

SEVENTEEN

Lily

I woke up tucked against planes of taut muscle and knew from the warm, musky scent filling my nose that it was Ruin's sinewy arms wrapped around me. He was really making a habit of this sneaking into bed with me thing, even though I'd gotten the impression that Nox had told him off the last time.

From the slow rhythm of his breaths, he'd slipped in here long enough ago that he'd fallen back asleep himself. This time he'd eased under the blanket, though not the sheet, and the heat of his body engulfed me as much as his arms did.

It was kind of like having a very large cat suddenly take up residence in my home—the persistent kind that'd squirm into bed next to you and purr like a chainsaw in your ear.

I should be glad he didn't bat at my nose to wake me up or yowl about how hungry he was. Because he probably was hungry. The guys all seemed to be at any given moment unless they were already in the middle of the meal, and Ruin's appetite topped them all. Somehow he'd only seemed to get leaner since taking over Ansel's broad-shouldered frame, though.

The mysteries of ghostly resurrection.

I didn't let myself think too hard about that. Why shouldn't I be able to simply enjoy the exuberant affection he offered so easily without worrying about how it was possible or who he'd been before?

The truth was… no one had ever *wanted* to be this close to me, to watch over me like this, before the guys I'd thought were imaginary had crashed back into my life. Marisol had loved me, but I was the one who'd watched over her. It'd always been me acting as her shield against the rest of the big, bad world.

Now I had four shields of my own. Somewhat unhinged shields with no apparent moral compass, but who was I to complain?

Ruin stirred and stretched with a brief yawn. He gazed at me with eyes still heavy-lidded from sleep. "Good morning, Angelfish."

My lips twitched upward at the silly nickname. I guessed I'd earned all the water references after swimming my way out of my childhood near-drowning. "Good morning."

He gave a pleased hum that amplified the feline impression and nuzzled my temple. My heart skipped a beat, and parts of me lower down woke up twice as much in anticipation of a repeat of yesterday.

Ruin only pressed a quick kiss to my forehead and drew back. His stomach grumbled loud enough for me to hear. He grinned. "How about some breakfast? What do you want me to bring you today?"

He made it sound like he could have scrounged up a banquet if I'd asked for it. I decided not to aim quite that high and test the limits of his admittedly supernatural abilities. "I wouldn't mind something with eggs."

He snapped his fingers. "Eggs it is. Lots and lots of eggs. The chickens will be all out."

As I snorted with laughter, he loped out of the room.

A minute into my shower, the pipes started groaning, as if protesting the quadrupled work load they were now getting. I wondered exactly how in violation of my lease I was by moving in four additional tenants. Was it possible to double-plus evict someone? I doubted my landlord would buy, "But they aren't even technically alive!" as an excuse.

By the time I emerged, the apartment was full of the smell of buttery fried eggs. Based on the takeout boxes cluttering the table, there really might not be a single egg left in all of Lovell Rise.

I found scrambled eggs and poached eggs, deviled eggs and hard-boiled eggs. Thankfully Ruin hadn't gone totally egg-crazy, so there was also an entire loaf of bread in toasted slices dripping with butter and a big serving of bacon and sausages too.

My stomach just about burst from looking at it. The guys had all already grabbed plates and started digging in. I grabbed a little of everything and savored it bite by bite.

This part of the whole undead gangster invasion thing I could totally get used to.

It didn't take long before the guys were hassling each other in their usual companionable way.

"It's breakfast, not a work of art," Kai told Jett, who was rearranging the bits of food on his plate with a studied eye.

The other guy raised an eyebrow. "It can be both."

Nox was staring at the copious amounts of hot sauce Ruin was splattering on his meal. "You're going to burn right through your gut like that."

"As long as it tastes good," Ruin replied cheerfully, and started forking the stuff into his mouth without even sitting down.

I sat on one of the rickety chairs by the table and soaked up both the breakfast deliciousness and the comradery that thrummed between my new roommates. It felt like being surrounded by a family. A real family, not my old fractured one with Wade's judgmental gloominess and Mom's pathetic attempts to mollify him, while me and Marisol were shunted off to the side as an afterthought.

And I was part of this family too. Even though I

didn't add much to the conversation, the guys all glanced my way regularly, as if checking that I had everything I needed.

Just for the moment, I kind of did.

Nox watched me the most, his usual cocky attitude somewhat subdued this morning. There was a fierce grimness in his dark gaze, like he was prepared to take on a whole world of trouble. Hopefully there wasn't a whole lot more than I was already aware of.

When all of the food had somehow vanished between the five of us—and mostly not me—the former Skullbreakers boss set down his plate with a thump. "We need to get Lily back with her sister. And that means we've got to find out what happened when they sent her away."

I gave him a crooked smile. "I want to know as much as anyone, but it's not that easy. I've tried all kinds of things to remember, and the only people who could tell me anything are keeping their mouths shut."

"You didn't have us helping you before," he insisted, which was both reassuring and ominous in one.

"I appreciate that," I said, "but I'm not sure how much you can help at unlocking something in my own head."

He was silent for a moment and then jerked his hand toward the front door. "Come on. I think we need to take a road trip."

We all marched out to where he'd parked Mr. Grimes's old car. Nox didn't disguise the wrinkling of his nose as he opened the driver's side door, but he tossed the keys into the air with a satisfied jangle. "Lily rides shotgun."

I wouldn't have cared either way, and all of the guys could have used the extra space more than I did, but the other three immediately piled into the back without complaint. I plopped down in the seat next to Nox, studying him as he revved the engine.

What was he up to? And how did he think this trip was going to unravel any of the uncertainties that loomed over my life?

Ruin squeezed between the front seats to fiddle with the radio until Nox swatted his hand. "Not this time. No distractions."

"Distractions from what?" Kai asked.

"With all your brilliance, you haven't deduced it yet?" Nox teased.

Kai grunted and poked at his glasses. "I'll take that challenge." He gazed out the window, the mid-morning sunlight glinting off the panes over his eyes.

Nox took one turn and another. Kai's lips slowly pulled into a smile. "Ah."

"*Ah* what?" I demanded.

"Practice your patience, Minnow," Nox said, giving my knee a quick, playful squeeze that shouldn't have sent a bolt of heat up my inner thigh. But it did. I swallowed hard and yanked my gaze away from the brawny hand that'd delivered it.

It was wrong to find all four of these guys attractive, right? But Nox had somehow transformed my bitter professor into a stud. I mean, Mr. Grimes had been a hardass, but not in the literal sense.

Nox veered onto the country highway that ran along the outskirts of town perpendicular with the marshlands. About halfway down it, he pulled off onto the shoulder. A hush had fallen over all of the guys. *They* clearly recognized the significance of the moment.

All I saw in front of us was a discount housewares store called Dishes for Dollars. Maybe they were very special dishes?

"Is this a hint that you're not happy with my selection of dinnerware?" I asked.

Nox gave me a baleful look. Then he lifted his chin toward the building. "That used to be the Skullbreakers' clubhouse."

I blinked and stared at the store again. "You ran your gang out of Dishes for Dollars?"

He snorted. "No. It was there, and after those other pricks wiped us out, someone took over the land, bulldozed the old place, and built this pathetic thing. But the clubhouse is still there underneath in every way that matters."

"I can feel it," Ruin said softly.

"Like we never left," Jett agreed in his low voice.

"How many fucking dishes can they be selling all the way out here anyway?" Kai muttered. "Stupid place for a low-rent shop."

Nox's gaze stayed fixed on the building. His voice came out all heated determination. "It won't be theirs for long. Now that we've returned, we're going to take our property back. Make them an offer they can't refuse. Raze that place to the ground and rebuild what's meant to be there, even better than before."

I really hoped that by "an offer they can't refuse" he meant because it'd be so much money, not because the current owners would fear for their lives. It could go either way with these guys. But a tingle ran over my skin at the same time that was much more excitement than apprehension.

In that moment, I could almost see the old clubhouse too, a vague, boxy shape where the guys had planned their dark deeds... and where Ruin had bounded around to blaring music, Jett had smeared vivid paint on the walls, and Kai had whizzed through reading material like he was trying to set a record.

I could picture Nox there too, the presiding king, calling out orders and grinning fiercely as he laid out their next moves with all the same passion I'd just heard ringing through his words. Another, deeper tingle raced through me, setting off a fresh flare of heat between my legs.

I kind of wanted to know what it'd be like to have him ordering me around. To find out what he'd like to order me to do. There was obviously something very wrong with me after all.

To avoid dwelling on that possibility, I started talking. "Why did you want to show me this?"

Nox turned to me. The fervent intensity in his eyes stirred up the emotions I'd been trying to stifle twice as hot as before.

"You've been through a lot, but the truth about what happened that day is in you somewhere," he said. "It hasn't gone away—it's only buried. We'll unearth everything that matters in your past just like we brought ourselves back, just like we'll resurrect the clubhouse. And your mystery we can get started on right now."

He shifted his gaze to the windshield. The air rushed out of me as he released me from the pressure of his gaze. "You'd say we should start at the beginning, wouldn't you, Kai?"

"That generally makes the most sense," the other guy said from the back. "What's the last thing you remember before it all goes blank, Lily?"

I didn't even have to strain my mind to answer. I'd gone over those shreds of memory so many times in the past, searching for answers in them. "I'd just been down by the marsh—wandering around... with you guys... making up some random song, braiding flowers. I was bringing one of the chains back for Marisol. It was the middle of the afternoon, but it was pretty dark—it was going to rain soon, lots of clouds. I looked up at the house and noticed the light was on in Mare's bedroom." I stopped. "That's it. There's nothing between that and the hospital."

Nox had started driving again without my noticing. He was taking the route toward the house. "You don't even remember going inside?"

"No. For all I know, I didn't."

Kai hummed thoughtfully. Nox gunned the engine, and we roared through the lonely streets until we passed by the lane that stretched all the way to the desolate property that'd once been my home.

To my relief, he stopped several feet down from the lane in a spot where we could only see the house with its weathered white siding and gray shingles at a distance. "You were here," he said. "When you look around, does that jog anything else loose?"

I peered across the scruffy grass and patches of weeds for a minute, but nothing else emerged, so I shook my head. "No. It didn't when I went right up to the house the one time either—and I don't think it'd be a good idea to try that again." Mom's threat to call the police was fresh in my mind. Trespassing was a criminal offense, no matter how much of a dick the accuser was being.

Ruin's voice went uncharacteristically somber. "I don't understand how they can treat you like it's not even your home."

"That's just... how it always was." I guessed I'd never really explained it to the guys when I'd thought they were imaginary—I'd assumed they knew everything I did, since theoretically they'd come out of my head. They'd figured out the gist of it, but the details wouldn't have been obvious.

I sucked in a breath and went on. "When my mom was pregnant with Marisol—I was four—our dad took off. After that, once every couple of years he'd send a postcard from wherever, but nothing else. Having him ditch us felt like shit, and it hit Mom even harder than me. She met Wade like a year later and fell head over heels, so she did whatever she could to make him happy... I think she was always afraid she'd piss him off and he'd leave like Dad did."

"Not exactly relationship goals," Jett remarked.

"No. She wasn't necessarily wrong about him, though—that he had one foot out the door. Wade wasn't all that keen on the fact that she already had kids. I always got the impression he only tolerated us because she buttered him up and doted on him so much. And then after trying and never managing to have kids of their own... He went more and more from tolerating to full-out resentment. So that was fun."

I'd kept my tone dry, but it was hard to squeeze all the emotion out of it. These days that emotion was more anger than anything else. I'd given up on being sad about my family situation ages ago.

The guys were silent for a long moment. Then Nox said, in more a growl than anything else, "We will take care of him. One way or another." When I opened my mouth, he added, "I know. Not yet. Not until you're sure your sister is safe. But he's going down."

I couldn't bring myself to argue with him. Instead, I rubbed my hand over my face. "What now?"

"If you were picked up by the cops on your property, then they'd have driven along this route away from there," Kai piped up. "I think the typical procedure would be to take you into custody at the nearest station and then arrange transport to the hospital. We could try following that route."

"Sure. Might as well."

Nox put his foot to the gas again. We cruised more slowly down the country road and onto the larger thoroughfare that I knew would eventually take us to the county police station halfway between Lovell Rise and the next town over. I'd come this way for other reasons before, but not the slightest flicker of what I might have seen from the back of a cop car came to me.

When we'd passed the station and Nox pulled over again, I shifted in my seat with a wordless grumble of frustration. "There's nothing." The mark on my arm prickled with a sudden itch. I scratched at it, frowning. "I don't understand. I've never forgotten anything else like this before."

"Trauma," Kai said. "Intense mental or emotional overload. It happens."

Nox reached over and grasped my knee again, letting his hand linger there this time as he caught my gaze. Heat coursed through my leg from where his palm rested, but what called to my heart were the words he said.

"We'll get there. No matter how deep it's buried or how much has been built over top, we'll dig it up. I fucking swear it."

Right then, with part of me wanting to melt into his touch, I believed he'd fulfill everything he promised—and more.

eighteen

Kai

I t seemed somehow fitting that Lily's stepdad Wade owned and managed a sporting goods store. He was a dingbat with a stick up his ass, after all. Maybe I'd get the opportunity to stick a real bat up his actual ass before my mission here was over.

I pushed my glasses up my nose and sauntered in, keeping a casual air but scanning every inch of my surroundings. You never knew what minor details might fill in the blanks when trying to figure out a person.

Not that I cared about finding any kind of sympathetic harmony with the prick. I just wanted to know what *he* knew about the incident that'd sent Lily away to the psych ward.

The place held no obvious surprises at a glance. He'd

arranged the aisles by sport, including some that a lot of people with too much time on their hands would have debated calling a sport at all but that were necessities in this kind of town, like fishing and hiking. A faintly sweaty odor hung in the air as if some of the merchandise had already been used for its intended purpose.

A tinny announcer's voice carried from a little TV mounted over the front counter where a football game was playing. Its wiring ran along the wall to a junction box mounted near the ceiling that'd clearly seen better days. I'd read a few books on electrical work, and despite being nothing close to an expert, I could spot a couple of irregularities at a glance.

But I wasn't here to search for code violations. The man who was the focus of my visit stood behind that counter in a self-satisfied stance, ringing up a customer who'd bought an armload of pool noodles. Even *I* was pretty sure there weren't any sports you played with those, but I didn't think either of them wanted to hear my opinion on the subject. I ambled closer, running my fingers over a rack of ski poles, and eyed my target surreptitiously.

Wade Locust was the kind of guy who gave dweebs a bad name. His taffy-brown hair had thinned to the point that you could see slivers of pale skull through his combover, and both his chin and his nose jabbed out at sharp points. He wore a baseball jersey that was a little too tight on his stocky frame but maybe had fit years ago when he'd bought it. One glance at his hand told me he still regularly chewed on his fingernails.

One glance at his smile as he waved the customer off told me he'd never said anything he wasn't willing to take back.

I already hadn't liked him before I'd properly met him, and he'd somehow dropped from the bottom of my esteem to unplumbed depths I doubted he'd ever return from. Had he been more of a catch when Lily's mom had gone gaga for him, or did she just have really crappy taste in men?

I was going to assume it was a heaping portion of both.

Now that he wasn't occupied anymore, I meandered over to the counter and nodded at the TV. "Quite a game."

I had no idea whether it was at all remarkable or not, but Wade happily agreed. "Sure is. Can I help you with anything?"

"I need to get a new rod," I said, motioning to the fishing aisle. "Not sure what'd suit me best. Can you make any recommendations?"

"Happy to help."

He hustled from behind the counter with more enthusiasm than he'd offered either of his step-daughters in their entire existence. "What kind of fish are you looking to catch?" he asked.

"Pike," I said, picking the first fish name that came to mind that I was reasonably sure lived in the waters around here. I'd actually gone fishing approximately zero times in my life.

Wade gave me a bit of an odd look, but I was used to people finding me strange, even if it usually wasn't because of my preferences in aquatic animals. I barreled right on to the real conversation I wanted to start.

I patted the beige shelving unit as if it was somehow impressive. "So this is your place?"

Wade puffed up his chest a bit, which only emphasized the straining of the jersey. "Yep. Started this baby twenty-five years ago and grew it from the ground up."

I nodded to his left hand with its thin band around the ring finger. "And you're a family man. Living the dream."

A shadow crossed Wade's face. "In some ways. We do all right."

He'd sounded ten times prouder talking about the store than the human babies he'd had a hand in raising. Although maybe "raising" wasn't the right word for it when he'd spent more time wishing Lily and her sister would die than teaching them how to live.

"Kids?" I asked conversationally, contemplating the array of rods.

Wade frowned. "A daughter," he said grudgingly.

Singular, not plural. The fucker. I let myself look straight at him then, widening my eyes as if I'd just remembered something. "Oh, yeah, weren't you— I heard some of the guys at the college talking about it—

There was some kind of incident with a girl named Lily…?"

The man's face shuttered in an instant. If he thought that'd stop me from picking up on his cues, he was shit out of luck. His hands twitched with obvious anxiety. Something about the subject made him *nervous*. Because he didn't want that reputation associated with his store, or was there more to it?

"She's gotten the help she needs," he said brusquely. "I married into the family—she probably got it from her birth father. Now, for a fish the size of a pike, I'd normally recommend something in this range." He motioned to several of the poles.

"Isn't she back in town, though?" I said as I picked one up. "I thought she was at the college. I guess you'll be supporting her transition from the hospital."

Wade's entire face twitched that time. He looked like he'd swallowed a lemon—whole. Abruptly, he leaned his hand against one of the shelves and narrowed his eyes at me. "Are you here to check up on me? Because he should know that nothing's changed— there's no reason to worry."

Now *this* was interesting. I folded my arms over my chest. I'd get more by playing along than revealing I had no idea what he was talking about. "And what if he did send me, and he's not satisfied with that answer?"

"If he runs into any problems, he can take them up with me. Himself, not any go-between." He motioned to the door, his mouth twisted between disgust and what I'd swear was panic. "If you're not here to buy, I think you'd better go."

"Not open to browsers, huh?" I couldn't help remarking. "I'd say that's bad for business."

"You know that's not what this is about," he hissed, and came as close to shoving me down the aisle as he could get without actually assaulting me.

"Maybe he'd be more satisfied if you explained right now how you're so sure that everything's under control," I suggested, fishing in the way I was much more comfortable with.

Unfortunately, the prick had decided to shut his mouth to me as well as his store. "Just go. We had an agreement."

Frustration flickered up inside me. I'd gotten something, but it didn't feel like anywhere near enough. And everything about this idiot made me want to end him. How did he deserve to keep breathing after the way he'd treated Lily and then kicked her aside?

My hands clenched, and an odd energy crackled through my veins. Suddenly I was sure that if I'd wanted to, I could have short-circuited his heart on the spot. My spirit wasn't fully fused with this body yet—maybe it never would be. I had at least a little of my ephemeral energies at my disposal.

But Lily hadn't wanted him dead—and he did know more than I'd been able to find out this time.

I bit back the worst of my rage, and my gaze snagged on the junction box again. I kept my expression impassive, but inside I started smirking.

I knew exactly how to deliver maximum agony without touching a hair on his body.

I kept walking, squeezing the doorframe just for a second as I stepped outside. My fingers shot a surge of energy through the wall straight to that bundle of wires.

The first sparks hissed as the door swung shut behind me. I was nowhere near it, so Wade definitely couldn't accuse me of setting it off. I'd made it halfway down the block when his smoke detector started wailing loud enough to reach my ears. Then I let out my smirk.

Wade burst out of the store a moment later, hollering, "Help! Does anyone have a fire extinguisher? It's—it's catching all over." Then he shouted into his phone, "Can't you get here any faster?"

I was absolutely certain the rinky dink small-town fire department wouldn't get here in time to save even half his merchandise. Poor Wade.

Resisting the urge to watch the destruction play out, I turned the corner to head toward Lily's apartment. She should know what I'd found out as soon as I could tell her. But I'd only made it a couple of blocks when a car pulled up alongside me.

A guy poked his head out of the window. "Hey, Zach, where've you been? What the hell's been up with you, man?"

Lord deliver me from this dimwit jock's idiotic friends. "What's up is I'm making some life changes," I informed him. "I'm done with football, remember?"

"You can't be fucking serious. The coach is going to

kick you off the team if you don't show up to practice soon."

"That'll be hard when I've already quit." I stopped for just long enough to fix them with a hard stare. "I've got better things to do than hang around you dumbasses anymore. So fuck off and leave me alone. How much clearer can I say it?"

They hurled a bunch of curses back at me, but they did drive off. I shrugged and walked on. Plenty of people hadn't liked me in my time. It didn't particularly sting when it was those bozos. It was time they got used to the new Zach who wasn't Zach at all.

Really I was doing him and his reputation a favor.

At the apartment, I opened the door with one of the spare keys we'd had cut and walked in to find Lily cuddled up with Ruin on the futon. Or, well, cuddling might not have been quite the right word, but she was sitting with her legs stretched toward him while she took notes from one of her textbooks, and he'd taken it upon himself to pull off her sock and give her a foot massage. Because naturally Ruin could never keep his hands off anything.

The unexpected bolt of jealousy that shot through me came with a hormonal flush that raced through my body straight to my groin. Over seeing her naked foot, for fuck's sake. I closed my eyes for a second to get a hold of myself.

Why the hell had I gone and picked the youngest of our possible hosts? This dude had only been nineteen, and he had idiotic hormones flooding his body at all the wrong times like he was a freaking baboon. My twenty-five-year-old soul and its much more self-controlled influence hadn't calmed down *that* part of his physiology anywhere near enough yet.

We were here to help and protect Lily, not fuck her. I'd never *needed* to fuck anyone, even if I had from time to time because it'd been a change of pace and burned off some steam. I wasn't becoming a slave to teenage horniness.

"Are you okay?" Lily asked as I opened my eyes again. She'd twisted around on the futon at my entrance and now was looking at me with eyes way too wide with concern.

I switched gears to a much more acceptable topic. "Yes. Better than okay. I just had a little chat with your stepdad."

"What?" Lily's forehead furrowed. "I told you guys that *I'd* deal with him."

I held up my hands. I'd kind of figured she'd be pissed. The trick was turning her initial judgment around.

"I didn't do anything to him." His store was another matter. "I just wanted to see how much I could get a read on him." My smirk came back. "And I did find out one interesting tidbit."

Lily's expression wavered between annoyance and hope. Ruin sat up straighter, already bringing out his grin. "That's awesome!" he said.

"Maybe." Lily nodded to me. "Fine. What did he say?"

I could respect a woman who didn't retract her first reaction right away. I settled into one of the wobbly chairs by the kitchen table. "I couldn't get a lot of specifics out of him, not during this first run. But he did give us a clear sense of direction. After I mentioned you, he got thinking that someone might have sent me. A mysterious 'he.' Whatever happened that day, it must have involved more than just your family, unless you have a secret brother or uncle you've never mentioned."

Lily shook her head slowly. Her gaze turned distant and pensive. "I don't remember anyone—but I don't remember any-fucking-thing." She sucked in a breath with a frustrated hiss. "Marisol acted like she was worried about someone other than me too. I figured it was probably Wade or my mom, but maybe that's all connected somehow."

"It must be." Ruin glanced from one of us to the other, his eyes alight with eagerness. "What do we do now?"

I let my smile grow. Mission accomplished. "Lily can keep focusing on getting all the crap she's taken on done and being a good influence over little sisters everywhere. The rest of us are going to look into everyone who's ever had any dealings with Wade Locust."

nineteen

Lily

I should have known that Peyton wouldn't let the water bottle incident slide forever, even if it'd have to take plenty of mental gymnastics to blame me for it. When I walked into a class I shared with one of her friends the next morning and felt the girl's gaze jabbing into me, maybe I should have been more on guard.

But there wasn't much I could have done to avert disaster anyway.

My mind was too taken up with questions about Wade and the unknown "he" my stepdad had mentioned to Kai to bother worrying about Peyton's friend much. I simply sat at the opposite end of the room and pretended she didn't exist.

Too bad for me, she didn't extend me a similar favor. Just as the professor walked in, she got up and snagged an empty seat behind me.

I dutifully got out my notebook and pen, planning to do nothing but take notes on the lecture. For the first several minutes, it seemed like I might get away with that. Maybe she was hoping she could literally shoot daggers into my back with her eyes, and that was as far as she intended to go.

No such luck. About quarter of the way through the lecture, a faint tap radiated through my chair. After the third iteration, I realized she was kicking the back of it. Lightly enough that it didn't make a sound, but firmly enough to be deeply annoying.

The Skullbreakers guys were clearly a bad influence, because the first response I imagined was whirling around and snapping her ankle in two. Not that I knew how to break bones with my bare hands anyway. Not that I *wanted* to.

I gritted my teeth and kept writing, tuning out the erratic rhythm of her swinging foot as well as I could. I only had forty-five minutes to get through. She wasn't going to fray my nerves that easily.

But of course she didn't stop there. Something pattered against my back—she was tossing little bits of... tissue? Pencil shavings? Had she brought popcorn to class? Flicking whatever it was subtly enough that the professor still didn't clue in.

I could picture my antagonist's reaction if I spun around and accused her. She'd play all innocent, and

I'd look like a lunatic having delusions. No, thank you.

There was about a half hour left when something jabbed into my tailbone so hard and unexpectedly I shot out of my seat with a yelp. Instinctively, I jerked around to see what Peyton's friend had done to me—and just as I swiveled to face her, her desk toppled over, clanging into the back of my chair.

She must have flipped it purposefully. But she stepped back with her hands held up and her eyes wide with a shocked expression, as if she had no idea how it'd been upended. Her act was so convincing that even I felt a flicker of doubt. Had something happened like with the water leaping from Peyton's bottle?

The girl's voice pealed out with words that sounded so rehearsed any doubt I'd felt vanished. "Sir, she knocked my whole *desk* over. I don't know why she's bothering me, but I can't work like this."

The professor was already frowning at both of us. His gaze zeroed in on me. "Miss Strom—"

"I didn't do anything," I protested. "She—"

But how crazy would it sound to say that the girl had tossed her own desk over just to make me look bad? He'd probably see the excuse as proof that I had it in for her.

As I scrambled for the right response, he pointed to the door. "Disruptions like this are unacceptable. Take a walk and cool down. If we have any more incidents in the future, I'll have to talk to Student Services."

Embarrassment prickled over me, but I didn't know

how to argue his decision without looking like an even bigger problem. Resisting the urge to glare over my shoulder at Peyton's friend, I stuffed my notebook into my shoulder bag and hustled out of the room.

My biggest mistake was thinking getting me kicked out of class was the ultimate goal. I was so peeved I barely paid attention to what was waiting out in the hall —or rather, who.

The door thumped shut behind me, I veered out of the alcove into the wider hall, and two pairs of hands clamped around my arms.

I twisted automatically to try to break their hold and caught a glimpse of Peyton's cold eyes and haughty nose as she kicked my legs out from under me. While I stumbled, another girl yanked open a door across the hall.

"This'll give you lots of time to think about why you should never mess with me or Ansel again," Peyton hissed at me. Then she and her other friend hurled me through the doorway.

It opened to a flight of concrete steps. My hands flailed out, snatching at the railing, but the girls had shoved me too hard for me to catch myself. I tumbled over and slid most of the way down on my side, flinging my arms up to protect my head.

I hit the floor at the bottom and jostled to the side, and my elbow smacked into a pipe so hot I'd swear I heard my skin sizzle. Searing pain shot through my arm.

I rolled in the opposite direction, a cry crackling up my throat. From above, an ominous scraping sound reached my ears, followed by a heavy click. A sadistic snicker filtered through the door. Then there was only silence.

Well, not exactly silence. The dark room I'd fallen into hummed, whirred, and clinked in a cacophony of mechanical sounds. I might have enjoyed the orchestra if my arm hadn't still been throbbing and the rest of me aching in all the places I'd have bruises tomorrow.

At least I didn't appear to have broken anything. I sat up tentatively, testing my limbs. My right shoulder twinged when I rotated it, and my probing fingers found a scrape on my shin, but otherwise I was uninjured.

Even though I was on the basement level, the air that closed around me was thick and hot. That and the noises tipped me off—this must be the utility room.

And I was pretty sure Peyton and her friends had trapped me in here.

I pushed myself to my feet, confirmed that my legs could hold me just fine, and stomped back up the stairs that'd battered me. As I'd expected, when I jerked at the door handle, it refused to budge. Probably this room was locked most of the time. One of the girls must have pilfered a key from the maintenance staff so they could toss me in here... and then seal me away.

I felt all along the door for anything that'd let me unlock it from the inside, but I came up with nothing. Shit. Squeezing my hand into a fist, I banged on the door. "Hey! Can someone get me out of here? Hello?"

No sound reached me from the other side. Classes

let out on the hour—there'd be a flood of students in the hall in twenty minutes or so. I just had to wait for that.

If any of them bothered to answer my call for help. If they even could. Hopefully someone would at least notify the staff so someone could come by with a key. I didn't think Peyton was such a criminal mastermind that she'd have stolen all the means to unlock this room or melted the keyhole or some ultra nefarious move like that.

All the same, I didn't love the idea of being rescued in front of a sizeable portion of the student body. Grimacing, I pounded on the door again. If I could get someone's attention before there was a whole crowd of witnesses, that'd be ten times better.

As my hand fell to my side, it occurred to me that I had another option. My phone was still in my pocket. Nox had come with me onto campus today, glowering at anyone who so much as glanced at me. He'd meant to prowl around the college while he waited for my class to be over, but he'd be nearby.

Calling on him like I was a kitten stuck up a tree made me wince, but it was the best of my bad options. Not that he'd have a key either. But anything my classmates could figure out, he could too.

Or something completely different. Less than five minutes after my hasty text, the door handle jiggled. There was a metallic groan and a faint screech, and then a clanking sound as if the whole mechanism had fractured into pieces. Which for all I knew, it had. From what I'd seen, the guys had never met anything they wouldn't happily bash given the excuse to.

Nox yanked open the door, all fuming menace. When I squeezed out into the cooler air of the hall, he loomed over me, checking me over for any fatal injuries I might have forgotten to tell him about.

"Who did this?" he snarled. "When I get my hands on them—"

His gaze caught on the burn—a strip of mottled pink skin from my elbow to halfway down my forearm —and he bared his teeth like he was ready to chomp someone's head right off. "Who did this to you?" he repeated in an even more ominous voice.

The fury radiating off him sent a shiver through me —not an entirely unpleasant one, I had to admit, but with enough apprehension that my answer stuck in my throat. I was pissed off at Peyton, but that didn't mean I wanted to see her eviscerated. And from the looks of things, that was exactly what I'd be sentencing her to if I let her name slip.

"It doesn't matter," I said. "It's over now. They let out their anger, and now they'll leave me alone."

I didn't totally believe that, so I couldn't blame Nox for his scoffing laugh. "They'll do something worse next time. I'm not giving them the chance."

"I'm *fine*," I insisted.

"You're not," he growled. "They hurt you, and they're going to pay. *Tell* me who it was."

His voice was getting louder. The squeak of moving chairs carried from a nearby room, and my pulse hiccupped. "Everyone's going to be leaving class in a moment," I said. "This really isn't a good place—"

With another growl, Nox swept me right off my feet into his arms. I wasn't the tiniest girl ever, but he hefted me like I was made of air. Air and glass. I might have protested harder if he hadn't tucked me against him so gingerly before he marched off down the hall.

"What the fuck are you doing?" I grumbled.

"Taking you someplace else where I expect you to give me some answers," he retorted, and hurtled on up the stairs to the second floor.

"You could put me down and let me walk there."

"This is faster."

I couldn't deny that. Or the fact that the well-muscled planes of his chest felt awfully good against me. My heart was still thumping hard, but it wasn't all nerves now.

A metallic, smoky scent rose off his skin, as if his brawny body had been forged out of fire and steel. Some strange part of me wanted to know how it'd taste.

Nox fished a key out of his pocket while balancing my weight with one arm seemingly effortlessly and barged into a room I immediately realized was Mr. Grimes's office. The space wasn't much bigger than a walk-in closet, with an overladen bookshelf along one wall, a narrow window with crooked blinds, and a large metal desk scattered with papers and books.

Nox shoved the mess onto the floor with one swipe of his arm and set me on the edge of the desk, my legs dangling. Then he leaned in, his nose nearly touching mine. "Who locked you up in that room? Who hurt you? We're staying right here until you tell me."

In that moment, with the heat of his body wafting over me and his smell flooding my lungs, I couldn't say that sounded like much of a threat.

"I'm not telling you," I said, staring right back at him as my heart thumped on. "You're too worked up. You're going to do something crazy."

"It's not *crazy* to look after you. It's crazy that you don't think you deserve it. Anyone who touches you is fucking *dead*."

He wasn't exactly making a case in his favor, but another quiver ran through me at his words. A hunger woke up inside me as if I'd been craving this vicious devotion my entire life and never known until now.

Of its own accord, my hand rose up, my fingers curling into the fabric of his shirt and brushing the muscles flexed underneath. A voice that hardly sounded like my own spilled from my lips as if the words were being pulled out of me by a magnetic force.

"Instead of making them feel worse, why don't you make *me* feel better?"

Desire flared in Nox's eyes. He looked down at me, his jaw working, and slowly raised his hand to my chin. His thumb grazed the seam of my lips, torturously light.

Somehow that delicate touch set off so many sparks in me I had to swallow a whimper. All at once, the office felt hotter than the utility room had.

"You aren't a minnow anymore, are you, Lily?" Nox said, his baritone dipping even lower. "You're a goddamned siren." He brushed his thumb over my mouth again. "You liked having Ruin all over you."

A pulse of heat between my thighs agreed with that assessment. It only fueled the wildness that'd come over me. "Maybe I'd like you too. Is that a problem?"

He sucked in a breath. "Hell, no," he muttered, and then his mouth crashed into mine.

If Ruin's kiss was all bright exuberance, then Nox's was total darkness. A pure, intoxicating darkness like the headiest of liquors, drenching me from head to toes in an instant. Just like that, I soaked my panties.

He nudged my knees apart so my legs splayed around him, pushing in on me where I was perched on the desk. The feel of his solid thighs between mine only drove me wilder. My hand stayed clamped around his shirt. The other wrapped around his shoulders as if I could pull him right into me.

He claimed my mouth so thoroughly that all I was aware of was the brutally blissful pressure and his body aligning with mine. One hand cupped my jaw, his thumb stroking my cheek, while the other squeezed my ass and tugged me even closer against him. The bulge behind the fly of his jeans collided with my sex, and a moan tumbled out of me.

Nox drank in the sound and pressed another scorching kiss to the crook of my neck. "You're a good girl, aren't you, Lily?" he murmured, every word like a flame. "No one's treating you fucking right. But I've got you. I'm going to make you sing again."

I was too dazed to wonder what he meant until his

fingers slipped over my hip to delve between us. They rubbed over my clit through my jeans, and I trembled against him with the flurry of pleasure the one small gesture provoked.

Nox growled, but there was nothing angry in the sound now. "That's right. I can't wait to see you unravel for me. I'm going to take you so high, baby."

He captured my mouth again, devouring me with searing lips and a flick of his tongue while his hand worked over me below. Each press of his fingers brought a more potent surge of bliss.

I couldn't stop myself from squirming, rocking into him as if I needed to urge him on, while I kissed him back just as hard. My breath slipped out of me in little hitches and gasps between the melding of our mouths.

I *had* needed this. I hadn't known it, but I'd been starving for it, and now the flood of giddy satisfaction was sweeping me away.

When my body started to shake with the pulsing of Nox's touch, he drew back enough to watch my expression. My muscles were turning to jelly, wave after wave of delight washing through them. A smile curved the former gang boss's lips, so heated it sent me spiraling faster toward my release.

"You're fucking gorgeous like this," he said. "So fucking beautiful when you're moaning for me."

He hooked his fingers at just the right spot against me, and I shattered with the moan he'd been asking for. A whirlwind of pleasure whipped through me, thrumming through every nerve and leaving me breathless. I clung to Nox as I came down from the high.

But with the release, some of the wildness that'd brought me here washed away too. My ears picked up the chatter of voices filtering in from the hall outside—students and professors in conversation. All at once, the objective reality of my situation sank in.

To anyone else's eyes, I'd just been all but finger-fucked on a desk by one of my professors. What if someone had heard those moans—what if they saw us coming out together—

And even if no one had, I'd just hooked up with a guy who'd been swearing to commit murder on my behalf a few minutes ago. What the hell had I been thinking?

I hadn't been thinking, that much was clear. And it got harder to think again when Nox teased his hand up just high enough to finger the button on my fly.

"That was just an appetizer. Wait until you get the main course."

A whole lot of me screamed *hell, yes!* but my momentary panic overwhelmed my hormones. I jerked away from him.

"No," I said in a voice that was way too breathy. "No, I think we'd better stop there. I—I need to get some air."

"Lily?" Nox said as I slid off the desk. Then a hint of a growl came back into his voice. "You still haven't told me—"

"Just—just leave me alone for five fucking minutes!"

I said, the words tasting sour and unfair even as I spat them out. But they worked, at least for long enough that I could make my getaway. I hurried out of the office and down the hall, and no footsteps thundered after me. In the stairwell, I paused for a second and pressed my palm to my forehead.

I wasn't crazy. I *wasn't*.

But right now I felt like I was teetering way too close to the edge.

twenty

Lily

I didn't go back to my apartment that night. I couldn't have said whether I was more embarrassed by how I'd stormed off on Nox or scared of how I'd feel when I saw the guys, but either way, I wasn't ready to face the way-too-literal ghosts of my past.

My phone had been blowing up with calls and texts since about ten minutes after I'd left Nox in the professor's office. I'd ignored all of those, texted Ruin—who seemed the least likely to totally blow his top—to say I needed a little space to get my head on straight and they should let me have that. Then I turned off my phone altogether.

After my closing shift at the grocery store, I curled up on the armchair in the corner of the stock room that doubled as the employee lounge and managed a stretch of broken sleep. A couple of times, I heard the rumble of a car engine outside, but no one banged on the door. It might not have been the guys at all.

I ducked out the next morning before the first shift started, feeling not a whole lot saner than I had the night before. Squirming in front of Fred's rearview mirror, I combed my fingers through my hair, smoothed the wrinkles out of my shirt with some strategic dabs of water, and applied a quick swipe of lip gloss so I didn't look like a total disaster.

Still, I was enough out of sorts that I drove right down Main Street on my way to my morning class instead of avoiding the strip that held Wade's store like I normally did.

I remembered awfully fast when I saw it didn't hold Triumphant Sporting Goods anymore. At least, not the building I remembered. Instead, there was only a blackened frame with fragments of charred wall here and there. I stared at it as I cruised past, my mouth going dry.

Kai's smirk from when he'd told me about his conversation with my stepdad floated up through my memory. I was going to guess he'd done a little more than just talk after all. My stomach twisted, but my horror was as much at the sense of approval that'd rushed through me as at the destruction itself.

Maybe I wasn't teetering on the edge after all. Maybe I'd already gone so far off the deep end that the pool drain I was getting sucked down into simply looked like an edge.

I arrived at the college an hour before my first class and immediately determined that move had been a mistake. As I left the car behind to cross the parking lot, as I popped into the campus café to grab a cherry danish for breakfast, as I meandered across the lawns nibbling at it, every glance shot my way felt even warier than before.

Was I imagining it, or had those freshmen veered to the far edge of the field to avoid me? Was that bunch of girls peeking my way between their furtive whispers?

If people here had found out about my stepdad's store, word had probably spread that I'd done it. It'd fit the picture they'd drawn of me, right? The police obviously didn't think I was responsible, or they'd have been knocking at my door two nights ago, but facts had never gotten in the way of juicy campus gossip before.

Or maybe I'd been spotted rushing out of Mr. Grimes's office all flushed and recently ravished, and they were gossiping about that. Hell, it could even be both. Whatever the case, I had the feeling my reputation had gone from in the toilet to sewer level.

The best way to keep it from sinking any lower seemed to be keeping my head low. I slunk in and out of class without saying a word, and no one got in my way. I did my reading under a tree out in the lonely reaches beyond the greenhouse that belonged to the

Environmental Studies department. After my last class of the day, I meandered back toward the parking lot feeling adrift.

It was only mid-afternoon. The guys were probably still hanging out at my apartment—or prowling around town looking for other ways to avenge me. The one time I'd turned my phone on, the massive number of notifications had horrified me enough that I'd shut it right back down. I was lucky I hadn't run into any of them on campus. And at the same time, some stupid part of me was *disappointed* that they'd followed my request for space.

I'd had great plans when I came back to town. I'd done everything right, or as right as I could. So why did it seem like every step forward I took, I slid five more backward?

I walked over to my car because I didn't want to stick around campus any longer than I needed to, taking a small bit of comfort from the rhythm of my sneakers smacking the pavement. Then my gaze caught on the unnatural glints of reflected sunlight sparking on the asphalt around the junker's tires.

As I hurried over, my chest clenched up. Whoever had it in for Fred—and me—had really gone to town this time. Holes had been punched in all of the windows, including the windshield, leaving glass shards scattered on both the seats and the pavement. The window frames were full of jagged chunks, fracturing any view through them into a kaleidoscope of shapes.

Something inside me cracked apart as if echoing the

scene in front of me. All at once, I couldn't bring myself to give a fuck.

This was what I was working with. Screw everyone who thought they could pull shit like this and I'd roll over. Underneath all the crap, I had one mission here, and it didn't even have anything to do with this school or the asswipes who went here.

I grabbed the emergency blanket from the trunk and wrapped it thickly around my arm before smacking away the remaining knives of glass lodged in the window frames. It wasn't like the windows were doing me any good the way they were, and I'd see better without the broken bits in the way. Then I brushed off the driver's seat, since the situation was enough of a pain in my ass without me having literal shards poking my behind.

As I sank into the driver's seat, a sense of certainty settled over me. I'd been avoiding the thing most likely to get me answers because I'd been afraid of the consequences. But consequences kept raining down on me no matter how carefully I played the game. So, fuck the rules. It was my life. I deserved to know how it'd been ruined.

That didn't mean I was going to be an idiot about my quest, of course. I drove slowly out within view of my old house but far off the lane that led right up to it and peered across the scruffy fields. The breeze passing through the open windshield frame rushed over me with an aquatic tang from the marsh.

Neither Mom's car nor Wade's was parked next to the house. That was a promising sign. I couldn't imagine either of them letting Marisol borrow their vehicle, so it meant they were both probably gone too.

Marisol would still be in school. Mom should be at work in the dental office where she was a receptionist. I didn't know what Wade was doing now that his store was in cinders, but I'd guess he had all kinds of insurance claims and who knew what else to sort through.

That meant I had no way of predicting when he'd be home, but I'd take that chance. This had been my house for years before it'd been his. I knew the ins and outs. I'd just keep my ears pricked for the sound of the engine.

I crossed the field on foot, the overgrown grass hissing against my calves. Nothing stirred in the windows or around the house. When I was close, I circled to the left so that I could approach it on the trampled path that led toward the marsh—the way I'd have been coming the day everything had gone wrong.

I stopped there for a moment, looking up at the house and superimposing my remembered image of it from that day in my mind's eye. Then I walked slowly up to the side door I'd usually entered through, all my senses alert for any twinges of recognition.

Nothing came. The side door was locked, which it'd rarely been back then, but Mom and Wade hadn't changed their usual tricks much. I checked a few stones along the edge of the flowerbed nearby and found the key under the third.

As I eased the door open, a frog hopped up beside me with a faint croak. I raised my eyebrow at it. "You stay out here."

I shut the door behind me but didn't lock it in case I needed to make a hasty escape. The smell of the place washed over me, familiar and yet not.

My mom still used the potpourri that was mostly cloves. A sour note of lemon cleaner trickled through it. She'd fried bacon this morning—a little of the greasy odor laced the air alongside the rest.

I hadn't breathed in that concoction of scents in seven years. It no longer gave me the immediate pang of *home*.

It didn't jostle loose any stray recollections either. I walked through the kitchen, where the table was clear and dishes were drying in the rack—Mom always kept everything as tidy as possible so Wade had nothing to complain about, not that it stopped him complaining. Then on into the dining room and down the hall past the living room. I'd never spent any more time on the first floor than I could help. After Wade had moved in, the only part of the house that'd really been mine was my bedroom upstairs.

When I reached the staircase, a frog jumped out of nowhere to land on the steps ahead of me. As I cocked my head at it, another sprang after. They literally leapfrogged after each other all the way up to the second floor. I watched them go, wondering what crevice they'd slipped in through—and why they'd bothered.

"You do you!" I called after them. "Just stay out of Wade's closet, or he might turn you into frog-leg soup."

They'd made the trip more eloquently than I could. The stairs creaked under my feet loud enough that I winced. But it wasn't as if anyone could hear me from all the way out in town.

At the top, I took a left—and discovered that even my room wasn't really mine.

It wasn't a surprise. I'd been gone all those years, and Wade had wanted me gone for way longer than that. But somehow it still hit me like a jab to the gut, seeing the sunny yellow walls hidden away behind piles of storage boxes.

I mean, I'd never been a sunny girl, but the room had always given me the sense that maybe I could be, even as the paint faded. Wade had turned the space into a combination junk yard and pawn-shop depot.

I spotted one of those stupid singing fish poking from the top of one haphazardly stacked box, and a wooden goblet that looked like it should have belonged to a Viking, not my weaselly stepdad, protruding from another. There was a jumble of pipes in one corner that could have been a modern art installation, half of them old and rust-blotched, half shiny and new.

It was like they'd stuck everything they didn't want anymore but couldn't be bothered to actually get rid of into my old room. If that wasn't an appropriate metaphor for my life here, I didn't know what would be.

I couldn't even tell if my bed or any of my other furniture was still stashed away amid the heaps. I didn't have time for a full-on excavation, and anyway, there was no guarantee those fossils of my childhood existence would provide any insight. Nothing about this house had made a lightbulb go off in my brain so far.

I toyed fleetingly with the thought of dumping a bunch of this junk on Mom and Wade's bed and seeing how they liked being relegated to trash, but common sense won out. It was way better for everyone if they never realized I was here.

Backing away from the doorway, I found myself eyeing the room at the end of the hall. Marisol's bedroom door was closed. Even though I knew she wasn't behind it, even though I'd already seen her in her sixteen-year-old state, part of me stared at it with a tickle of conviction that if I yanked it open, I'd find her nine-year-old self sprawled on the floor on the other side. She'd glance up from where she was doodling farting unicorns and dimpled dragons with her markers and grin at me. *What're we doing today, Lily?*

As that image receded, a strange flash of emotion came over me. There was something—I had to—She *needed* me.

I'd taken three steps down the hall before I caught myself. She wasn't *here*. Yeah, she needed me, but walking into her empty room wasn't going to accomplish that.

But for some reason, a deep trepidation gripped me as I grasped the doorknob, as if I were going to swing open the door and find a monster on the other side—and not one of the shaggy, cuddly ones with fanged smiles that'd been in her drawing repertoire.

I shoved the door wide and peered into the space, braced for the worst.

But there was nothing. Nothing except the same old bed and dresser she'd had before, more flakes of the white paint worn off to show the pale wood underneath. The walls were bare now, none of her drawings tacked up. *Did* she even draw still?

I thought of how I'd stopped singing, and my stomach clenched up.

The two frogs hopped past my feet, seemed to consider the room, and hopped back out again. "It was nicer before," I informed them. Back when I'd been here with Mare.

The mark on my arm itched, and I scratched it as I gave the room a long, careful look. No further emotions stirred. The anxiety I'd felt moments ago dwindled. Had it just been a trick of my head, or did it mean something?

It'd sure be nice if my internal states came with a secret decoder ring.

My gaze settled on a lump of bundled fabric nestled beside Marisol's pillow. There was something oddly familiar about it. I took a couple of steps closer and then realized why.

It was my old hoodie—the purple one with the

raincloud pattern that I'd adored so much I'd worn it even when I was frying in the summer heat, back when I was thirteen. I hadn't had it on the day I'd been taken away because Marisol had asked to borrow it the night before to help her sleep, and she hadn't been up yet when I'd left the house in the morning. I had a vivid memory of tucking her into bed with it enveloping her skinny nine-year-old frame.

Seven years later, she was still keeping it close. A lump filled my throat. I couldn't have asked for better proof that she still needed *me*. All she'd had was this scrap of fabric instead of her actual big sister.

Swallowing hard, I shut the door again and turned toward Mom and Wade's room. As little as I wanted to go sticking my nose quite that far up their asses, it was my last chance at finding some clue about what else had gotten up Wade's ass—and why he'd thought Kai had been sent by someone to hassle him. I couldn't help Marisol if I didn't have the answers I needed.

But I'd only crossed the hallway as far as the top of the stairs when the thrum of a car engine penetrated the walls, way too close outside to be heading anywhere but here.

My heart flipped over. I dashed down the stairs and to the side door—and then crouched there behind the counters, listening. I couldn't make a run for it now without whoever was driving up seeing me.

If I'd been anyone else, maybe I'd have felt like a super spy. Instead I had the impression of myself as a naughty child shirking the punishment to come, like I'd left muddy fingerprints all over the walls or something.

I didn't stick around to find out what my punishment would be. The second I heard the front door click open and footsteps creak inside, I slipped out into the yard. Then I took off for the span of trees that stood between our official property and the area near the marsh as fast as my feet could carry me.

As soon as I was in the shelter of the trees with no accusing shouts lobbed after me, I followed the line of trunks until I was parallel with my car and headed back to Fred. There, I flopped into the driver's seat and exhaled.

I'd done it. I'd done it… and I didn't have any more answers than I'd had before.

I wet my lips, tasting the marsh on the air that flowed through all the glassless windows around me. A pang that was almost like homesickness formed in my abdomen, which didn't make a whole lot of sense, considering I'd just been closer to my theoretical home than I'd gotten in seven years before.

But it wasn't that house I was missing. Or my dreary apartment. No… I was aching for company.

I looked off toward the town where the four guys who'd risen from the dead for me were waiting. The sensation around my heart tugged harder.

I *missed* them. I missed having them around, with all their banter and laughter, their proclamations and their growls for vengeance. Even their craziness.

What was the point in denying myself that, really?

Either *I* was crazy, or I wasn't. Being around them wasn't going to change that. Look what I'd done all on my own.

I wet my lips and pulled out my phone. This might be the most idiotic decision of my life, but it was *mine*.

twenty-one

Jett

The bar was loud, smelly, and totally lacking in artistic stimulation. Flat dun-brown paint coated the walls, and smooth, pitch-black tiles covered the floor. The most interesting thing was the formica tabletop, also black but with a mottling of scratches and dents, but the other guys kept grabbing their drinks every time I moved them into an appealing visual composition.

Someday I was going to teach them that you could get buzzed on art just as much as alcohol.

I guessed I couldn't blame them though, because I knew what they were like—and this was our first real night out with Lily. She sat kitty-corner to me at the cramped rectangular table, nursing a dark ale and somehow looking radiant even in the dim bar lighting. Maybe it was just that her pale hair and skin stood out against the dark furnishings to the point that she practically glowed in comparison.

It was almost like she was the ghost among the bunch of us.

That thought would have amused me more if it hadn't come with a weird twinge of guilt. I'd had a cramp in my stomach since Nox had driven us out to look at the indignity our old clubhouse site had been subjected to. I was trying not to examine that cramp too closely. My left hand ached from the little cuts where I'd drawn blood for an epic painting this morning, trying to work all the lingering uneasiness out of me.

It hadn't worked, but the result hadn't been bad. Almost inspired. If I could just find that one missing element...

Ruin clapped his arm around my shoulder and leaned in. "Don't look so gloomy, Jett! Do you want some of my wings?" He grabbed another off the heaping plate he'd ordered.

The cramp in my stomach hadn't stopped me from getting fucking hungry all the time, but I eyed Ruin's order skeptically. He'd always gone for intensity, and based on how he'd been acting in our new lives, that habit had only gotten stronger. The sauce slicked across the wings made my eyes burn just looking at it. Lord only knew what it'd do to my tongue.

It might make an interesting medium, though. I unfolded my napkin to its full size and took a wing to set it at one corner. The neon orange sauce stung my skin in the process. Better keep that away from the bandaids on my other hand.

Kai sensed my hesitation. "We could order some nachos," he suggested from the other side of the table, where he was leafing through yet another book. With all the speed-reading he'd been doing the past few days, you'd think he'd be all caught up already and well into the future of mankind by now. "That's the most recommended item in the reviews for this place."

Of course he'd read those too. I shrugged and downed a gulp of my Jack and Coke. "Doesn't matter. I ate before we left."

Kai peered at me over his glasses in that irritatingly knowing way of his. "But you're hungry again, and you value your tongue enough not to sear it off with those wings."

"I'm fine," I grumbled, and started dabbing the spicy sauce onto the rest of the napkin. The blotches looked like the figures all around us, at least how they appeared to my eyes—so many jumbles of color and motion. Nothing artistically appealing about any of *them* in here.

Which was fine, since it made it easier not to pay attention to them. No one really mattered except our little group… and Lily.

"You're a little hungry too," Kai said to her—still a know-it-all, but a little gentler in tone with her, I'd noticed. "Nachos? Or we could get the stuffed jalapenos. Maybe those would have almost enough kick for our spice-demon here." He shot Ruin a baleful look.

Ruin huffed and moved from me to peck a kiss to Lily's temple. "Lily can share my wings too."

Lily laughed. "I tried one little taste and I'm not sure my mouth will ever recover. Nachos sounds fine, as long as you guys are eating too." She paused. "You're okay for money, right?"

Nox stretched out his legs where he was sitting at my other side. "Don't worry about that. We've got it covered."

The truth was we'd burned through all the cash we'd originally had in our wallets, but Kai's host had been dim enough to write his bank PIN code down on a sticky note, and Ruin could get into his account using the fingerprint recognition on his phone. He'd sent himself a bank draft that we'd immediately cashed. From the size of that posh dude's savings, that should keep us going for a while. But I suspected Nox was a little annoyed that he hadn't been able to contribute from the professor's stash so far.

Of course, he found his own ways. His gaze settled on a pinball machine at the other end of the bar, and his eyes lit up. "Tonight is on me," he announced, shooting Lily a cocky grin, and got up to saunter over to it. From the gestures he made at the figures standing around it, he was arranging bets.

Kai flagged down the waitress and then watched our boss's progress. "He'll bring in enough for tonight and another couple besides, it looks like," he said.

Lily cocked an eyebrow. "He's that good?"

"Nox is the *best*," Ruin declared. "He once kept the ball going for five hours straight."

"The guys he bet against had already paid up and left for closing," Kai added. "We had to hold the owner at gunpoint to stop him from shutting Nox down." When Lily's eyebrows jumped even higher, he raised his hands. "It was either that or let Nox shoot him for throwing off his game."

"He takes his pinball *very* seriously," I muttered, and added another streak of sauce to my composition.

"I see," Lily said, blinking, but she didn't look as disturbed as the average woman might. But then, I'd already known she wasn't an average woman.

She scooted her chair over to take a closer look at my napkin. Her elbow grazed my arm, and my nerve endings flickered into sharper awareness of her presence.

"That's amazing," she said with an awed little laugh.

"You think so?" I studied the image that'd come together with the smudges of sauce. It was a tree sprouting from a haze, the orange hue making it look as if it were made out of fire.

"I'd hang it on my wall, if my wall was worthy of it," she said. "What you're doing always looks so simple, but then it comes together into this image that just hits me." She brought her hand to her chest and then shook her head. "And you managed that with hot sauce on a napkin!"

"I've seen him use weirder materials," Ruin said with a chuckle, and Kai grunted in agreement.

The picture still felt like it wasn't quite *there*, but with Lily's praise beaming over me like sunlight, I didn't totally care. The guys had never said anything about my art like that. It just didn't really register for them. They were more interested in the scenes I could create with a gun and a knife. Which, okay, I did enjoy too.

But Lily's smile made me want to paint every surface in the world just for her. I *should* be able to create something epic with a muse like this. Having her next to me, I had to believe she could fill those empty spaces inside me that I'd never been able to satisfy on my own.

I managed to smile back at her, a gesture my mouth didn't form without conscious effort. Then my senses prickled with a twinge of apprehension.

My gaze slid away from her and settled on a lanky collection of shapes crammed into a booth halfway down the bar. When I focused in on him, his features gradually came into sharper focus: a knob of a nose, puffy lips, and beady eyes that were fixed right on our woman.

My hackles rose automatically. The man's posture oozed slimy and his expression screamed predator. I'd like to stuff a few of Ruin's wings down *his* throat.

A second later, the guy caught me glaring at him. His head twitched to the side, the leer that'd twisted his mouth snapping away. It appeared I could spare Ruin's food from the dire fate I'd pictured.

The nachos arrived, and we all dug in—including Nox, who returned flush with cash that he tossed on the tabletop. Ruin got Lily up to dance, even though no one else was boogeying, but she followed him anyway and giggled as he spun her around in the strip of clear floor between the bar and the tables.

The bartender rolled his eyes, and I contemplated removing them from his head.

The slimy creep stalked over to a woman sitting on her own at the smallest table. He bought her a drink and another, his hand lingering on her wrist even when her shoulders tensed up a little. Every now and then, he glanced over at Lily, so I kept glancing at him.

When Lily started yawning, Nox took one look at her and declared that it was time to get home. I tossed my napkin painting on the nachos platter with the rest of the garbage—I'd do better next time, and in a medium that wouldn't start to stink—and considered the creep once more.

"I've got to take care of a couple things," I told the others. "I'll meet you there."

"Is everything okay?" Lily asked with a furrow of concern on her forehead, as if *she* needed to be worrying about me.

"No big deal," I told her.

"Jett *always* looks like the world's about to end," Nox informed her, tucking his arm around her waist as the four of them headed out. "You'll get used to it."

I didn't have to wait long. It couldn't have been more than five minutes of lurking outside the bar when the creep came sauntering out with his hand locked around the woman's wrist. She was wobbling on her feet, obviously drunk. He led her down a couple of blocks, around a corner, and then hauled her into a narrow alley there. She was only aware enough to let out a confused mumble of protest.

I didn't know her. She had no bearing on my life. But I knew pricks like him—and I knew he was about to do to her what he'd *wanted* to do to Lily. I was just taking care of a little trash.

They disappeared into the shadows farther down the alley. There was a gasp and a little squeal quickly muffled by the clap of a hand over a mouth. I pulled out the knife I'd outfitted myself with using the last of the nerd's cash.

I hadn't done the job all the way to the end the one time it'd mattered most, but I wasn't going to make that mistake again.

The man was too busy wrenching at the woman's panties to notice me stalking over behind him. I plunged the knife right into his jugular and shoved him toward the end of the alley. The woman gasped and staggered away. Her uneven footsteps pattered into the distance. No shouts of alarm. She was just glad to get out of here.

The creep gurgled and sprayed the grungy walls with his blood. I traced the lines with my eyes, tempted to direct him a little further but holding myself back. I needed him dead, not pretty.

He slumped right over on the ground. After a few minutes, he stopped twitching. I checked his pulse to be completely sure he was a goner. Then I swiped his wallet, because a little extra cash wouldn't hurt, and that way it'd look like a mugging. We could dodge the police, but it was easier if they weren't looking for us in the first place.

The creep had created a sort of bloody snow angel on the pavement. I committed the image to memory as I wiped the knife on his pants and stuffed it back in my pocket. It could make a nice painting someday.

But there was too much threatening Lily in this town, and I'd only dealt with a little of the danger. We were going to have to step up our game.

twenty-two

Lily

"Of all the crap we missed in the last twenty-one years, this Bennifer thing has got to be the weirdest," Kai remarked as I drove toward Mart's Supermarket, twisting his phone in his hand as if looking at it upside down would make the news easier to swallow. "The two of them don't make any sense together, so how are they a couple *again*? Wasn't the first time enough?"

My lips twitched with amusement. "I thought you were getting caught up on actual news, not celebrity gossip."

"All news is 'actual.' You can learn tons of things about how people think from the superficial stuff."

I glanced over at him as I slowed for a red light. By

their own special methods, the guys had found someone to replace all Fred's windows overnight, so we weren't taking a blast of wind in the face like we might have yesterday.

"Is that what you want—to figure out how people think?" I asked.

He shrugged, still eyeing his phone. "The better grasp I have on the psyche of the average human being, the better I can manipulate them. I got a lot done for the Skullbreakers that way."

I guessed that explanation made a sort of sense. I didn't have much chance to ponder it, because as I cruised around the next bend and the grocery store came into view, the scene in the parking lot seared every other thought from my mind with a shock of panic.

Two cop cars were parked outside the store entrance. It must have been a slow day for the county's tiny police force, because that might have been all the cars they had in the whole department. A few men in uniform were standing in a semi-circle around Burt Bower, who was motioning to the front of the store—

"Oh, fuck," I said under my breath as my gaze traveled that far. Kai's head jerked up.

The entire face of Mart's Supermarket, from the bold-lettered sign up top to the tall windows that stretched out on either side of the glass doors, had been marked with broad slashes of red spray paint. Mostly they cut across the panes and pale siding seemingly at random, like cuts gouged into the store by giant claws. But here and there they formed more coherent patterns… like the words *FUCK YOU* blazoned right across the door right next to a jutting illustrated dick.

For just a second, I thought of Jett and his affinity for paint, but this crude mess looked way too rough and amateurish to be his work. And I couldn't see any reason he would have attacked my workplace this way. Burt had been a bit of a jerk, but Jett didn't know that, and the guys were all aware of how much I needed this job.

Why would *anyone* have messed with the grocery store like this? Had my manager made unexpected enemies among an underground punk gang?

I drew into the lot tentatively and parked several spots away from the police cars. The lot was mostly empty—the store didn't open for another half an hour—but a few other vehicles had pulled in on the far side, people watching the scene through the windows. In Lovell Rise, this incident definitely counted as major news. It'd keep the gossip channels going for weeks.

As I stepped out of the car with Kai following, Burt waved toward me. The cops turned to inspect my approach. I tamped down on the prickle of nerves that rippled through me.

It was possible one or more of these officers had been involved when I'd been hauled away seven years ago, but I didn't remember any of them. No reason to assume they'd recognize me. They should have bigger things on their minds right now than a thirteen-year-old's mental breakdown nearly a decade ago.

"What happened?" I asked, focusing on Burt. Where we even still opening today? I had a feeling he'd want to get the paint cleaned off rather than have people walking through the doors with a giant erect dick pointing at them.

One of the cops puffed out his chest as he looked me up and down and said, "We were hoping you could tell us about that."

I blinked at him. "I'm sorry?"

"Yes, you should be," Burt snapped, in a tone so seething I was surprised smoke wasn't billowing out of his ears.

Neither of them were making any sense. I turned to the puffed-up cop. "I really don't understand what you mean. I only just got here."

One of the other cops let out a disbelieving grunt and jabbed his thumb toward a few figures I hadn't noticed who'd gotten out of their car. "We've received a report from witnesses who saw a woman fitting your description leaving the scene with a paint can in your hand."

As I took in my accusers, my blood went cold. Peyton shot me a tightly triumphant smile, her skinny arms folded over her chest. The guy next to her was another of Ansel's friends, the one my guys had hung from the dock post a few days ago. He glared more at Kai than at me. And beside him was some dude I'd never talked to before but who I thought I remembered from the football field when Zach and his teammates had harassed me.

"Yeah, that's her all right," he said. "She did it." The others nodded.

My jaw dropped. "I—You've got to be kidding me." I glanced from one cop to another. "I swear I had nothing to do with this. I haven't been at the store since my closing shift two days ago." Well, technically I'd been here the next morning after sleeping in the lounge, but that wasn't relevant. "I don't even know where I'd *buy* spray paint."

The first cop scoffed. "I'm going to have to go with the eyewitness report on this one. You'd better—"

Kai cleared his throat to interrupt, tucking his phone into his pocket and stepping forward so he was right beside me. He pushed up his glasses and gave the police officers an incisive look through the panes. "Even when the eyewitnesses are heavily biased?"

The lead cop's brow furrowed. "What are you talking about?"

Kai raised his chin toward my trio of accusers. "A bunch of Lily's fellow students have been harassing her for several days now, including those three. I'd bet they defaced the store so that they could pin the blame on her. I know *she* didn't do it, because I was out with her and then at her apartment all night."

"This guy and his... friends have been harassing *us* because of her," Ansel's friend retorted.

The cops looked between us and the other group with increasingly put-upon expressions. They must have been starting to think they'd been caught up in a petty college-student squabble, but there'd still been an actual crime committed here. They still needed to find the perpetrator.

Kai ignored the other guy's statement and motioned to a security camera mounted by the front door. "Your camera must have caught the person who did this. Have you even looked at the footage?"

Burt raised his chin. "Of course. There was only one person in view, and she was wearing a hoodie. She never turned her face toward the camera, so she can't be IDed from that alone, but it definitely could have been Lily."

Or it could have been Peyton, or even a slim guy, with all the shadows obscuring the image.

Kai wasn't deterred. "What time did this all happen?"

"Just after midnight."

A hint of a smile curled the former gangster's lips. "No problem, then. We left The Deep Dive around twelve-thirty last night. I'm pretty sure the bar has security footage too. One quick check, and you'll see Lily couldn't have been here making this wonderful art, unless you're going to claim she can clone herself."

His know-it-all tone clearly raised Burt's hackles, but facts were facts. The cops stepped aside to mutter with one another, and Peyton's crew tried to murder us with their eyes. I wondered if it was possible to charge someone with attempted assault by death glare.

One of the cops got on his phone, I guessed with the bar. After he nodded to his colleagues, the lead officer turned toward me. "We're going to check out your alibi. If your friend here is telling the truth, there shouldn't be any trouble. But I don't want you leaving town in the meantime."

"I wasn't planning on it," I said, doing my best to sound agreeable and not snarky.

From his expression, I only half succeeded, but that was enough for them to leave. Peyton and co drew back to their car to hash out the situation among themselves, and Burt swiveled to face me. His peevish expression made me tense up all over again.

"Are we opening the store?" I ventured.

His scowl deepened. "Not for the moment. And you won't be opening it at any point. I'm going to have to let you go."

I stared at him. "But—I didn't *do* this. I didn't do anything wrong. As soon as the cops check with the bar—"

He was already shaking his head. "It doesn't matter either way. This incident clearly had something to do with you, one way or another. You're bringing too much trouble to this store—after just a couple of weeks on the job. You can pick up your paycheck for the hours you did work on Friday."

With that, he stalked across the parking lot to his own car, leaving me standing there with my heart plummeting to my feet. The other spectators were driving away too, the excitement having dwindled with the cops' departure. In a minute, it was just Kai and me near the doors and Peyton's group by their car.

Kai gave my shoulder a quick squeeze. "We'll figure something else out."

I swallowed hard. "It's going to be all of ten seconds before every employer in town hears about this—and half of them will probably only get the part of the story where I was spraying dicks on my workplace's door. Damn it."

As I stood there, momentarily adrift, a jeep pulled into the parking lot. It rumbled over to stop next to Peyton and the others, and five more guys got out—a couple of them people I'd seen hanging out with Ansel, others who might have been footballers, at least one I had no clue about whatsoever. Apparently the sport of ganging up on Lily had become a free-for-all.

The pack of them marched over to us together, Peyton staying off to the side but looking as fiercely eager as the others. I backed up a step instinctively, but Kai held his ground, his shoulders squaring.

"Not so confident when it's just you on your own, I bet," one of the guys sneered at him. "You think you're so tough. Time we taught you a lesson."

Kai chuckled, not sounding remotely fazed. "The lesson that it takes seven of you to come at one of me? I already knew you were wimps."

The guy who'd spoken let out a growl and stomped forward. But at the same moment, two more engines roared into hearing behind us.

First came the car that'd once been Ansel's, with Ruin behind the wheel and Jett braced in the passenger seat. As it jolted to a halt next to us, a motorcycle whipped into the lot with Nox poised on its seat. His teeth were bared in something half grin, half snarl.

He'd finally gotten the bike he'd wanted so much, some distant part of my mind registered. Kai must have texted for them to come before he'd started debating with the cops.

The guys leapt out of the car, and Nox hurtled off the motorcycle. Even though they still had nearly twice the numbers, our opponents fell back, their threatening expressions turning comically uncertain.

One of them broke and ran for the cars. Kai whipped a switchblade from his pocket and flung it across the pavement so fast it was a blur—until it slammed into one of the tires. The air groaned out. Jett hurled a knife of his own at the second vehicle.

"You're not going anywhere until we're good and done with you," Nox said. "And probably not even then."

"We shouldn't kill them," Kai piped up. "The three of them have been connected to Lily just now in front of law enforcement. Adding murder to the mix might be dicey for her."

Nox let out a huff of disappointment, but his eyes flared. "Fine. We'll just make them very, very sorry."

He stalked toward the bullies with murder radiating from every pore.

twenty-three

Lily

My bullies weren't stupid. They could obviously tell they were about to be dead meat, or at least the closest thing to that without actually meeting their ends.

The group broke apart, the assholes scattering in every direction, Peyton dashing around the side of the store. But my guys were faster.

Nox caught one of Ansel's friends and hurled him right through the spray-painted windows. The guy crashed to the floor with a cacophony of breaking glass. Ruin wrapped his arms around another in a deadly bear hug and whipped him after his companion. Kai tripped one and sent him rolling. Jett flipped another over his shoulder and flung him through the broken window.

The two of them grabbed their knives from the sunken tires.

Peyton had vanished, but there was no escape for the others. At the brandishing of Kai's and Jett's knives in between them and the other end of the parking lot, the remainders fled into the store after their friends, maybe hoping they could find a back entrance to flee out of. Of course, that door would be locked.

The Skullbreakers charged after their foes. Yelps and squelches emanated from within the grocery store. My whole body had gone numb, but I managed to move my feet to step through the window and witness the fate my accusers were meeting.

The grocery store had transformed into a whirlwind of violence. Over in the produce aisle, Jett was pelting two of the guys with potatoes, hard enough for each strike to land with a meaty thunk and a pained gasp from his targets.

Kai had toppled another dude. He swept a heap of grapes off the display onto the guy's back and then leapt onto him to mash the fruit in with his stomping feet. At the guy's whimper, he smirked. "That's right, we're making a little whine."

Down the other aisles, Ruin had grabbed two bottles of his favorite hot sauce. He squirted it at the faces of three guys who tried to hurtle past him, and they stumbled into the shelves, groping at their eyes. As he cackled, Nox cracked a frozen pizza over the last bully's head. Pepperoni rained down, sticking to the dipshit's cheeks like clown make-up.

Ruin snatched a jug of apple juice and heaved it right into one guy's groin. The lid popped open on impact. The dickhead doubled over, juice sloshing down his khakis as if he'd wet himself. From the look on his face, he might have done that too.

Jett had rushed in on one of his targets. He scooped him up and rammed him headfirst into a pre-packaged meat display. The guy rolled off the shelves, bleeding from his head and smeared with ground beef and bits of porkchop as if his innards had popped right through his skin without breaking it. Jett gave him another kick to the head for good measure.

At a choking sound, I spun around to see Kai ramming a handful of hotdogs into the other potato-pelted dude's mouth. They poked from the guy's swollen lips like a meme about chowing down on dicks. Kai straightened up and pushed them deeper with his heel.

A hysterical laugh bubbled in my throat. I couldn't decide whether I was more horrified or amused. One thing was for sure—these fucknuts were never going to forget *this* beating.

Over by the cash registers, Nox had now knocked down two guys. He had them both pinned with a knee on each gut, stabbing them with spikes of dry spaghetti so they were gradually turning into human porcupines. At their groans and hisses of pain, he glowered at them. "If there has to be a next time, I'll be stabbing these right through your intestines. Keep that in mind."

Ruin dashed by, shoving a guy into a tower of canned veggies and then smacking the rest to rain down on him, bashing the douche-nozzle's head and chest. "Best possible use for lima beans!" he crowed.

Jett leapt back into view, his knife in one hand and a Pop Tart in the other. He slashed out at the last guy still on his feet, cutting sliver-thin cuts with the knife and broader gouges with the corner of the breakfast pastry. When the jerkwad slipped and sprawled face-first in a puddle of sour juice from a pickle jar someone had smashed on the floor, Jett leaned over to carve the words *PICKLE PRICK* across his shoulder blades. He let out a dark laugh. "Your dates deserve fair warning."

The sounds of the mayhem swirled around me, grunts and gasps, sloshes and crackles. It filled my head with a weird, wavering melody that begged for words. Crazed as it was, there was something so brilliantly orchestral about the maelstrom of violence...

The hum I'd felt before expanded through my chest as if to match that strange harmony. My nerves quivered, and my stomach lurched. I'd felt that sensation right when Peyton's water had started jumping around—

Kai glanced over at me, and a gleam lit in his eyes. He grinned at me as if I'd done something fantastic, even though I hadn't done anything except stand here staring for the last several minutes. Then he noticed one of the guys half crawling, half sliding through the mess on the floor toward the stock room. He bared his teeth. "Oh, no, you don't. You don't know *half* of what we're capable of."

Neither did I, it seemed. Kai slammed his hand

down at the edge of the wet streak, and sparks shot across the mess of liquid. The guy's body seized and spasmed as if he'd been struck by lightning.

Ruin, watching, let out a whoop. "Can we *all* do that?" he asked, and spun on a guy sitting in a puddle of hot sauce before Kai even answered. At the smack of his fingers, his foe jolted on his ass, teeth rattling.

Holy shit. They hadn't lost all their supernatural powers when they'd dived into their new bodies. What were my bullies going to make of that?

Nox cocked his head with curiosity and sent a zap through a pool of juice toward the two guys who were slumped in it. At the twitch of their bodies, a satisfied smile curled his lips.

"You stay away from us, and you stay away from Lily," he bellowed to the store at large. "This was us playing nice. You don't want to find out what mean looks like." Then, apparently determining that their work here was done, he motioned for the others to tramp with him over to the broken window where I was still standing frozen.

The rising hum inside me had faded. The bottom of my stomach had fallen out, leaving me uncomfortably empty and more than a little dazed. I wobbled out of the store, images and sounds still whirling in my head, and my gaze caught on the camera that had factored so much into the accusations against me. My heart stopped.

"The security system!" I said. "The owner hasn't bothered with alarms"—because things like this didn't happen around here, not in Lovell Rise—"but we'll be on camera." It didn't matter if Nox had scared the scumbags out of tattling on him and his men if the video footage told the story for them.

Kai made a dismissive sound and clapped his hand to the doorframe below the camera. With a sizzling noise, the camera gave off a few sparks and sagged slightly. Kai wiped his hands together with a triumphant air. "I fried it all the way to the hard drive that's storing the footage. There won't be anything to look at except our redecorating efforts." He glanced at the wrecked store with an arch of his eyebrows.

I looked at it too, and my chest constricted. My daze was washed away by a flood of panic.

The guys had gotten revenge on my bullies, sure, but how much did that really change? They'd given away so much about what they were and what they could do, while leaving a trail of wreckage in their wake.

How much of my life was about to get so much worse?

I swept my fingers back into my hair, my breath coming short. "I lost my job. I don't have any way to make more money. People are going to be talking about me all around town as it is. If anyone realizes I was at all connected to what just happened here—"

"They won't," Kai said calmly. "The police will clear you of the graffiti, which'll make it obvious that your accusers were the real criminals. Who knows what else they might be mixed up in to end up like this?" He waved toward the store. "Things that have nothing to do with you or us."

He sounded utterly confident, but I couldn't quite wrap my head around it being that easy. *Nothing* had been easy since I'd gotten back here.

"There could be something we haven't thought of," I said, the words tumbling out of me. "I can't come back from this. Everything's—everything's gotten turned upside down. How'm I supposed to get back to Marisol when I'm mixed up in this mess?"

Nox set his hand on my back. "Let's get you back home," he said firmly. "We don't want to hang around here now that we've taken care of those dolts. Then we'll have a real conversation. It's all going to be fine. We've got you now, no matter what comes."

He hopped onto his new motorcycle with a nod to the other guys. Ruin escorted me over to my car. He nudged me into the passenger seat and got in behind the wheel. I let him take the keys, sinking into the lumpy padding and closing my eyes.

Had I made a mistake letting these guys into my life? Had they always been this wild, or had death left them even more unhinged than in their original existence?

Who was going to protect me from *them* if they got too crazy? They might only want to protect me, but that didn't mean it'd work out that way.

Ruin switched the radio to a station that was more noise than melody and turned it up loud enough that conversation would have been impossible anyway. He tore through the streets so fast that it only took the length of one song to make it back to the apartment. After he parked, he came around to my door, and I got the impression that he'd have carried me inside like Nox had hauled me into his office the other day if I didn't show I could manage it on my own.

I pushed myself to my feet, willing my legs to stay steady, and trudged down the steps to the apartment door. Inside, I flopped onto the futon and immediately slid into the dip in the middle. I couldn't summon the resolve to clamber back out.

The guys gathered around me as they followed us in, Nox sitting on one side of me and Ruin on the other, Jett and Kai dragging over chairs from the table.

"What's bothering you?" Nox asked, with an edge to a tone that suggested he hoped it was something he could shoot or stab.

I bent over, pressing my hands against my face. "I was trying to build a normal life so that Mom and Wade wouldn't have any excuse to keep me away from Marisol. But that's all gone to hell, hasn't it? Everything's just a mess."

"You couldn't let those pricks keep treating you like a punching bag. They weren't stopping just because you weren't fighting back."

Ruin rubbed my arm. "*They're* the ones who screwed things up. You deserve to have someone defending you."

"You should let us wipe them out completely," Jett muttered.

I tensed. "People *dying* isn't going to make the situation better."

Kai leaned forward. "If you won't let us crush the bullies completely, then *you* need to put them in their place. Show them you won't be a target anymore. There'll be others like the pricks we dealt with today. Rolling over for them wasn't working, so it's time to stand up."

I raised my head to stare at him. "How am I supposed to do that? Go around punching and knifing anyone who makes a nasty comment at me?"

He smiled, his eyes glinting behind his glasses. "I think you can do something better than that. You just need to let loose that power inside you. I could feel it back at the grocery store. You could have all these assholes shaking in their designer sneakers if you let yourself."

"Power?" I repeated, but my hand rose to my chest at the same moment, thinking of the hum that'd resonated there. Of Kai looking at me as the vibration had filled my torso.

Ruin sucked in a breath. "I noticed it too! You've got some kind of energy in you—kind of like ours." He looked down at his free hand. "But *you* were never a ghost."

"She almost was," Nox said into the sudden silence. "We don't know how close she got to crossing over—close enough that her spirit called out to us." He caught my gaze. "Maybe you came out of the marsh with more than you went in with."

"It's hardly typical science, but that possibility seems plausible to me," Kai said. "There's definitely *something* more to you than you're letting out."

A shiver ran over my skin at the thought of some unknown power inside me. "I don't even know what it is. If there's some special magic inside me, how'm I supposed to control it? How can I bring it out when I actually want it?" I dropped my head back into my hands and shook it. "Fuck. This is too insane."

Maybe Mom and Wade hadn't been wrong to shut me away with the psychos after all.

twenty-four

Nox

Lily's pose, so hopeless and terrified, made me want to burn the world down. Although I had the feeling that would make her more upset, not less.

Why couldn't she see that the strangeness that shone in her made her something *more* than any regular human being, not less? That she could rise above all the assholes who wanted to crush her under their heels and put them in their places instead?

I'd lost my crew once and gotten them back, but now I felt like I was losing her too, after all the lengths I'd gone to so I could be here for her. What was the point of any of this if the pricks like those college bullies and her stepdad won in the end?

A growl formed in the back of my throat, but I held it in. She'd spent too long having all those living voices around her telling her she was worthless, nothing but an inconvenience. Our ghostly chorus hadn't been enough to drown them out. And now, with the four of us braced around her, maybe we were suffocating with our own expectations.

I stood up abruptly. "Out!" I barked at my friends. "All of you, find something else useful to do with yourselves. I'm going to talk Lily through this alone. She doesn't need all four of us breathing down her neck at the same time."

Ruin's arm tightened around her with a possessiveness that rankled me. "But—"

"*Out*," I repeated, and he didn't rebel any further. He pressed a quick kiss to Lily's forehead and got to his feet. Kai caught my gaze with a questioning glance, but when I jerked my head toward the door, he went. Jett followed the two of them with his usual brooding silence.

When the door clicked shut and it was just me and Lily, she stayed sitting there with her face in her hands. Her long, pale hair fell forward like a veil. She looked *small* somehow, and that wasn't right at all.

It occurred to me that I had no idea what to do next. I ruled the Skullbreakers, so I should be the one to tackle this problem too… but it wasn't anything I could threaten or batter into going my way. Lily's greatest enemy was something *inside* her that was freaking her out, and I wasn't going to let myself break her trying to get at it. Not when all I wanted to do was put her together into the stunning woman she should have already known she was.

Maybe I should have let Ruin handle this. What the hell did I know about being gentle? I flexed my hands at my sides, groping for the right thing to say, the right thing to do.

"Come here," I said finally. Without waiting to see if she'd listen, I scooped her off the couch and carried her into her bedroom.

Setting her on the edge of the bed, I knelt in front of her. The frame was so low that position brought us eye-to-eye.

It should have felt awkward being on my knees in front of anyone. But with Lily, the pose didn't feel like any kind of humiliation. I was showing her we were on the same level. Could be that was the best place to start.

I brushed my fingers over her cheek and into her hair, unable to resist giving it a playful tug. "You didn't let the marsh swallow you, and you're not letting whatever this is beat you either," I informed her. "What's really the problem here? Why do you give a single shit what any of those people think of you?"

Lily drew in a wobbly breath. "A few of those people are standing between me and my sister. A lot of the others could get me in trouble with the first people if they complain about me enough... or even with the cops. I can't get sent back to St. Elspeth's. I don't know if the doctors would ever let me back out."

"*We'd* break you out of there if it came to that," I

said, my jaw tensing at the thought. "But it won't. You've got us now, and you've got *you*. You don't have to let any of them get between you and your sister."

"But—"

"You've got the strength to shove them aside and take what you know you're owed," I went on before she could dismiss my words. "That's how we live. Fuck the rules. Fuck catering to assholes' judgements. If you let yourself stop caring what the people who don't matter want, *nothing* can get in your way. Can't you feel that power Kai was talking about in here?" I tapped her chest.

Lily shivered. "It doesn't feel like power. It feels like… like I'm going to lose control, and I don't know what'll happen then. I don't know who I might hurt. And what if I *want* a life that's at least kind of normal? I've got to follow the rules then."

I raised my eyebrows at her. "Do you actually want something normal, or are you just scared that you'll be punished if you carve your own path?" I guessed me and my bros weren't the best example of that. *Our* paths had been cut short by other pricks who hadn't liked the rules we made for ourselves. But we were back, and we weren't going to let anyone get in our way now.

And I'd rather live free for a short while than be tied up in some straitjacket of politeness for an eternity.

"I don't know," Lily whispered. "Marisol needs me. I don't want to let her down."

I pushed myself straighter and leaned in so my face was just inches from hers, teasing my fingers into her hair again. Her intoxicating scent swept into my lungs, wild and sweet, and suddenly the correct path for me right now stretched out in my mind, perfectly clear.

"I think the reason you feel out of control is that you're not used to using your power," I said. "You didn't even know you had it. But you've got all kinds of power, Minnow. Do you have any idea how much power you hold over *me*? You're my siren. You're the reason I'm here at all. The things you do to me, just having you so close…"

Just saying the words, desire flickered through me like a flame over kerosene. It'd been too fucking long since I'd gotten to indulge these bodily urges, since I'd had a body to indulge them with, and my nerves screamed for more. I held myself back with a fraying thread of self-control.

What I wanted wasn't the important part. Lily needed to be the one who crossed the line this time. She needed to *take* instead of being taken.

She reached up, her soft fingers tracing along my jaw and lighting more flames in their wake. "I really mean that much to you?"

"To all of us," I said, reluctantly but honestly. I owed that much to the guys who'd stood by me. "I'm going to rebuild the Skullbreakers and remake our name —but I came back for *you*. I already had one life that was all about me. In this one, you come first."

She inhaled with a little hitch of her chest that sounded more awed than anxious. I grazed my fingers over her scalp and pressed my advantage while my hardening cock pressed against the seam of my jeans in tandem.

"Why don't you find out what it's like working some of that power on me? Get a little practice in. See just how much you can rule even when you're letting go."

Lily hesitated just for a second. Then, thank the Devil, she tugged me toward her to capture my mouth with hers.

It wasn't the epic collision of our first kiss, but the tender eagerness of her lips sliding against mine sent a rush of satisfaction through me that was just as heady. I let her take her fill of me, kissing her back but not taking over, running my fingertips up and down the side of her neck as I did. She let out a pleased murmur and kissed me harder with a passion that had me rigid as rock down below.

She'd spent a lifetime being told she wasn't good enough for anyone. I had to show her with every gesture and word I could offer how fucking cherished she was now. How much she was really worth. Until I convinced her. And then I'd keep reminding her so she never forgot.

I eased my other hand under her shirt, tracing her smooth skin up to the curve of her chest. Her bra was thin enough that her nipple poked through the fabric when I swiped my thumb over it.

Lily made another sound that was more of a growl, scooting even closer, and a smile curved my lips against hers.

"Every part of you drives me crazy," I murmured, trailing my mouth along her jaw. "Your mouth. Your cheeks. Your fucking *ears*." I nipped her earlobe, and she gave a tiny gasp. "This neck is goddamned delicious." I teased my teeth down the slope of it, bringing out a perfect whimper of need.

It was a miracle being able to touch *any* woman like this again. My veins were on fire. But the fact that it was Lily made it ten times sweeter. I hadn't known we'd careen toward each other like this—had never looked at her this way in the times before when she'd only been a kid—but now it was nothing short of perfect.

No other woman had ever held a candle to the inferno she'd set off in me.

"I want to see you," Lily said abruptly, her hands fisting in my shirt.

I was more than happy to oblige. I peeled off the Henley and pulled her tee over her head in turn. She sat there on the bed without the slightest hint of self-consciousness about being bared to her bra in front of me, her attention fixed on my torso.

I'd grown into this body that hadn't been shaped quite right to fit me when I'd first possessed it. The muscles that'd filled out my chest and shoulders were almost on par with what I'd sported back in the day. I might still be a few inches shorter than my former glory of height, but I'd just have to make up for that with an even more massive presence.

Lily trailed her fingers over my pecs, and I had to clench my hands to stop myself from yanking her right to me. "Is this how you looked before?" she asked tentatively.

"I'm getting there," I said. "No professor bod is going to get in my way for long." I glanced down at myself, taking a measure of the terrain. "My tattoos haven't reemerged. I guess they weren't inked right on my spirit. I'll have to get them done when I don't have more important things occupying me."

She swiveled her thumb over one of my nipples, watching my face to catch how my eyes blazed at the quiver of pleasure. A growl crept into my voice, but it wasn't remotely angry. "I love having you touch me almost as much as I love touching you."

And because I was a man of action, I followed that statement up by reaching around her to unclasp her bra. I ducked my head to lap the peak of one breast into my mouth and worked it over with my tongue and teeth until Lily was moaning and clutching my hair.

"That's right, baby," I said as I moved to worship her other breast. "I've got so much more for you. You taste so good."

I'd bet she tasted even better farther down. As I sucked on her nipple, bringing another gasp to her lips, I flicked open the fly of her jeans and tugged them down her legs.

Her panties were soaked. Approval thrummed through my chest as I stroked her through them.

"Good girl. So fucking wet for me. Do you have any idea how hard I am for you? You make me want to explode. But I'm going to look after you first."

I wrenched her panties down too and buried my face between her thighs.

Lily gave a shriek that was all pleasure. I devoured her, flicking my tongue over her clit and delving it right into her pussy, drinking up those sharply sweet juices that flooded out of her at my call. Hell, this was the best meal I'd had since I'd gotten back my mouth.

It was a fucking crime that no one had ever worshiped her the way she deserved until now.

As I suckled her harder, her breath broke into stuttered pants. She tipped back on the bed, her head resting against the wall, her hips rocking to meet the thrusts of my tongue. I focused my mouth over her clit and brought two fingers up to hook inside her. With a few testing strokes, I found the special spot inside her that made her shudder.

It only took a few pulses of my fingertips against that place alongside the pressure of my mouth to bring her to a quaking release. Her pussy clamped around my fingers and her back arched up as the sweetest moan in existence reverberated out of her. I'd taken her even higher than I had the other day on the professor's desk.

Part of me wished I'd drawn out her gratification even longer, but a bigger part was desperate to fuse my body to hers in the most primal possible way. I gave her pussy one last lingering kiss and loomed up over her, fumbling in my pocket for the condom I'd thankfully had the foresight to carry. I had no idea if possessed swimmers swam well, but after all the weirdness of our ghostly union with these bodies, I didn't think knocking our woman up with ghostly jizz was a smart idea.

Lily undid my fly for me, freeing my cock into her waiting hand and then gazing up at me with heavy-lidded eyes. I practically came just looking at her. As she swiveled her fingers around my straining shaft, a groan tumbled out of me.

"God, I want you so fucking badly. You're my universe, Lily. You defied death and dragged me back to life. There isn't anyone in their right mind who should mess with you."

A glow lit in her face that hadn't been there before. Maybe I was getting through to her.

I kicked off my jeans, pausing every now and then to hiss a breath and pump into her stroking hand. As she tugged my boxers down, biting her lower lip as she did, I knew just how to take this final step.

I slicked the condom over my rigid cock and sank down onto the mattress on my back. When my own hand worked up and down my shaft, making my balls ache, Lily's gaze followed the movement. She licked her lips, and my dick twitched.

"You want this?" I asked in a low voice.

Lily lifted her head to meet my eyes. Her cheeks were flushed from her first orgasm, all of her absolutely radiant. "Yeah," she said, soft but certain. "I do."

I grinned. "Then come and get it, baby."

And fuck me if she didn't clamber right onto me, straddling my hips. I pushed myself up on my elbow, and she bent down to claim my mouth. Her tongue cautiously slipped between my lips and then tangled with mine. I hummed encouragingly, massaging her ass with my free hand.

She lined herself up over me and sank onto my cock, impaling herself with that jutting length. Her slick cunt closed tight around me, and sparks went off behind my eyes. I couldn't hold back another groan— but why should I? I wanted her to know how much she affected me.

"Your pussy feels so good around me," I muttered. "So fucking good. Take me all the way—I know you can."

She eased lower with a rock of her hips, and I gripped her ass to steady her. Giddy heat flooded my entire body, with the tightest knot of need at the base of my groin. "Oh, yeah. Just like that. I can't wait to make you scream."

She let out a mewling sound, and I took that as my cue to move. As her hands braced against my chest, I bucked up to meet her, thrusting even deeper inside her.

Lily swayed with the rhythm, arching her back and pumping up and down over me at the same time. Her eyelids fluttered shut. Her lips parted to form a gorgeous O. I'd take her to an even better one.

"Keep doing that, baby," I said, massaging her thigh. "You feel fucking incredible. You ride me so good."

A whimper spilled out of her, and then a sound that

wasn't the scream I'd been searching for but something so much better.

She was singing. In a pale, whispery voice that rose and fell with the colliding of our bodies, but it was the first melody I'd heard from her lips since she'd come back into our lives.

"So high... soaring all the way to the sky... Never felt, never knew... that it could be so bright..."

She made up a song just for me. For us and this sweaty, blissful moment. Somehow or other, I'd managed to heal that one part of her that'd been broken. I'd done something really fucking right.

My heart swelled nearly as much as my cock. I was right on the verge.

Squeezing her ass, I plunged up into her with a swivel of my hips, seeking that perfect spot she needed. On the second try, a shudder wracked her body.

Her head dropped back, her whole body tightening against me with the spasm of her pussy, and my cock erupted. My vision sizzled with the force of my coming.

Lily bowed over me with a hitch of breath and a small, sly smile. As she nestled her head against my shoulder, I wrapped my arms around her and smirked at the thought of all the bastards who were going to pay when she showed them just what she was made of.

twenty-five

Lily

Something had shifted in the air. When the rest of the guys came back to the apartment with Chinese takeout, when Nox ran a possessive hand down my back and Ruin slung a companionable arm around my shoulders, when I snuggled in the bed that still smelled like heavenly sex while the sound of their sleeping breaths filtered through the wall, every motion I made and every sound that stirred around me blended together into a giddy sort of harmony.

It sang through my nerves and tingled over my skin every place Nox had touched me. With his adoring words in my ears and bliss rushing through my body, I'd felt as if I really was as powerful as he said. A goddess who could bend the world to her will.

The thought seemed a little silly now, but the sense of weightlessness remained. No one was going to hold me down. I could make the world I wanted to live in… Insist on a life where Mom and Wade couldn't keep me from Marisol… Ward off anyone who tried to trip me up or insult me. Even the music that wove from the world into me felt right, like it would be okay for me to put a voice to it again. Like I deserved a chance to let out the songs that tickled up through my mind.

But that sense only stayed solid while I was in the bubble of my apartment with the guys. Outside under the mid-morning sun with the crisp fall breeze in my nose, reality came crashing back in on me.

I paused on the sidewalk outside the side lane that led to my apartment steps, inhaling and exhaling, wondering what the police were saying about me now after the mess they'd have found in Mart's Supermarket yesterday. What the whole town was saying about me. A shiver of uncertainty rippled through my previous confidence.

Ruin slipped his arm around my waist with his usual warm affection and nuzzled my temple. I was pretty sure all the guys had been able to tell what Nox and I had gotten up to, but if it put off the cheerful former gangster, he hadn't shown it.

"We can all go with you," he suggested. "Walk you right to class. Make anyone who even looks at you funny sorry."

A despairing chuckle fell from my mouth. Imagine what my classmates and professors would think of me having that devoted an entourage—and one composed of a guy they still recognized as a professor and students who'd never had anything to do with each other before.

But that wasn't really the point, was it? If I'd wanted the guys with me, then I shouldn't care what anyone else thought about it. These men could handle any backlash that came their way.

What mattered was that they'd been right about one thing: I needed to stand on my own two feet. As long as they were doing all the defending, the people who wanted to push me around would just keep doing it when they felt they could get away with it.

I had to show them it wasn't worth it even when they were only dealing with me.

I still wasn't totally sure how I was going to accomplish that or that the attempt wouldn't go horribly wrong, but enough resolve condensed inside me that I raised my chin. "No. You can come with me to campus, but I'll go on my own from there. If anyone comes at me, I'll figure out my own way of changing their tune."

"That's my girl," Nox said, and I wondered if the new baritone quality to his voice had gotten even deeper overnight. It sent a pleasant shiver through me, which amplified when he glanced around at the others and corrected himself. "*Our* girl."

"Our *woman*," Ruin said with a grin, and sought out my lips for a kiss so brilliant that all of a sudden I was much more concerned about when I could drag *him* into bed for more than just a cuddle than what challenges waited for me on campus.

I glanced back at the apartment. "I'm still going to need rent money and the rest. I have a little savings from the work placements I got through St. Elspeth's, but that won't last long."

Kai's eyes glinted behind his glasses. "Don't worry about it. If you can find a job with a boss who's not a prick, go for it, but we have our own ways of getting the bills paid in the meantime."

I wasn't sure I wanted to ask what those ways were.

I insisted on driving out to the school in my own car while the guys followed behind with Nox on his motorcycle and the other three in Ansel's old sports car like a bizarro presidential motorcade. Fred's engine grumbled and sputtered a few times, but it got me to the college parking lot just fine. I found a spot closer to the campus buildings than was usually free and decided that was a good omen.

"If you need us, you know how to call on us," Nox reminded me, with a flare of heat in his eyes that suggested he'd have liked to take a page out of Ruin's book and steal a kiss for himself. But I wasn't throwing caution to the wind so much that making out with a supposed professor in broad daylight seemed like a good idea, no matter how much the former gangsters' covers were already blown at this point.

I strode across the lawns and into the building for my first class of the day braced for the worst, but I didn't even hear a whisper of derision. I took my notes and managed not to nod off when the professor got particularly drone-y about Organized Criminal Behavior, which I was starting to realize he knew shit-all about. No one kicked my chair or tossed any beverages in my face. It was shaping up to be a pretty okay day.

At first. Between classes, I ducked into the restroom. When I came out of the stall, Peyton was standing by the sinks, looking no worse for wear after yesterday's confrontation but still just as pissed off with me.

I froze in my tracks, glancing around. We were alone in the bathroom. I willed someone to walk in to act as a witness, but no one came. I could have made a run for the door with my germy hands—ew—but she probably wouldn't have let me get that far anyway.

I settled for walking to the farthest sink from her and lathering up as if I didn't give a shit that she was glaring daggers at me. My nonchalance must have pissed her off even more, because I'd swear she sharpened those daggers in mid-stare.

"You're a menace," she spat out. "Everyone knows it, even if those guys you've roped into fighting your battles for you are beating them into silence. Funny how you're never so tough on your own."

I turned toward her, crossing my arms. My nerves jittered, but I kept my voice steady. "Maybe that's going to change."

"Oh, yeah? What are you going to do when I smash your head into one of those toilets? Seems like fair payback for what you brought down on all those guys yesterday. For what you're making Ansel do." She sucked in a harsh breath. "There are no cameras in the bathrooms. I could shove your head underwater until you drown, and no one would be able to prove a thing. I'd just be cleaning up the college and setting those men free."

I raised my eyebrows even though my pulse was thumping so hard I was surprised she couldn't see it vibrating through my stance. That deep, dark hum that was becoming familiar started to resonate through me, swelling in my chest. "It's funny hearing that coming from a girl who's tossed me down a flight of stairs, falsely accused me of a crime, and gotten me fired. From where I'm standing, the only menace here is you."

"I've only been protecting this school and the people in it from *your* nasty influence," Peyton shot back, and came at me with her hands raised.

The hum inside me blared louder, with a whooshing sound in my ears like I was plunging through a waterfall. A flicker of panic shot through my veins— what was going to happen if I gave it free rein?—but I squared my shoulders and stepped back into a defensive pose. "You don't want to do that."

"Why not?" Peyton taunted, squeezing her hands into fists. "Are you going to pout and cry out for your boys at me?"

My jaw clenched. "I can do something way worse than that." I just… wasn't totally sure what that was. But we were both about to find out.

I focused on the thrumming within, and for the first time I urged it farther, higher, louder. It spread through my whole being, reverberating along my cells as if I were a church organ being played to grand effect.

I'd expected the energy to go surging out of me, but instead it only condensed with a growing, silent peal, like every note was a war horn being sounded, calling... something... to battle.

And something was coming. I could feel it in every inch of my skin. Peyton swung a balled hand at me and snatched at my wrist, I jerked out of the way—and the small window behind me rattled.

Peyton froze for just a second, and in the same moment, the pane burst open. A flurry of green flashes cascaded through it. More were rushing in under the door. It took a second for my mind to wrap around what I was seeing.

Frogs. A flood of frogs, flinging themselves toward Peyton from both sides.

I'd summoned an army of fucking *frogs*.

Maybe it wasn't actually normal for people to run into the croaking creatures all over town. Maybe they just liked me. Huh.

The sleek green bodies hurtled at Peyton with a cacophony of croaks. They leapt off the floor at her legs and bounded off the sinks to land on her chest and shoulders, a few even clinging onto her hair.

I couldn't imagine they were doing a whole lot more than sticking themselves to her, because it wasn't like they had claws or teeth or anything that would have been remotely painful. But Peyton reacted as if she was being swarmed by stinging hornets or chomping mice.

She screamed, whirling around with her legs and arms flailing in a frantic dance. But for every frog she shook off, two more jumped up in its place. They swarmed across the floor now, ribbiting merrily and bouncing about as if they were having the time of their lives.

A laugh burst out of me. Peyton howled and pawed at her head. I felt a little sorry for the frogs she swatted, but they didn't seem bothered by her hysteria.

"What the fuck did you do?" she shrieked at me. "Get them off me! This is insane!"

My heartbeat had slowed to a steady, even rhythm. I smiled at her and took a step toward the door through the narrow clear path the frogs had left for me. "What else do you expect from a psycho? Trust me, you don't want to find out what else I can do."

I wasn't sure I even wanted to find out, but I didn't have to mention that.

Peyton wailed and continued her desperate dance of frog-revulsion. "You can't just… just do things like this to people. I'm going to tell security—the dean—"

I snorted, cutting her off. "Tell them what? That I sicced a horde of frogs on you? Who are they going to think is insane then? It's not like there are any witnesses. After all, there are no cameras in here, just like you wanted."

I spun on my heel and walked out without looking back, leaving her to her new amphibious friends.

twenty-six

Lily

When I met up with the guys after my last class, I found a very different array of escort vehicles around my car in the parking lot. It appeared they'd all taken a page out of Nox's book. Each of them stood beside a shiny new motorcycle.

Jett's was bulky and muscular-looking like Nox's. Kai had gone for one sleek and compact as a greyhound. Ruin's had flashes of neon trim, because of course it did. It probably also had a hot sauce dispenser.

"We figured it was time to get back into the Skullbreaker groove," Ruin said with a grin as I checked them out. The bikes, not the guys. Although I might have ogled the guys a little too. I had to admit they looked pretty hot sitting astride those beasts.

I patted Fred, even if my growing affection for the heap of junk was kind of ridiculous. "There are some benefits to car ownership. More storage space, for instance."

Nox looked me over, appreciation gleaming in his eyes as he must have taken in my lingering sense of victory. "You've been busy."

I couldn't stop a smile from curling my lips. The hum of power inside me had died down, but the exhilaration of the moment when I'd shown Peyton just who she was trying to mess with still tickled through my veins.

It'd been crazy—what I'd done, the fact that I could do it at all. I was a little scared to think too hard about it. But at the same time... maybe crazy was the real way out of this. Maybe it simply wasn't possible to be sane enough to make all the assholes around me satisfied anyway.

"I don't think I'll be having any more trouble with my classmates," I said. The Skullbreakers had already put fear into the worst of the guys, and Peyton had been the ringleader among the girls. And if anyone else decided to get mouthy or handsy, I knew now that I could set them straight.

Kai's eyes glinted too. "Excellent. Did you zap a few souls?"

I laughed, thinking of the supernatural power their spirits had brought into their new bodies. "No. It seems like whatever energies I can draw on, they're more... marshy."

He made a thoughtful sound. "Fascinating. I suppose you took a little of the marsh with you when it didn't manage to take you. I look forward to seeing you in action."

"What now?" Ruin asked eagerly.

I ran my hand over the car's hood, and a jab of certainty I couldn't deny lanced through my gut. "I need answers. I need to know what really happened seven years ago and if there's anything I need to do to make amends with Marisol."

And there were only two people I was sure knew the full story—the two people who'd sent me off to the loony bin to begin with.

I considered confronting Mom, but something in me balked. She'd been a crappy mother, and I'd rather have eaten worms than make nice with her, but she'd been in a crappy situation. Dad's abandonment had screwed with her head and wrung her out until there was barely any of herself left.

It was Wade who'd let her get so small and meek. Wade who'd encouraged her simpering and berated her if she ever disappointed him by not catering to his every whim. I had no doubt it'd been his idea to threaten to call the police on me.

And he was the one who'd been talking about some

mysterious other person who might somehow be involved.

As so often, Kai picked up on my thoughts before I said them out loud. "We're going after your stepdad."

Jett let out an approving grunt. "Let's crush that motherfucker."

I sucked my lower lip under my teeth to worry at it. "I guess he won't be at work, since he doesn't have much of a workplace anymore…" I gave Kai a pointed look, and he just smirked. "I might as well start with the house and then expand the search from there. Marisol won't be home from school yet." I didn't know exactly what was going to go down between me and Wade, but I suspected I'd rather she didn't witness it as her first introduction to the stranger parts of me.

The mark on the inside of my arm itched. I scratched at it idly and considered the guys. "I have to do this by myself too. I want him to know he can't intimidate me even when I'm on my own." And if I could help it, I didn't want him making more trouble for the guys than they'd already gotten into, not that I thought they'd accept that reasoning. They seemed to think the protecting could only go one way around here.

Nox nodded. "We'll follow you out there. Make sure you don't run into any problems along the way—and be ready as backup if anything goes wrong."

"Fair." I dragged in a breath and went around to Fred's driver's side door. "Here goes nothing."

It didn't feel like nothing, though. It felt like… well,

everything. Like the whole world and all the hopes I'd had for my life in that world were weighing down on my shoulders as I drove toward the house where I'd lived for the first thirteen years of my life. I guessed you could say I came with a lot of baggage.

But Wade was the one who'd put most of it there, and I was about to unload.

The guys roared around me on their bikes, zipping ahead and then falling back behind as the whim took them. Every now and then Ruin gunned his engine as hard as he could and soared into the distance like he'd taken off on a jumbo jet. I suspected he enjoyed the extremes of speed just as much as all the other extremes he'd been indulging in, from flavors to sound.

He drew up beside me as we reached the lane that led to the old house. Wade's not-particularly-posh sedan sat in the driveway. A quiver of anticipation ran through me.

I might finally unlock the mystery that'd been haunting me for seven years—more than a third of my life. Suddenly it seemed so simple. But I wouldn't have had the courage to confront him like this—I wouldn't have believed it wouldn't ruin my chances even more and get me nowhere at the same time—until the friends who weren't so imaginary after all had barged back into my life.

Friends who weren't exactly just friends, either. After I'd gotten out of the car, Nox tucked a few stray strands of my hair behind my ear with fingers that left a trail of heat in their wake. Ruin grasped my hand and squeezed. This wasn't the place for a PDA, but a palpable ripple of devotion passed from them into me even with those small gestures.

"We're right here if you need us," Nox said.

"I know." I drew up my chin and marched to the front door of the house.

It was hard to believe I'd been here just a couple of days ago in much stealthier fashion. The house looked somehow bigger approaching it from the front, but also shabbier, as if it'd gotten more run-down in that time.

There wasn't anything so imposing about it, even if I'd been banned from the premises. In ways Wade could never erase, it was mine, tied to my history and my childhood.

I rang the doorbell and held myself still and straight while I waited. It took a while before I heard footsteps creak toward the front hall. There was no peephole, so my stepfather had no idea who was waiting for him on the other side until he swung the door wide.

Wade's posture went rigid, his gaze snagging on me and sticking there. Then he started to sputter. "What the hell are you doing here? Your mother said she warned you—you're not welcome on this property—"

"It's my house too, Wade," I interrupted, sharp and firm. "And I say I am. We need to talk. Why don't you step inside so we can do it like civilized people?"

"I'll have the cops here in a minute—"

He pulled his cell phone out of his pocket. I snatched it out of his hands and hurled it over my shoulder.

Wade stared at me, his eyes going even wider and a little of the color draining from his face. He wasn't that much taller than me, really, even if he had at least fifty pounds more pudge. In the past seven years, more crow's feet had formed at the corners of his eyes, and frown lines had dug in at the corners of his mouth.

Looking at him with an adult's eyes rather than a kid's, it was hard to believe I'd ever found him intimidating. He was pathetic. A miserable weaselly man who'd made himself feel bigger by bullying literal children. Who probably continued to do that when it came to my sister.

That last thought set my teeth on edge and brought the first hint of the unnatural hum into my chest.

Wade moved as if to push past me, and I shoved him backward instead. He hadn't been expecting that, and he stumbled a few feet before catching himself. His face went from pale to ruddy with a furious flush. "Who the hell do you think you—"

"I think I'm Lily Strom, and this house was mine before it was ever yours, and you're going to tell me what the hell happened here seven years ago that you used as an excuse to ship me off to the psych ward."

Wade's mouth tightened, but his eyes darted back and forth with an anxious twitch. He wasn't much of a physical fighter. I'd never challenged him this openly before. He might even have heard some of the stories about what'd been happening to people who messed with me lately.

His gaze slid past me to the guys on their

motorcycles parked outside and then focused on me again. He wet his lips. "Fine. You're not going to like it, but fine. Come to the kitchen and we'll talk."

I had the feeling he'd picked the kitchen because that was where the phone with the landline was located. I followed him there at his heels and grabbed the cable before he could so much as reach for it, tugging it out of the outlet. "We wouldn't want any interruptions."

Wade pursed his lips. He leaned against one of the laminate counters and narrowed his eyes at me. "It's a short story. You should have heard it already. You had a total mental breakdown. You went wild, throwing things around, attacking us. Your sister was terrified. We put you away for your own good. Lord only knows why they let you out. You're obviously not much more stable than you were back then." A trace of nervousness crept into his tone.

I *had* heard that story before. It was the one everyone had been telling me in bits and pieces since it'd become obvious that I couldn't tell *them* what'd gone down. But the doctors had heard it from Mom and Wade. They didn't know any better. There had to be more to it.

The hum expanded through my veins. I restrained a shiver. Resting my hand on the counter beside the phone, I started to drum my fingers. The sound fell into rhythm with the subtle but familiar creaks of the old walls and the warble of the rising breeze outside the windows.

The steady tempo formed by that unexpected

symphony smoothed out my nerves. It didn't diminish the growing swell of energy within me, only seemed to hone it, as if it were more a weapon I could wield than a surge of random power.

"That can't be the whole story," I replied, focusing on my stepdad more intently. "*Why* did I go 'wild'? What made me upset?"

Wade's jaw wobbled, so minutely I might not have noticed if I hadn't been watching him closely. He didn't want to tell me that part. "None of us did anything," he insisted. "And nothing could have justified—the fit you had—"

A flare of the anger I'd been suppressing so long under shame and doubt spiked to the surface. He was dicking around with my fucking *life* here. He'd stolen seven years of that life from me, and he couldn't even bring himself to tell me why?

I smacked both my hands on the counter. "*I'd* like to be the one who decides what was justified. What the hell happened?"

Wade jumped, but his mouth clamped tighter shut. The hum inside me rose to a roar, but the melody I'd latched onto wove through it, keeping me steady.

I didn't want frogs this time. I wanted—

My mind leapt to the marsh, to the sensation of sinking down into the sluggish current with slimy weeds tangling around my six-years-old legs—and the sink faucet gurgled to life. Water sprayed from the tap hard enough to splash Wade where he stood a few feet away.

As he jerked away from it, it gushed even harder.

The pipes in the walls groaned. My mouth set in a grim smile, and I let the power thundering through me sweep from my body like a tsunami.

And a tsunami it was. The pipes burst, bits of plaster flying with torrents of water careening out in their wake. The blasts whipped up and around rather than falling straight to earth.

One slapped Wade across the face with a wet wallop. Another pummeled him in the gut, sending him toppling onto his ass. Smaller jets smacked him back and forth like a boxer's fists toying with an opponent.

He cringed there on the floor, a thin whine creeping from his throat. His arms swung this way and that in an attempt to fend off the assault, as if it was something more horrifying than the same water he drank and flushed down the toilet every day.

"They didn't fix you," he babbled. "They didn't fix you at all. You're *crazy*. This is crazy!"

The truth clicked in my head with a wave of shock. This wasn't *his* first introduction to the stranger parts of me. What I was doing right now, or something like it, was what he'd meant by going wild.

I'd brought out my powers once before, all those years ago... and somehow I'd forgotten.

How could I have forgotten? I wasn't an elephant, but sudden marshy magical abilities seemed like the kind of thing that'd stick in your mind.

And I still didn't know what'd stirred me up enough for me to let them out.

The water kept pouring across the floor in an erratic

waterfall, but the more punishing streams eased off. I sloshed over and bent down in front of Wade, grabbing his soaking shirt collar in my hand.

"It is crazy," I said in a menacing voice. "But whatever set me off must have been even crazier. What. Fucking. Happened? Or do you need me to drown you a few times before you'll think about answering?"

I didn't have enough faith in my ability to inspire dudes to rise from the dead that I actually meant that threat, but Wade started to blubber like a toddler. Maybe the sight of my crazy powers had sent his mind into meltdown mode.

"I don't know," he wailed between hitches of sobs. "You came down and you started yelling at me and your mother, and I told Eleanor to leave so she didn't have to hear, and then... and then all of this..." He gestured toward the broken pipes weakly. But there was still something hesitant in the twisting of his mouth.

"Don't hold back on me," I snapped. Behind me, a swell of water arched up like a wave captured in mid-tumble. "I came down from where? What was going on with Marisol during all this? Why don't I *remember*?"

"I really don't know. He—he just wanted—I was only trying—I can't—"

"Who?" I shouted, shaking him. A faint mist rained down on us as the wave loomed higher.

A shudder ran through Wade's body, and his answer tumbled out in a gasp. "Talk to the Gauntts. They handled everything. They— He wanted to see your sister. I didn't badger him about why. I didn't— Ask *them*, and keep me out of it."

The Gauntts? I frowned, groping for why that name was familiar.

Thrivewell Enterprises. They were the family that owned the company, weren't they? The company with a name that'd chilled me for no obvious reason when I'd heard it last week.

How the hell were *they* connected to my life?

"Which one?" I demanded. "Who's 'he'?"

Wade shook his head, but the name tumbled out in a trembling whisper. "Nolan. I told you everything I know. Please."

I let go of him with a shove and stepped aside. The wave released, crashing over him but without any additional force than gravity. All it did was dislodge his comb-over so it splayed over his forehead and drench him even more than he'd already been.

The Gauntts. Nolan Gauntt. They had something to do with Marisol—something that'd sent me into a supernatural rage at thirteen years of age. I didn't think Wade had absolutely *no* idea what that might have been, but when it came to men and little girls, I could put all the horrible pieces together well enough on my own.

The rest I was better off getting straight from the source.

"No more threats about calling the police on me," I said to the sopping man who was cowering at my feet. "And if I want to see Marisol and she wants to see me, you're not going to stop me. You're going to tell my mom not to get in the way either. Understood?"

"Yes," Wade mumbled with a cringe.

"Good. Looks like you'd better invest in a good plumber." I turned on my heel and walked out of the house dripping but with twice as much resolve as before.

twenty-seven

Lily

As I tramped into my apartment with the guys half an hour later, still damp but not uncomfortably so, Nox looked around and let out a gruff sigh. "We are *definitely* getting you better digs than this. No arguments."

I wrinkled my nose at him. "That might be a little difficult considering I have no idea how I'm going to afford even these digs going forward."

"We told you not to worry about that."

"Fine." I flopped onto the futon. "I'm a lot more worried about these Gauntt people."

"Well, for starters, they should probably eat more," Ruin suggested.

The other guys all rolled their eyes at him, and he

held up his hands with a grin. "Hey, with a name like that, they're just asking for it."

"You should stick something in your mouth and chew instead of talking," Jett muttered.

"Excellent idea. I was getting kind of hungry." Ruin bounded over to the fridge.

Nox's gaze followed him with an expression that seemed to say, *When is he not?* But then the boss tossed out, "Throw me some leftover dumplings or something, will you?"

They'd better come up with some kind of income source, or they'd eat through their hosts' savings in another few days.

"You could talk to your sister again now that you put Wade in his place," Jett pointed out.

I hesitated. Marisol's obvious anxiety when I'd come near her was still clear in my memory. "I want to, but I think I need to have a better idea what we're dealing with first. If these dickheads have been threatening her, I have to be sure they can't actually hurt her." The underside of my arm itched, and I scratched at it absently as I pondered our options.

Kai had whipped out his phone the second he'd gotten off his bike. His thumbs pattered away on the screen. "Let's see, then. The Gauntts… Thrivewell Enterprises… Hmm."

I'd filled them in on what Wade had told me when I'd returned to my car outside the house, but then, other than the name, Wade hadn't told me much at all. All I knew about them was what I'd picked up at the rally—and that the name Thrivewell made my skin shiver in ways that weren't at all promising.

I leaned forward on the cushions. "What did you find? Who's this Nolan guy? I mean, other than probably a creepy pedophile."

Ruin coughed from over by the fridge. "Um, it looks like I already ate all the leftovers. Well, maybe not just me, but—probably a lot of it me." He shot us a sheepish smile. "I'll go out and grab some more. It's almost dinner time anyway."

"Fine, fine," Nox said with a dismissive wave. "Just make sure you don't eat it all on the way back. And ask for the hot sauce *on the side*!" he added in a holler as Ruin vanished into the stairwell.

"Nolan Gauntt is the current patriarch of the Thrivewell Enterprises empire," Kai said without missing a beat, as if the conversation had never veered off course. "He shares joint responsibilities with his wife, Marie. No specific age given, but from the looks of them, they're in their 60s. There haven't been any scandals big enough to make the news, but who knows what's been covered up."

"Do they still live in Mayfield?" I asked. "Can we—"

My question was cut off by a thump and a loud clatter from above—the kind of thunderous clatter you'd expect if an entire motorcycle toppled over on its side. The hairs on the back of my neck stood on end.

"Ruin!" Jett rasped, and all three guys launched

themselves out of their seats and toward the stairs as one being.

I ran after them, close enough behind them that I burst out the door on their heels. In the lane at the top of the stairs, a man was poised, so burly and bearded that if he'd been wearing plaid instead of polka dots, he'd have passed for a lumberjack.

He had Ruin shoved face-first against the side wall of the building, arms yanked behind his back and a pistol pressed to his forehead.

"Ansel Hunter," he was rumbling, "you've got a lot to fucking answer for."

Did you wonder what Lily's guys got up to while she was taking a little space from them in chapter 20? Grab a bonus scene from Ruin's POV by going to this URL or using the QR code below: https://BookHip.com/TNSAQGT

about the author

Eva Chase lives in Canada with her family. She loves stories both swoony and supernatural, and strong women and the men who appreciate them. Along with the Gang of Ghouls series, she is the author of the Bound to the Fae series, the Flirting with Monsters series, the Cursed Studies trilogy, the Royals of Villain Academy series, the Moriarty's Men series, the Looking Glass Curse trilogy, the Their Dark Valkyrie series, the Witch's Consorts series, the Dragon Shifter's Mates series, the Demons of Fame Romance series, the Legends Reborn trilogy, and the Alpha Project Psychic Romance series.

Connect with Eva online:
www.evachase.com
eva@evachase.com

Printed in Great Britain
by Amazon